The
HIGH CITY

BOOKS BY CECELIA HOLLAND

The Serpent Dreamer
The Witches' Kitchen
The Soul Thief
The Angel and the Sword
Lily Nevada
An Ordinary Woman
Railroad Schemes
Valley of the Kings
Jerusalem
Pacific Street
The Bear Flag
The Lords of Vaumartin
Pillar of the Sky
The Belt of Gold
The Sea Beggars
Home Ground
City of God
Two Ravens
Floating Worlds
Great Maria
The Death of Attila
The Earl
Antichrist
Until the Sun Falls
The Kings in Winter
Rakóssy
The Firedrake
Varanger

FOR CHILDREN

The King's Road
Ghost on the Steppe

A TOM DOHERTY ASSOCIATES BOOK
New York

The
HIGH CITY

CECELIA HOLLAND

This is a work of fiction. All of the characters, organizations, and events portrayed in this novel are either products of the author's imagination or are used fictitiously.

THE HIGH CITY

A Forge Book
Published by Tom Doherty Associates, LLC
175 Fifth Avenue
New York, NY 10010

www.tor-forge.com

Forge® is a registered trademark of Tom Doherty Associates, LLC.

Library of Congress Cataloging-in-Publication Data

Holland, Cecelia, 1943–
    The high city / Cecelia Holland.—1st ed.
        p.   cm.
    "A Tom Doherty Associates Book."
    ISBN-13: 978-0-7653-0559-6
    ISBN-10: 0-7653-0559-3
    1. Istanbul (Turkey)—Fiction.   2. Basil II, Emperor of the East, ca. 958–1025—
Fiction.   I. Title.

    PS3558.O348 H54 2009
    813'.54—dc22

                                                                    2008038019

First Edition: February 2009

Printed in the United States of America

0 9 8 7 6 5 4 3 2 1

This book is dedicated to
CHARLES BROWN.

The
HIGH CITY

CHAPTER ONE

He understood nothing of the talk around him, only the orders: pull, now, together, stop. Faster. Steerboard, backboard. Now they had the sails spread and rowing was easy work. The ship, square-bottomed, shallow in the keel, clunky as a log, carried two triangular sails rigged crosswise of the mast and spread on booms. They used the wind better than square fore-and-aft sails. The wind now was out of the east and felt dirty. There were only seven other rowers, the captain being miserly with his wages, but the ship was packed with cargo, so there was no room anyway.

Raef was just going, moving anywhere he could, blind as a baby. His home was on the far side of the world and he had no idea how to get there. He had striven at first to go north from Kiev but with the winter coming on the only travel was bound south, and so he went south. He had found this little trading ship in Chersonese and in seven days she had moved him nearly to the western end of the Greek Sea. Beyond, down a narrow corridor of water, was another sea, smaller, closer to where he was trying to get to, but still, a long way off. He was crawling sunwise along a chain of water, wide and narrow, like a string of jewels.

He tried not to know that he knew this, how the expanded edge of his mind bent and folded with the water ahead of him into the gullet through the land, churned and heaved as the water did to crowd through the choking narrows. He wanted to know nothing. He was jumpy anyway, his back itching, a sense of doom close on him, and he wanted not to notice this either. He longed to be like the other men, who could joke and drink and gnaw their crusts without dread.

Inside him was an endless echoing pit. He sank over and over into memories, of black-haired, gray-eyed Conn, his cousin, his heart's brother, gone now, his life over, a hero's life. Lived in a fury, as if he knew all along how soon it would end. Now Conn lay still at last, deep inside the yellow cliff under Kiev, and Raef turned steadily from the living men around him, toward that memory, that inward place where Conn remained, immortal.

The captain roared at him—he had missed an order—and slapped him across the back with his switch. Raef bent to the oar, his teeth clenched. He hated Ruskas, the captain, who beat him and made fun of him because he could not speak Greek. Not speaking Greek, Raef had to endure it, ignore it, like a yoked ox. He knew Conn would have fought back with his fists. Would have taken over the ship by now, Greek or not.

Raef swung the oar around, matching his seatmate's pace. The ship wallowed through the sea before the bracing wind. He felt his back tingle and wanted to look over his shoulder, to see what was coming. He closed his eyes, losing himself in the hard work.

The captain laid them by for the night on a long thin white beach on the southern seacoast, just a shelf at the foot of the first inland hills. The sky overhead shone clear but the air to the south was hazy with smoke. Ruskas pretended to forget to give Raef his measure of bread and drink, until Raef's seatmate, Markos, spoke up for him, gesturing, and made Ruskas hand over the flat doughy loaves, the cup of raw cloudy liquor, which even watered down was much stronger than wine. Markos shouted at him, as if

Raef would understand better if he were deafened, "Good puller! Good puller!" and patted his shoulder like a dog.

That he knew, understood, to row well, to meet the sea with the blade tipped, to sweep the wave away behind them, twist the oar flat on the return. Now, sitting idle among them on the sand, he was a clod. They diced and talked and laughed and drank and he was outside it all. He sat as if in darkness while they were in the light. Sometimes one shouted at him, got angry because he could not understand. He made no effort to respond. If he didn't understand it didn't matter anyway.

He kept his mind always turned inward, toward the memory of Conn, lying in the cave under Kiev. Conn, who had died saving him.

The raw sea air made the winter cold more harsh. He slept, huddled together with the rest, bundled under sails and blankets and anything else they could find to ward off the chill. A hawk soared through his dreams, her scream like an edge in the wind. He had seen her before. When he woke, he tried to remember what she had looked like, and could not, but he still heard the thin shriek of summons, or reproach, or warning.

Ruskas was bawling at them to get up. The ship pitched and tugged at her anchors, and just getting back on board was hard work; several of them dunked into the cold sea. The eastern sky was murky with clouds. The wind swept out from under the clouds in a fitful blast that ruffled the water dark and ugly. Ruskas was in a rage to get on, his face red, his eyes bulging. He bellowed at them to set the sails. Raef shut his mouth against the warning in his throat; the captain had sailed here much. He had no way to talk to him anyway. They rigged the two sloping yards and let the sails out, and Ruskas turned them out to sea. The rest of them sat down on the benches to row.

Raef put his hands on the oar, its grip wrapped in frayed rope, and a shock went up through his arms. He felt the sea rise under him like a monster coming out of the deep. A cold terror gripped him. Markos sat beside him, cheerful as a bird, still eating a piece of bread, while under them the world slipped and gave and opened like a maw. Ruskas called out, "Pull!" Stiff with fear Raef bent forward, the oar dead wood in his hands.

They swept across the water, light as thistledown in the wind. Swiftly, ahead of them, the sea pinched down to nothing, its flat blue edge meeting the steep shoreline, overgrown with trees. Only in one little space the hills came down straight into the water, and white wings of surf marked the sides of the strait.

Raef could feel the sea churning wild under him, buffeting through the narrows in both directions. The strait ran north to south, and the water ran both ways, a rush of water southbound on the top, beneath that a slow, saltier surge north into the Greek Sea. The banks of the sea-neck ahead twisted and turned, and reefs stirred the streams, so they coiled up and down, and broke each other around into eddies. It was like some vast music played on the harp of the world. The wind roared in icy-edged, breaking the choppy surface into flecks and scuds of foam, driving the ship on. Now they were running between the white plumes of the surf, sailing and rowing into the mouth of the strait, cutting off far to the north where the current went best, and well out of reach of the rocks on the south. Maybe Ruskas knew what he was doing.

As they ran deeper into the narrows the highlands on either side broke the wind down. From either side, harsh gusts suddenly slapped the ship, like fists punching, and the sails fell flat slack against the mast and then abruptly cracked open again.

Markos, beside Raef, shouted at Ruskas over his shoulder. Raef leaned into the oar. The wind plastered his salty hair to his face. He smelled the green pine of the land. In spite of his fear the sea's wild ceaseless tumbling made him joyful, as if he were part of it, as if he would never end while the sea rolled.

Markos shouted again, and Ruskas roared back a long string of words, the two of them talking over each other, Ruskas trying to sound calm, giving what Raef knew for an explanation. Markos howled at him, unconvinced.

They were well inside the strait now and the wind suddenly died. The sails luffed and drooped. Raef scraped his sodden hair back off his face and looked up at the sky, like a field of boulders overhead. He could feel the fitful breeze against his face, and then against his ear, and again on his back, bouncing in along the steep rocky coasts so near on either hand. He leaned forward and thrust the oar into the water and boosted them forward, toward whatever safety Ruskas was convinced they could reach. Then, abruptly, the wind roared back and slammed hard across their steerboard quarter, and the ship heeled over.

Clinging to the oar, Raef slid sideways into Markos; somebody screamed, somebody else swore. The wind howled around them in a maniacal laugh. The mast creaked and bent, and one of the yards carried away, streaming its rigging like hair. The other sail ripped and frayed in an instant to a flying web of threads. Ruskas was shouting but Raef could not make out the words.

The wind roared in his ears. He felt the sea yawn open to swallow them. Yet the ship, deep-ballasted with cargo, struggled upright again, and he tried to row, to get her some grip on the water, and the wind smashed into her again and laid her over again. A body crashed into him from above and knocked him into Markos and icy water flooded over them all.

The cold shock made him gasp, but his head was still above water, so he drew in only a great lungful of the air. He let go of the oar, flailing with his arms for something solid, his feet too solidly caught under the bench. Hands clutched him. The ship pitched under him, and he went down, the ship rolling all the way over this time, throwing him down under her, pushing him down into the throat of the sea.

He held his breath now. His foot was trapped under the bench. Underwater, he clawed at it, panicked, his lungs already trying to breathe. Somebody banged into him, kicked him in the shoulder. With one arm pushing that body away, he reached up with the other hand and grabbed the edge of the bench. His foot slipped from his shoe, and he twisted and dove away.

Dove down. Out from under the sinking ship. His lungs hurt. He had to breathe, far underwater, in the dark and cold. Distant over his head, a patch of pale sunlight glowed in the sea, and he kicked and stroked, struggling toward it. A little water trickled into his throat. His head was bursting. Rising toward the glow, blind with desperation, he hit something in the water so hard all the sense flew out of him and his lungs opened and the sea flowed into him.

Somebody gripped his arm and pulled, and he followed, groggy, and his head broke up out of the sea into the windy air.

He sobbed, trying to breathe. His chest sloshed and it was hard to move his lungs. The sea rose around him in dark mountainous waves. Rain struck him, the wind harsh in his face. He was clutching somebody's arm with both hands, and he looked up at the man who had saved him.

It was Ruskas, his free arm wrapped around a floating yard, the sail and much of the rigging drifting around it like a big sea-anchor. Raef at first could not make himself let go of him. Patiently Ruskas shoved him toward the yard, and with an effort of will Raef reached out one hand, gripped the round spar, let go of Ruskas, and transferred all his weight onto the yard and lay there, coughing and heaving. Water spilled from his mouth and nose. His chest burned. The inside of his nose felt scoured.

The yard tipped up, riding up a wave, and the crest broke over his head and he inhaled more water. He clung to the yard, coughing when he could, the rain beating on his back. Another of Ruskas's sailors had hold of the yard, on the other side from him; he had pushed himself up so that most of his chest was out of the water. He was shivering up and down his body, shuddering with cold. Mumbling something over and over, probably a prayer. Between him and Raef the sail's boom hung down into the sea, dragged down by the brass fitting at the other end, and Raef guessed that was what he had hit, coming up. The side of his head hurt. But he was breathing again.

He turned back to Ruskas, who had saved him. Ruskas was still working to save somebody else, had managed to unknot and coil up some of the rigging line, and was throwing it out into the wave. Raef could hear a voice nearby screaming. Ruskas hurled the rope out and it dropped uselessly on the upslope of a mountainous wave rising between him and the screeching head out there. The captain coiled the rope again, to try again.

Raef held out his hand. "Give me the end." He spoke

dansker, gibberish to Ruskas. The captain glanced at him, waved him off, took the coil back over his shoulder, and as the wave carried them up and up over the top he flung out the rope toward the man sinking there in the trough.

The rope fell well short. Raef swam after it, sliding down the backslope of the wave. It was Markos out there, the round head bobbing on the rain-pocked surface. With a gulp, the curly black head sank down under the waves and then reappeared, arms thrashing. He could not swim. Raef had reached the floating end of Ruskas's rope and he took it in one hand as he paddled by. The crest of wave lifted Markos up ahead of him, a black lump in the swirl of white foam, and then carried him away out of sight. Raef kicked up and dove through the moving hill of the sea and on the backslope came to Markos.

The Greek was exhausted, his face gray, his body lying floppily on the wave. Raef reached him in a stroke and passed the rope around him, under the armpits. At the touch Markos came to, rolled around, clutching at him, screaming again, his eyes wild. Raef swam out of his way before he could drag them both down. Still holding the end of the rope, he stroked back toward Ruskas, who had the other end fast.

The rope tightened quickly around Markos, and Ruskas began at once trying to reel it in, so that Raef had to wrap his end around his wrist to hold on. The taut length of line sliced through the wave, kicking up a little wake on either side. Raef swam to it and tied his end around it, closing the loop around Markos. Markos was lying on his back now, letting the rope tow him along. Slobber ran down his chin. Raef swam back to the yard.

His other shoe was still on, cumbersome, and he nudged it off with his bare foot. The ship was gone. Each wave carried him up enough to see all around them and there was no ship anymore. A few bales of the cargo floated low in the water here and there. Something that might be a body. He leaned on the yard, glad of it, tired. When the wave carried him up he could see the tree-shrouded coast to the south, much closer than the northern one. He thought within a few days the currents would dump them out there, but if they waited for that, they would all be dead of the cold.

Beside him, Ruskas had reeled Markos close enough that the other oarsman, weary and half-drowned, could get one arm over the yard and cling to it.

The sky was still low and lumpy with clouds, the wind slashing, but the rain had slackened. A few feet off to his right, Raef could hear the fourth man whispering his prayer, his body bunched up on the spar. Ruskas said something, and Raef turned toward him, understanding none of the words. The captain was staring at him. Again he spoke, and waved his arm to the south.

Raef wiped his hand over his face. He guessed what Ruskas had said, and nodded. "The beach. Yes. Land. Yes. That way." He waved south.

Ruskas leaned toward the man just beyond Raef, endlessly gabbling, and spoke something sharply to him. That man made no answer, only his constant sobbing prayer. His lips were blue with cold.

"Petros!" Ruskas said. "Petros."

No answer. With a shrug Ruskas turned to Markos, on the far end of the yard, still retching and coughing, his head laid against the wood like a pillow, his hair all over his face like seaweed. His eyes glazed, Markos lifted his wobbling head and nodded.

Overhead abruptly a hot glare of sun came through the black clouds. Ruskas went hand over hand down the yard to the knot end, and began trying to undo the sail stay. Raef felt along his belt for his knife, still in its sheath after all the rolling, held fast by the rawhide loop. He went to help the captain free them from the drag of the sail. Eventually Markos joined them. Slowly, kicking and pushing, they began maneuvering the yard in toward the shore.

⟶⟵

Ruskas said, "I wish I had drowned. This is a disaster."

Markos said nothing; he was enjoying sitting there in the sun on the beach and not being dead. They had come out on a tiny rocky stretch of pale brown sand at the foot of a steep rise covered with trees. Petros lay sprawled next to him like a corpse. Ruskas glared at him. "Go on down there and see what you can find. We have to get something to eat."

Markos grunted at him. Ruskas's head turned, looking around him, his face furrowed with care. "If I could have gotten that cargo to the City, you know what it would have been worth? I could have paid all my debts. Even with what the Eparch would take. Paid off the ship. Kept plenty for myself. Got Irene something nice to wear. Now what is there—nothing, nothing." He flung his hands out, empty, useless. "I'm ruined. While you, you fat lazy bastard, you won't even get off your fat lazy bottom and look for something to eat."

Markos glanced over his shoulder, his gaze going the other way up the beach. The stupid Scythian was trotting off obediently. All Ruskas had had to do was point at him and point at his own eyes and point a third time up the curving shore. Now Ruskas thought he could give orders to Markos on land, too.

He looked up at the captain, who was also his cousin, as these things went. He said, "I'm not moving, Ruskas. I just almost drowned out there, and I'm tired." He crossed himself. "I'm cold. If anything I'm going to build a fire." He didn't want to think of the rest of the crew, gone down with the ship. He nodded at the dark shapes bobbing in the surf. "Go look down there, maybe some of it's salvageable."

Ruskas turned and stared at the bits of his cargo coming in with the waves. A few bales of fleece were drifting into the surf, and he went down along the shore, wading into the curling edge of the narrow sea, to recapture a little of his wealth.

The sun was baking Markos a warmer crust, and his stomach felt pinched. Probably it was a good idea to look for food, some help, some idea where they were. He got up and ambled after Ruskas. He said, "Where are we? Is there a village up here somewhere? We can't be all that far from Chrysopolis. I told you you were an ass trying to beat the storm there."

"What exactly did you think I should have done otherwise?" Ruskas snarled. "Hauled to? Where?"

Markos said, "You're the captain, not me. You got us into this."

Ruskas's face sagged, accepting that. "Irene will tear me to pieces." He was dragging a half-soaked bale of fleece in toward shore. "Nothing we could eat of course is going to float. All that wine." He peered out toward the sea. "It's likely right there, on the bottom. We're only a little way from Chrysopolis. If we'd just gotten around the point—if the wind had held one half hour longer—"

"Here comes the Scythian," Markos said, and backed up onto the dry beach.

The Scythian was running into view around the bend at the eastern end of the beach. He was tall, whip-thin, with white-blond hair hanging almost to his waist, and a shabby blond beard. Markos had always taken for granted he was stupid but certainly he was strong, had muscled them steadily through the water into the beach. He trotted up to them, his gaze sweeping them, breathing hard.

Ruskas said, "Did you find anything?"

The Scythian's bright blue eyes fixed on him. "Now," he said, one of the few Greek words he had, and gestured with his hand for the captain to come. "Now." His body was taut with urgency, his voice harsh.

Ruskas said, "I've got to get this stuff in before it sinks. Markos, go with him."

The Scythian somehow understood that, or maybe just the tone, and the way Ruskas looked at the debris floating from the wreck. He turned to Markos, his eyes wide and unblinking. "Now," he said. "Pull." Markos took this to mean hurry. He went after the Scythian, who broke into a jog back up the beach.

The beach was narrow and sloping. Clumps of black rock broke up through the pale sand, in their lee ridges drifted wood and weeds in heaps. Markos swerved around a piece of a broken barrel. He ran a little to catch up.

He said, "What's your name?"

The blond man glanced at him and said nothing. Markos gave a little shake of his head, thinking it was useless even to try. He had to burst into a sprint every few steps to keep pace;

the Scythian moved fast. Nonetheless, he tried again. He patted his chest. "Markos Kallasides." Pointed to the Scythian. "You?"

The bleached pale brows drew together. "Raef."

"Ah, Jesus," Markos said, and crossed himself reflexively. "Not much of a name." Probably he lived in a den in the woods, wherever he came from. Ahead the beach pinched down to pass around the toe of a steep narrow hillside that plunged straight down into the salt water, and Markos let the Scythian Raef go ahead of him along the rocks above the waves.

As he came around the little cape, he let out a crow of relief. The coast bent away from him into a broad cove; beyond, the dark green, tree-covered hills came down almost to the water. Along the inside curve of the cove was a row of huts with red-tiled roofs. He thought at once of food, and started forward, but the Scythian had stopped and put his hand out to hold Markos back also. A moment later Markos realized the houses were empty, burnt, no one moving there, nothing growing around them, no boats, no nets hung. This place had been sacked, thoroughly, recently.

His guts knotted up. He turned; his eyes met the Scythian's. Raef gestured to him, and Markos followed him around the edge of the village, between the gutted houses and trampled gardens and the rising slope of the ridge, toward the dark forest and the hills inland.

Markos said, "What's going on?" He had a bad feeling about this; he glanced back at the burned-out village, and then looked down at the ground around them and realized Raef was following a trail of many feet on the ground. They came to the edge of the trees, mostly salt cypress, with twisted, wind-curled arms, where the trail continued.

It wound away through the trees, toward the higher, denser forest beyond. The surface was pounded to a thick layer of dust. Some of the branches of the trees had been snapped off. The wood was strangely silent, not even birds singing.

Without slowing his stride the Scythian went up this path. Markos hesitated a moment, but he looked behind, at the burned-out village, and knew that was a bad place to be. He followed Raef. Breaking into a run, he caught up to him, peering around through the trees, looking for anything to eat. The path wound up the hillside, and at the top, the Scythian stopped, staring ahead, and held out a hand for Markos to stop also.

Markos came up beside him, and looked out through the screening trees. Ahead the ground sloped down again, the trees thinned out, and in the distance, he saw people moving.

A lot of people. A town, he thought, seeing bright red roofs, a haze of smoke in the air. Then he went cold all over. Not buildings: tents. A mass of bright-colored round tents, people moving in and out, there, someone with a string of horses. A camp. An army camp.

"Holy God Almighty," he murmured, and crossed himself.

The Scythian Raef was watching him narrowly. When he caught Markos's eye, he raised both hands, made a circle with them over his head, and then pointed at Markos, his eyebrows raised.

Markos shook his head. "I don't think so. Not the Emperor—this must be one of the rebels." He crossed himself again. There had been uprisings for years, ever since the old Emperor died, leaving only the two little boys on the throne. Markos could not remember a real peace. Basil and Constantine were still on all the money; but there had been usurpers before and there could be another tomorrow. A big military force here, so close to the City, this was terrible. And they were surely enemies, rebels, possibly not even Roman. He realized they had burnt the village back there. He said, "Let's get out of here."

Raef patted his stomach and pointed toward the camp. Markos gave a bark of laughter. "No. They won't feed us, you idiot, they'll crucify us, to scare everybody else. Let's get out of here."

He turned back toward the path, but the Scythian did not follow him. Markos wheeled around, urgent, panic trembling in all his limbs. "No," he said, pointing toward the camp. "Bad. Enemies. Hurt. Bad. Come on, now." He stared at the Scythian a moment, not wanting to leave him, but he could see that the tall man was not following him. Finally he turned and jogged away down the path.

The Scythian stayed behind. Markos ran along the path, going downhill, and now, with the camp in his memory, he saw the prints of horses in the dust. He realized the whole wood was empty because it had been swept for firewood and food. He found a side trail that led him down the west side of the ridge, and followed that out to the beach. As he burst out of the trees onto the sand, he filled his lungs, to yell, to warn Ruskas and Petros.

He plowed to a stop in the sand, the shout choked off in his throat. Too late for warning. Ruskas and Petros stood down near the water, in the middle of a pack of armored cavalry. A miserable pile of salvaged bales of fleece stood nearby. Markos wheeled around, but the horsemen down there had seen him. He ran three strides and then a horse galloped up behind him and a blow knocked him sprawling. He lay on his belly, his breath whining through his teeth, and waited for the spear in the back.

But they did not kill him; they only dragged him back to the others, and bound them all in a line, and led them along the beach, to the enemy camp. Plodding along, he began to wish, like Ruskas, that he had drowned.

CHAPTER TWO

Raef watched Markos go back toward the beach and almost followed him. Almost called to him. He did not want to be alone. Even a Greek was better than nobody. He turned his eyes toward the camp in the distance, careful to keep within the cover of the trees.

He knew going back was witless. Whoever had burned the village would keep watch on it. They would be caught before nightfall. He studied the camp before him, putting together what little he knew about this place and these people.

Not the Greek Emperor's men, these. Then some enemy, and from Markos's reaction, a bad enemy. Back in Chersonese the Greek who bribed away their victory had told him something about a rebellion against the Emperor. He swallowed, trying to collect himself. He had the sudden feeling that everything ahead of him was coming loose and flying around like a great wind. Conn would have known what to do. He would not have been alone, if Conn were there.

His heart hammered, like something trying to get out. With Conn beside him, it seemed, he had never been afraid.

He knew that was untrue. He had never been brave, even with Conn around, he had always fretted, always unsure, gnawed by doubts and fears. And now he was alone. Without Conn, he felt like a shadow, a ghost, with no place in the world.

Conn would have found some way to attack this. To turn it into something he understood, something he could dominate. Raef could not do what Conn did. He wiped his hand over his face. All he had left was a ragged shirt, his leggings, the knife in his belt. He was hungry, barefoot, and cold, and this army was in his way.

Up there, westward, somewhere, not too far, was a town; he could almost smell it. Certainly he could feel it, a thick teeming clog at the edge of his senses, close to the water, almost riding on the water. That was all he had, this feeling, this sense, which he had always hated, his strangeness, like an extension of his nerves out into the world. He cursed himself for a coward, second-guessing, unsure.

It was useless to be afraid. Worse than useless. And he couldn't brood on Conn anymore. He had to stay up on the keen edge of his mind. Keeping close to the trees, he started to circle around the back side of the camped army ahead of him.

—⚬—

The camp filled the lowland along the shore, flowed up the skirts of the steep hills. As he went along the fringe of it, he came constantly upon wood gatherers, foragers, hunters, all poking around looking for something, making broad tracks through the wood and over the hillside, noisy and clumsy. Mostly they traveled in packs, with horses and mules, and he avoided them easily, hunkered down against a tree, behind a rock, waiting until they moved on by.

He watched for mushrooms, for berries, finding nothing. He passed by another little village burned empty as an old shell. His bare feet began to ache, and his belly griped with hunger. In among some rocks he sniffed out a spring and drank all he could. Broad-leafed plants grew along the water's edge, and he dug up their sweet fleshy roots with his knife and ate them. Old and withered yellow fruit hung on a scrubby little tree but it was too hard and sour to eat.

He watched a stream of horsemen go southward on a well-beaten path, big men, in padded, metal-plated breastplates, their horses clad in quilted armor. They carried spears in their right hands, swords in their belts, and helmets and little round shields that clanked on their saddlebows.

He saw how the armor covered only the outsides of their arms and the fronts of their legs, and how the breastplates stopped below their throats; a knife in through the armpit or over the collarbone, he thought, would get any of them. Hamstring them with a backhand slash. Kick them down. But they were soldiers, they had fought much. They fought together. They might beat him, head to head.

On the other hand, these were moving away from the camp, not into it. So there were two armies, maybe more.

He climbed steadily higher, into the last light of the day. At sundown he was on the brow of the highest hill behind the camp, and he sat down, and looked north over it all. The camp sprawled below him, filling the fingers of lowland in among the steep tree-covered hills. It stank of smoke and dust and filth, crawled with people and horses. At the north edge, pressed against the narrow strip of the sea, was a walled town, with tiled roofs, white walls, a white breakwater thrust into the water beyond.

The sun was sliding down below the horizon, the whole round rim of the world touched with rosy pink, and now, beyond the narrow water, at the limit of his vision, like a reflection in the sky, he began to make out another city.

This one seemed to float on the rise of the evening, in the last uptilted sunlight. He wondered if he was imagining it, half-visible in the haze, was he making it out of the shadows, the slanted light, the night mists? He could not see an end to it, or a beginning. Maybe it was only hilltops, trees. Clouds and palaces. A dome shone golden in the sunset, or it might have been the setting sun shining on a cloud. He thought he saw more domes and spires. Walls, he thought, climbed up and down the hills, through masses of trees, or maybe gardens, all blessed in the last of the day. Then his heart leapt, and he realized, That is Constantinople.

He realized he was stretching himself up, trying to see better, his whole body yearning toward it, his eyes struggling to bring it within reach.

That was why this army was here, not to burn little fishermen's villages, not to lay siege to a few huts on the shore. It was this they wanted, this half-visible glory, suspended between heaven and earth. His eyes ached. If he looked away it would be lost. He dared not even blink, or he would lose it, and now that he had seen it, even from far off, he could not bear to lose it. Clean and white, rich and beautiful, the high city of the world.

Then a surge of rage took him, that this clanking filthy army stood between him and it.

He started down the hillside. The night was creeping up from below, blue twilight, and the first cold of the darkness. His bare feet padded through the rocks and dust. He knew now where he was going. He felt the way ahead of him as if it were lit up with torches and he walking down the middle, like a king. He plunged down into the clamorous stink and darkness of the camp.

As he came down the hill, the tent city was spread out below him, rounds of striped cloth in rings and clusters, broad lanes flowing among them, everywhere busy with hundreds of people, walking, standing, carrying bundles and jars. A steep hillside bounded the camp to the west, but even there, in among scrawny trees and stumps, he saw black fire rings.

Then trumpets bellowed, and drums in an impatient thundering resounded. He stopped behind a thin twisted tree and watched the swarming settlement below him as all in an instant the aimless churning stopped, turned, and began streaming up toward the wall at the north end. Banners floated along the lanes between the clusters of tents. Rows of lances like porcupine quills. The people seemed to flow away from him through the camp as if they became one thing.

At the back edge of the camp, heaped up with garbage and pocked with cesspits, he waited a moment, looking for sentries, and saw no one.

Night was falling. In the open, with the sun gone, the air was turning cold and sharp, but at the edge of the camp it began to feel warmer, rank with the stink of smoke, rotting meat, and shit. He could hear shouting, at the far edge of the camp, and then a sudden roar of thousands of voices all at once. A hot yellow glow lit up the edge of the sky there. He wondered if they were fighting. If they had their enemies in front of them it might be that nobody would be watching back here. He remembered the armored horsemen riding away; they could believe they were covered. He walked straight into the camp, avoiding the lanes, winding his way quickly through the grouped tents.

On the broad lanes, off past the square outlines of the tents, masses of people were still tramping by, going toward the besieged city. Standing silent in the lee of a canvas wall like a stretched sail, he let them get well beyond him.

He came to the center of the place, a circle of tents close to the siege army. At the far side, beyond the last tent, hundreds of blazing torches cast their smoky yellow shine up and through a forest of upright spears. Next to every spear a round metal head. The lines of soldiers stretched on one side up to the slope of the hillside and on the other off out of his sight. Lurking between two tents he watched a troop of maybe forty men pass by, in neat rows and walking in step. They wore metal armor, even on their legs, and helmets like pots; the man leading them had a waving feathery crest on his. In the armor, their long dark cloaks, they all looked the same.

He watched them go along. In the solid tramp of their feet he felt how strong they were, all together. Under those ranks of spears, up ahead, were blocks of men like this. He drew back between two of the round tents; one, he knew, had a woman in it, asleep, but the other was empty. He slid around the curve of cloth to the door flap and let himself in.

The space was close, and low, so he had to stoop. The light was very dim but he made out the square corner of a bed, half-hidden under a jumble of gear and clothes, a stool, a chest with bread, cheese, and onions laid out on top, a half-full cup, as if somebody had been sitting down to eat when the trumpet sounded. He ate the food, found himself a warm tunic in the jumbled clothes, took a long red cloak hanging on the tent post, and tried on a pair of black sandals, but couldn't get the straps to fasten over the broad pads of his feet. He swung the cloak on. The dangling front flap bothered him, and he cast it back over his shoulder. There was a short spear tipped against the tent pole and on the way out he took that.

Staying away from the broad lanes, he slipped past a string of horses dozing over their hay and worked his way around more tents. He waited while two women passed, chattering together, baskets on their heads. Most of the tents were empty, not even guarded. Over a fire in the middle of a ring of the tents, a man squatted on his heels, making soup in a helmet.

Ahead, the shouting fell into a lull. In the quiet Raef heard voices, off to his left, and he went shyly behind a tent, feeling this out. Staring at the blank white cloth, letting his mind empty, he felt over there a horde of women, anxious, watching what was happening, afraid to go too close. A few called out men's names, but most were still, wringing their hands, trembling. Quietly he went off in the opposite direction, out of their way, and walked up closer to the fighting.

There was another thunderous roar of voices, and ahead, there was a harsh piercing whistle, which faded away into the distance, toward the town. He circled several wagons drawn up close together, wondering about the whistle, and because he was not up at the edge of his mind he turned in front of a wagon and was without warning face-to-face with a soldier in a helmet with a sideways crest.

The man blinked at him, startled, and for an instant he froze. His gaze went to Raef's new clothes, and his hand rose reflexively, as if he would salute. Not sharing this confusion Raef swung up the spear at his side in one short thrust, butt first into the man's throat, just above where the breastplate ended. The Greek staggered back and went down hard, almost under the wagon, and doubled up in pain, choking and gasping.

Raef pushed him all the way under the wagon, wrenching the crested helmet off as he did. The crest was only a stiff brush, not flowing and feathery, but it was the same color as his cloak. The rows of red bristles were set into a metal strip that ran crosswise of the helmet; he thought the other plumes he had seen had run front to back.

The soldier was still alive, his head rolling, his breath ragged and wet. Raef moved off around the wagon and hunkered down in the space between it and the next. He tried the helmet on. It was loose and uncomfortable and he took it off again quickly. Finally he wadded up his hair on top of his head and jammed the helmet on over it. The crest on it made him feel top-heavy but his hair cushioned it all and it fit better.

In the quiet, down behind the wagon, he thought over what had just happened. He had been right, all these years, to fear his strange sense, which would betray him if he relied on it, disappear when he most needed it. He was just a man, like everybody else, and he had to remember that. A few yards away the downed Greek soldier was stirring. Through the crisscross of axles and spoked wheels Raef could see his feet moving, pushing at the ground, but he was still on his side and made no outcry. Raef straightened and walked away, the spear on his shoulder, the helmet on his head, going toward the flickering glow in the air and the shouting.

Ahead of him the torchlight was bright enough to throw shadows. The fence of spears was ten or twelve rows deep and ran all across the front of the town wall, with its high square gate a little way down from him, hundreds, maybe thousands of men. Beyond the spears he could see the top edge of the wall, cut with arrow notches, and that was where the torches blazed, masses of them, their light glaring over the land just below. They were packed especially bright by the big gate up there in the middle. The defense was ready, up there, and would not be surprised, at least not from this side.

Another shout went up from the attackers, and again something whistled up into the air toward the town. This was a ball of flames, like a brief little sun. The light washed over everything, a wave of red glare, arched above the torch wall's light against the darkness of the night, fell into the town, and was gone at once. Against the inside of his eyelids he saw the top line of the town, a spiky mass turned light for dark, the sky above boiling with smoke, tiny shadowy figures moving along the wall.

He came to the crosses.

They stood in a row, facing the town. A prickle of heat went along all his nerves even before he saw what hung on them. Two of the bodies were old, bird-picked, the bones showing through rags of cloth and hairy skin, but the third, the one in the middle, was new, and it was Ruskas.

Raef felt him before he saw him; he had gripped Ruskas with both arms, when the captain saved him, and now his arms burned, all along their insides, raw with pain. Then he saw the face, what was left of it. One eye staring out wild as if it were still alive. The rest bashed in, matted with hair and blood and brains. He had been dead when they hoisted him up here. They had made sure of that, not quickly. He had seen death coming, the blow coming, inescapable, straight into his face.

Raef stood among the crosses fighting against his heaving belly, his mind shocked and empty. Ahead of him, suddenly, the great crowd gave another many-throated bellow, and they all surged backward, away from the wall, momentarily shattering their order. He jerked aware again. A shower of rocks clattered down all around, and the lines at once re-formed, each man shoulder to shoulder with the next, orderly as before.

Something in him recoiled at that, the monstrous unison.

He looked up at Ruskas, who had saved him, and whom someone else had done such evil to. It came to him that they must have Markos also. His temper blazed. He brought to mind everything he could remember about Markos, his curly dark hair, his pocky skin and merry eyes, his hand patting Raef on the shoulder like a dog. He began to think Markos was somewhere behind him, over a little rise to the west, in a tent. He turned, and followed up this trace.

—⚬—

Petros was still alive, but unconscious, his mouth open, the blood gurgling out each time he fought for breath. Each breath a little slower, a little fainter. Die, Markos thought. Die, will you, please die, stop hurting and die.

He had drawn himself up as close to the wall as he could, his knees against his chest, his head down. He should not will Petros to die, because then they would start on him. He was already splattered with Petros's blood. Everything in the tent was flecked with Petros's blood. Several lamps flooded the little room with light, glinting on the drops and pools. His skin felt cold. He was afraid to look at either of the two men sitting in the middle of the room. The third, near the door washing his hands in a bucket, had his back to them all. Markos had been sick already once and the nausea flooded him again, although his belly was painfully empty.

"How are they doing out there?" said one of the men sitting down.

The man by the door looked up, and out the flap. "Still volleying shot. They're trying to knock out the little catapult on the wall by the gate. Now they're switching to fireballs."

"We should attack," said the other sitting man. He wore a bright yellow dalmatic, elaborately worked on the hem. "We can storm the land gate. They have no soldiers. We have all the soldiers. This is the whole army, here, and at Abydos. Delphinas is a fool."

"Phokas will order it soon," said the first; he shifted on his stool, crossing one leg over the first. "There was a messenger from him this afternoon. Meanwhile we need to find out why Basil sent these men around behind us." He turned toward Markos, his eyes reflective. "Leo, get over here. Maybe this one will tell us what he knows."

"I don't know anything," Markos cried. "I swear, by the Holy Mother, I'm not a spy." Leo shook the bloody water from his hands and reached for the short, saw-toothed knife in his belt, turning, calm as a butcher. Markos whined, his whole body shivering. "I'm not a spy. I don't know anything." None of this had helped Petros, either. Ruskas they had simply beaten to death as an example.

Then, behind him, there was a harsh ripping sound. Leo's gaze twitched, aiming past Markos, his face falling open, startled. He yelled, indignant, "Hey! Whoever you are, use the door!" Markos felt his hands seized from behind him, the rope suddenly cut away. Before he could move, in past him strode a tall centurion in a red-crested helmet and a long red cloak.

"What in God's name—" said the man in the yellow coat. Leo let out a yell.

"Who are you? Guards! Guards—" He lunged, his little saw-toothed knife out in front of him.

The red-crested officer bellowed something at him, furious. He lifted his spear in both hands and took it straight into Leo, as Leo rushed at him, knocking the torturer's knife thrust aside with his forearm and butting the spear on the ground for the impact.

With both hands he thrust the spear deeper into Leo's belly, lifting the big man up so that his own weight slit him open.

The seated men were scrambling to their feet, shouting for help. One picked up the stool and held it like a shield. "Not one of us—he's not one of us!" Leaving the spear in Leo's gut, the tall officer wheeled around, gripped Markos by the shoulder, and pushed him on ahead of him, out the long slash in the wall of the tent.

"Pull!" he shouted. "Now!" Stunned, Markos recognized this voice.

He gave a yelp of laughter. Not one of them, they were certainly right about that. Behind him the tent flap flew back, and another soldier rushed in, a sword in his hand. Markos leapt through the gash in the cloth ahead of him, out into the dark cool freedom of the night, and ran.

CHAPTER THREE

He ran as hard as he could, the Scythian loping along next to him, guiding him with a hand on his arm now and then. The Scythian seemed somehow to know exactly where he was going. Always heading downhill, they dodged steadily along through a jam of wagons parked on a slope. Two drovers, dicing in a wagon bed, gaped at them as they went by but made no outcry. After the wagons they turned abruptly to the right, onto flat ground following but not on a road that ran parallel to the city wall. Beyond that road rank on rank of spearmen stood, with the light before them glowing over them, weaving their shadows together until they seemed like giants. Then abruptly the Scythian, whose name he had forgotten again, pulled Markos around toward the torchlight, toward this army and their spears.

Markos held back, taut. He saw that the lines of soldiers were ending; they were almost to the shore. Before him, ranged along the top of the coastal bank, stood a row of gigantic scaffolds. High as the town wall, they were made of wooden beams, broad-based frames narrowing at the top to a point. Something dark covered parts of the frames, like hide over bones. The torches along the wall lit them from bottom to top, and as his gaze fell on them, he saw that a limber arm tilted across the narrow peak of each scaffold, its long end slanting down toward him, its short, stubby end on the far side stuck up in the air.

An array of ropes dangled from a crossbeam at the end of this stub, and as Markos hung back, resisting the Scythian's pull, he saw a dozen men taking hold of these ropes. With a great yell they rushed all at once toward the rear of the engine, spreading out on either side of the frame to get room to keep running, hauling their ropes over their shoulders. Markos had to skitter sideways to stay clear of their rush.

The short beam swung down, and now just over Markos's shoulder, so he had to twist around to watch, the longer sling-arm of the stone-thrower rose up. A man waiting nearby for this stepped quickly forward with a torch and touched his fire to a lump on the ground, which instantly took flame. As the sling-arm lifted, Markos could see the doubled rope coiling away after it; the rope jerked tight, the arm flailed on, faster and faster, and the flaming sling lashed up along after it.

Flying around at the end of the doubled rope, the burning ball soared up into the black sky, its wide arc a perfect curve, much faster even than the wooden arm. Just past its apex, before the slower arm could brake it, one end of the rope came undone. Freed, the fiery load sailed off into the sky like a comet, crashing toward the city in ripples of flame.

Markos whined, afraid. The Scythian had him by the elbow, was pushing him on between that engine and the next. Markos dragged his feet but the Scythian was strong. On either side now there were swarms of soldiers. With a long rattling creak the arm of the first stone-thrower had swung back to rest, and its crew swarmed around it. That put most of them behind him, and with a sudden courage he scampered ahead of the Scythian toward the darkness.

A yell ahead of him stopped him, as much as the Scythian would let him stop. In front of them now was the second engine, ready to shoot, its load lying in the net of the sling, the rope loose between it and the low end of the arm. A half-naked man with a torch stood ready to light it. On the far side, a dozen men reached up for the dangling ropes. Nonetheless the Scythian strode quickly along past them, dragging Markos along, as if he and Markos were invisible.

Maybe they were, he saw, astonished. Nobody looked at them. It came to him that at first glance the Scythian would just seem to be a tall centurion with somewhere to go. Markos shook himself, strode along, trying to keep up, to look as if he belonged here. But his skin tingled.

The second stone-thrower began to fire. The men rushed away from him now, he was crossing the line directly in front of the frame, the air dusky with light from the torchlit town. When the wooden arm came forward, almost overhead, it squealed and bounced on the crossbar, and the rope whistled, and then, the sudden bright flare of the light washed over everything like a demonic lantern, hissing and howling.

But cutting through the array of stone-throwers they had circled the ranked soldiers. Now they were even past the war engines. Markos looked around, relieved. They were striding along a steep little slope, well away from the town. The brush here was trampled and broken and he nearly tripped on a knot of exposed roots. Suddenly at his feet the land ended in a six-foot drop. He bounded down to a narrow pebbly beach and backed up quickly into the shelter of the overhang, where nobody could see him. The Scythian dropped down next to him.

Markos bent forward, his hands on his knees, his legs shaking. "Are we safe?"

Beside him, the tall man said nothing. He pried the helmet off and his hair fell loose and lank over his shoulders. His long red cloak was very fine and the tunic under it was fancy enough for a domestikos. Markos said, "God, if you could please speak Greek." He remembered the Scythian coming through the tent like a lightning bolt, seizing him, killing Leo, and blazing out again. He crossed himself, whispered thanks to Almighty God. He would make some special prayers when he got home. He would devote a day every week to fasting. His ribs hurt. He wiped his mouth on his hands, listening to the uproar above them, muted by the overhanging bank.

Nobody was chasing them. He turned to the Scythian, trying to remember his name, and said, "Look, you probably don't even understand me, but thank you for helping me, back there. I thank God for sending you. I'm alive because of you. God's will be done."

The Scythian saw something in his look, and smiled. His gaunt face improved with the smile. He had the centurion's helmet in the crook of his arm, just like a real officer. Off just beyond his head, a little inland, a yell went up. Now Markos made sense of all the racket. He heard the squeal, the creak, and knew the great wooden engine was swinging its arm around forward, flinging its shot. Up above the edge of the bank, against the roiling sky, the flaming ball hurtled up and out and over the wall of the city, dragging its light like an orange skirt. Behind the rampart, a thready screech went up. Heads shrank down and away from the shot. The burning mass tumbled over them, trailing sparks and embers, and fell beyond into the city.

In the darkness after the gaudy spray of light, Markos shivered. He had escaped but only into this mess. He thought of Petros. They should have brought Petros. Except Petros was surely dead by now. He crossed himself. He was alive; for the second time that day, he could be glad of that. God be thanked. God be thanked. He thought of Ruskas, of Petros screaming with each cut, until they tired of that, and ripped his tongue out, and all at once it overcame him. He crossed himself and sobbed.

The Scythian touched his arm. When he looked up, the tall man—Raef, he remembered now—shook his head, waved aside his grief. "Pull. Safe. You, me." He pointed to the water, glittering in the light from the torches, and made motions with his hands.

"Swim for it," Markos said. "Swim. Swim." He turned, looking out at the water.

The narrow, rushing water sparkled where the torchlight struck. The wind blasted along it, true out of the west now, clearing away the storm. A fog lay low over the water, blurring the far side of the Bosporus, but abruptly he recognized this shoreline he stood on, the long shallow curve of the bay, the massive seawall on his left, the light tower at the far end. This was Chrysopolis. He was a mile from home. There was a battle of some kind going on, and he was stuck in the middle of it, but he was still nearly to his home. He rushed the few steps toward the water, glad, unreasoning, and bent down and put his hands to the surface. "No. I can't swim." He turned back toward Raef. "The ferry. In Chrysopolis." He turned and pointed, just as another stone-thrower on the bank above them fired its meteor shot into the air and dim red light spilled down over them like a bloody rain.

Raef was staring at him, his hands on his hips. "Swim," he said, tentatively.

Markos thrust his face at him, although there was a good hand's span difference in their height. "No. I can't." He settled back, thinking, again, This man saved my life. God sent him. He said, "I can't swim. I'm a sailor, I belong on top of the water." Somehow the joke didn't seem funny now. He said, loudly, firmly, "No. No swim."

Raef spoke to him in a long string of some garble. Markos

grunted at him. "Learn to speak Greek and I'll listen to you." He started off toward Chrysopolis, along the line of the shore, wondering how to get inside.

The tall Scythian went along after him. The bank on their left rose to just above their heads. On the flat ground up there men shouted and tramped, so that the bank trembled, shedding pebbles and sand. The stone-throwers went off one after another in their long slow rhythm. The town wall loomed before Markos, dense blocks of stone, built sheer down from the high ground, marching out into the water. He could hear the slap of the waves against the stones, out there, even under the crunch and trample of the fighting.

At the foot of the wall was a ditch, ankle-deep in scummy water, choked in rubbish, with a stench that made him gag. Dead things here. Half-burned, rotten, dead things. Markos stopped. Getting inside Chrysopolis didn't seem any better a proposition than being out here. He made himself accept they would be very unlikely to be operating the ferries. He was tired and hungry, but mostly tired; he had to crawl into some safe hole and sleep for a while. Another flaming shot sailed over them, glistening on the fetid puddles in the ditch, on smoldering garbage, a tree stump with jagged roots. The tall Scythian walked along the side of the ditch, looking up at the wall.

Afraid to leave him, Markos followed anxiously, wondering how to tell him they should be going the other way.

The ditch was climbing, shallower, and narrower. Up there the darkness gave way to a smoky dim light, where the arched bridge crossed this ditch to the land gate of Chrysopolis, all blazing with torchlight. Markos blinked, coming to the edge of this light, and drew away, toward the darkness. The Scythian was already moving back beside him.

The army was close above them, and with each shot from the stone-throwers the soldiers roared and banged their spears together in a thunderous acclaim. In the brief light of the fireballs he saw tangled bodies in the ditch, he thought he saw eyes, watching him, and yelled.

He looked wildly all around him. Just ahead of them, the light shone brighter, washing the whole ditch with its glare, and there were bowmen on those walls—on the land side, too, among the attackers. Once anybody up there saw them moving around down here they would be easy game. He shrank back, even farther, but the dark was worse; he could not tell now what was around him.

He reached out and grabbed the Scythian's arm. "Listen! We can't go in there—they're going to attack—they have no soldiers in there." He remembered what the men in the tent had said. The whole army was on the wrong side. The Scythian faced him, frowning. Markos said, "I'm tired. I want to rest. I'm tired." He scrubbed his hand over his face.

"Pull," the Scythian said thoughtfully.

"Is that all you can say?" Markos shouted. "I'm tired. I'm hungry." He put his hand to his belly. "Hungry. It stinks here. Let's go back. Go back." He grabbed the Scythian's arm and pulled him back toward the Bosporus, the cleaner air, the shore.

The Scythian went along easily enough with that, striding beside him, looking up at the wall with every step, as if he thought he could climb it. The bank beside them began to rumble. Markos shrank into the shelter of it, his hands on the earth. Pebbles and clods fell around him. He turned, gaping, back toward the bridge, where the army was attacking.

Bodies, armor, shields, spears, they packed the bridge, a column of soldiers, smashing into the gate, and ladders went up against the wall. On the wall archers appeared, a fringe of raised bows. The Scythian grunted. "No," he said. "No." He got Markos by the arm. "Go back," he said, and Markos hurried after him away down the ditch.

With a nasty thin whine something sliced through the dark past him and whumped into the ground. He yelped, jumped, fell, hit something soft and slick, and retched. Under him cold, stinking fur, maybe bark, smelling of blood maybe. A hand grabbed him by the shoulder and dragged him up and he stumbled and scrambled his way after.

—❧—

Out by the water, on the cool dark pebbly beach again, Markos lay down with his back to the bank, shivering, his eyes already closing. Raef dragged him over into the shelter of a rock, where he would be harder to see. Above them, far away, he heard the rumble and screaming of the fighting. It was useless, he had seen that at once, twenty men could hold the gate there if they had enough arrows. He stood watching the city; the air was smoky in the light of the torches but he saw no flames inside the wall. The stone-throwers were silent. For all their fiery excitement they had not worked. Whoever was leading this siege didn't know what he was doing.

He glanced over at Markos, who was sleeping curled up like a dog. The Greek was tougher than he had expected. It was funny, the way he talked, as if he could force his words into Raef's head, and yet he had: Raef understood more of what he said now.

They needed something to eat. Something to drink. He

folded his hair up again and fit the helmet on, and bounded up the bank to the top again.

The stone-throwers were still, their crews drawn up on the far side of the engines, so they could watch the fighting by the gate. Raef went along beside the huge silent wooden racks. He stopped a moment beside one of them, put his hand on a timber, looking the piece over. Hides covered the forward sides of the tower, to protect people when they moved them around, or to defend against fires. The hides felt oily. The short arm ended in a wide rack, from which the ropes hung. He stood looking it over, puzzled. The whole action worked too well for the length of this short arm. Then he saw how the crossbar with the ropes was braced, and realized it was weighted, not enough to overbalance the long arm, and so make the whole mechanism useless, but enough to get the long arm moving like a whip.

A great yell went up from the town gate, where the fighting was. He thought it came from inside the town. He thought the fighting wasn't going well for the rebel army. The packed mass on the bridge had not burst the gate open. They had brought up ladders to scale the wall but the rough ground hindered them. He could see men dropping off the walls into the ditch. The screams and howls from the people looking on sounded desperate. Raef went on up toward the pounded road along the edge of the camp.

That went bad right away. Someone behind him shouted, in Greek. He ignored it, strode on. But then ahead of him a soldier standing by the edge of the wagons turned, saw him, and shouted more Greek, and when he didn't answer, but kept on walking, drew a sword and turned his head and bellowed for help.

Raef dodged off toward the nearest tents and started running through the lanes between them. He was near the place where he had found Markos, and now there were soldiers all around him. Maybe they were still trying to find out what had happened then. He sensed a dozen armored men spreading out, getting ahead of him, on either side, all around. He pulled off the helmet with the sideways crest; still running, he stripped off the red cloak, warm as it was, and tossed them to either side.

Stooping, he crept in between two tents; he heard a yell out there, close by, somebody seeing the helmet, he thought. Somebody else shouted, crisply, an order, from the opposite direction. He was between them, and they knew he was close. On either side of him was a blank canvas wall but across the round space in the midst of the ring of tents was one that had been badly set up, the side riding up against poles spread too far apart. He stepped out across that space, dropped down on his back, and slipped in under the edge.

There was somebody inside. There was a light, in the front of the tent. He heard someone breathing harshly, and then a voice, calm, reassuring. He lay in the dark on the ground behind a litter of gear, a saddle, a chest, a breastplate of armor on a stand. With one hand he pulled the side of the tent down behind him as far as he could, not much, since he was afraid of making any noise. Outside a loud yell ended in an answering, louder yell.

Peering around the edge of the armor stand he saw a man lying on his back on a low bed, breathing hard, while another man knelt over him with a rag, cleaning his wounds. The younger man, the wounded man lying there, made a gesture with his hands, the one Markos was always making, which called on his god. He said something in a voice wheezy with pain. The man nursing him laid both hands on him, and spoke, calming, promising him something.

Raef lay still, rigid. A moment later on the far side of the canvas several tramping feet came by, brisk, marching. He could see the studs on the bottoms of their shoes through the gap at the bottom of the tent wall.

Inside, beyond the wounded man, a tent flap flew back, and two men bore in another, this one dragging his leg. The tall man went to help them lay him down, and while they were all busy Raef rolled back out through the gap under the tent wall and went the opposite way of the soldiers.

They had lost track of him. He felt them scattered around, looking in all directions around him. They called out to each other and stopped passersby. They still surrounded him but the net had lost its vigor. He worked his way out from their midst, from shadow to shadow. They were easy to elude. They made too much noise. They were safe here, and went carelessly. He let them drift by him, he slipped past groups of them in the lanes.

He needed a weapon, having only his knife. His slow passage through the tents brought him to the edge of the massed wagons, parked on the rising slope of a hill. He crawled in underneath, remembering the man he had shoved under here earlier in the night, who might have had a sword.

On his elbows and knees he shuffled through beneath the wagons, sliding under the axles, and squirming through the gaps between wheels. They were not parked in line, but however the slope let them, just getting them out of the way. The torchlight shone through in swaths and bars. He saw no sign of the man he had left here. At the far edge, near the stone-throwers, he saw feet marching by, sometimes so perfectly in time that for an instant he would see only one set of striding legs.

He crept backward again, going to his left, off away from the trampled road. Trumpets sounded, distant. A loud whoop of voices carried on and on. He reached the edge of the massed wagons and got up squatting on his heels, looking around. Here were horses tethered in lines, quiet, hay-munchers, uninterested in the battle lost and won. Near the head of one line, a sentry leaned on his spear, staring away toward the fighting.

Raef stayed where he was a moment before a horse nearby turned its head to look at him, and that alerted the sentry. Raef dodged back under the wagons. The sentry shouted in Greek, and came striding down the line of the wagons, gripping his spear. Raef waited until he was visible down a clear light of sight, where several of the wagons all came together, and stood there, and made sure the sentry saw him, and dodged away again.

The sentry came cautiously out into the nest of wagons. He poked with his spear into spaces and behind wheels. Raef, lying under the bed of a wagon, reached out and gripped him by both ankles and yanked his feet out from under him, and without even a cry the Greek fell headfirst into the wagon on the far side.

Raef squirmed out into the open, and lunged for the sentry's throat. The body under him was already limp. The front of the sentry's face had hit the edge of the wagon so hard it bent the nosepiece of his helmet. It was a round helmet, with no crest, and Raef pulled it off, not bothering with the chin strap. The nosepiece broke off entirely when he tried to straighten it, which made it easier to get his head inside. He undid the clasps of the sentry's cloak, and took his sword with its scabbard, and walked away from the wagons to find something to eat.

He moved straight off from the tent where he had found Markos, away to the ragged edge of the camp, where the inland hillside began. The battle had ended and all the soldiers flooded back to their grounds. Each campfire as he passed seemed more crowded. The broad lanes were thick with people, not lined up, not marching, filthy with dirt, their bodies drooping. They had lost, at least for now. A man in a crested helmet like the one that had gotten Raef in trouble walked up and down a stretch of lane, shouting and brandishing his fist. Nobody paid any attention.

Raef passed by one fire where a man sat gripping a bleeding shoulder, while another ranted and raved, his arms flying like scythes. Raef slowed his steps, watching; more people were gathering to listen, battered, filthy faces grim with defeat. When he felt too many of them around him he backed hastily out and went on.

The ground turned upward under his feet, climbing the hillside. Above him, on either side, the campfires shone through broken stumps of trees.

Now there were women among these people, a barefoot girl in a ragged gown helping a lame man walk along, two or three older women in black shawls carrying baskets of bread. Watching these women with their baskets, all coming from the same direction, he realized they were getting the food from the same place. The army was feeding them. He went backward along this trail, looking for women with full baskets, following the scent of fresh bread in the air.

CHAPTER FOUR

It seemed to Markos that he only dozed for a few moments, but when he started awake, he was alone, lying against the cold beach stones, and the Scythian was gone. Around him was mostly quiet. The bank behind him rose up into a crust of grass and roots that overhung him and hid him from the inland side. He could hear the patter and hiss of the waves on the shore, and not much else. The attack on Chrysopolis must have succeeded, or else failed. The stone-throwers had stopped, anyway, and nobody was shouting. He tried to judge by the stars how much of the night had passed and finally he recognized just the tail of the Big Bear as she went down beyond the northern edge of the world.

He had slept then for hours. He sat up, hungry. Then something dropped down almost on top of him, and with a cold terror he shrank back, seeing the round helmet, the soldier's cloak. But it was the Scythian. He pulled the helmet off and his long hair hung down over his shoulders. Out of a fold of the cloak he pulled several loaves of flat bread and some apples.

Markos gave a low cry, and seized the food. Stuffing his mouth full, he said, "What's going on out there, anyway?" Gesturing with his hands, very broadly. The bread was tough, sour, crunchy with chaff, and he could not eat it fast enough.

The Scythian shrugged. He fished a little flask also out of his cloak, turning away from Markos to keep it out of reach, and took a long drink. He pointed to the water again, turned to Markos, and said distinctly, "Swim. Swim."

Markos said, "No. I can't."

The Scythian jabbed one thumb at himself. "I. Swim." Pointed at Markos. "You." And handed him the flask in almost the same motion.

Markos grabbed the flask eagerly, and drank; it was bitter watery raki, but he was thirsty enough to drink anything. Wiping his mouth, he said, "No, you can't swim me. That's crazy. You're crazy. There has to be some other way." He looked east, up over the bank behind him. Past the top of the stone-thrower he could see the hills there distinctly now; the dawn was coming. "We could find a boat."

The Scythian said something in gibberish, but the tone was an unmistakable sneer. Markos said, "You idiot. You don't know what I'm saying to you, and I don't care what you say to me. And I've got the raki." He waggled the flask, which was nearly empty anyway. The Scythian scowled at him, but abruptly he stiffened, and his head turned, listening behind him.

Markos ate the last of the apples, even the cores. The Scythian went a few steps closer to the lapping water. Swallowing, his ears clear of the sounds of chewing, now even Markos could hear the noises coming across the strait, even, rhythmic splashing, like something with many feet walking on the waves.

He grunted, went up beside the Scythian, trying to see out there over the jumping wind-ruffled strait. The day was coming on stronger with each breath. The air around him was crystalline, transparent, blue, still shadowy, and on the crumpled surface of the water out there he could see long dark shapes creeping toward him.

At first he could only make out a few. Then, in a blink, as if they took form out of the blue shadows, he saw many more coming after the first, standing out to weather the tip of the seawall, a flock of beetles striding over the water, lunging on oars toward this shore.

Then, a rising yell of voices sounded behind him, up on the bank. A horn blew. There was a general calling of voices and running of feet, and then wood timbers squealed and creaked. Markos spun around. Above the level of the bank he could see just the top of the nearest tower, and as he laid his eyes on it, the high square framework swayed and turned. He could hear the grinding of some kind of winch. They were bringing the stone-thrower around to fire on the oncoming boats.

Steadily, as the light grew, and the sky turned pale as an eggshell behind it, he saw more. He saw how by fits and jerks the great cumbersome scaffold twitched around. He felt in his mind the completion of that arc. The boats were still far out there. The stone-thrower would get off a couple of shots, Markos saw, and by then, the rest of the great war-machines would be shooting, too, volleys of stones onto the helpless boats, crushing their beetle shells.

Even as he took this all in, before his eyes the Scythian was wheeling around toward the stone-throwers. With one hand gathering his long white hair and with the other jamming his helmet on. He had found a sword, somewhere, and he pulled it out of his belt. Markos, frozen with amazement, watched him tramp back up the little strip of beach toward the bank. He was going to take on the stone-throwers. The idea was mad; Markos expected him at every stride to realize this, to turn, to come back, to look for some other way, but then the Scythian bounded easily up the bank and was gone.

Markos yelled, astonished. He was alone on the beach, unarmed, unarmored, with the rebels just above him readying shot, and a tide of strangers racing in across the strait toward him. He ran across the beach and scrambled up the bank after the Scythian.

He came up onto the top of the bank almost directly in front of the great stone-thrower. The front of its high four-sided tower, wide at the foot and narrow on top, loomed over a dozen soldiers lining up before it. They were getting ready to fire it. Their arms reaching up grasped the veil of ropes hanging down, and a tremendous yell went up from them, from the rest of the crew, back behind the stone-thrower, from anybody around them.

The Scythian was running straight at the men on the ropes, the sword in one hand. The soldiers bent, gathering the ropes over their shoulders, pulling down the crosswise rack at the end of the short arm. The long arm began to creak, rising. Markos plowed to a stop, his mouth open to yell, and the Scythian bashed in through the row of soldiers on the ropes.

As he crashed through their midst, the sword slashed right and left, right and left, through the ropes, knocking them loose or cutting right through them.

Freed, the short, weighted arm hung a moment almost in balance with the long one, and then jerked upward again. The stumps of the ropes dangled down out of reach of the men on the ground. Staggered at the first, unexpected attack, the soldiers gathered at once, and launched themselves at the Scythian.

He had charged straight through them. Now he bounded up onto the bottom edge of the stone-thrower's tower, onto the crossbeam there, and slashed down with the sword, hacking the few ropes left within their reach, and the crew all pulled back out of his range.

"Get help!" one of the soldiers yelled. "Get a bow!"

All along the line of the great stone-throwers, the other

crews were dragging their machines around to meet the onslaught
of the boats. A single trumpet sounded, and then a whole screeching chorus of them. On the bank of the shore, Markos shouted to
his Scythian, "Run! Run!" and waved his arm, and the Scythian
with one last stroke of his sword to keep the crew back bounded
down off that tower and raced toward the next.

Nobody chased him. From inland trumpets were sounding
in wild peals, like alarmed birds. Around the crippled stone-
thrower, its crew was turning to look over their shoulders, out
toward the Bosporus. Marcos turned his head that way, and a
whine rose in his throat.

In the full daylight now, boats stuffed with men covered the
whole narrow water from this shore far over to the other. The
first were crunching into the shallows, and the men inside leapt
out to heave them up onto the beach. Big and bushy-bearded,
unkempt as animals, these men carried long-handled axes;
swarming off the boats they rushed up the beach and for an instant disappeared from his view behind the overhang of the
bank.

Down the shore a little way, among the first line of boats,
was a dromon, without its spur. As it grated onto the shore, a
single rider bounded down into the leaping surf. The horse was
black; the rider wore a black helmet, a black cloak, no badge,
no ornament. On his curved shield was a painted image, the
Virgin, by the colors, Protectress of Constantinople. He galloped through the surf onto the beach, wheeled and gestured,
and then bounded his horse up the bank, out of the range of
Markos's vision.

Markos made for the nearest cover, which was in around
the side of the crippled stone-thrower. These big axemen and
their black bat of a leader did not look Roman to him, in spite

of his icon. The army behind the stone-throwers looked more Roman. The crewmen on the stone-thrower. He wondered what to do.

That crew was shouting, pointing. One had climbed onto another's back, to reach a dangling rope, but now a yell of terror went up. The bushy tide off the boats was spilling up over the bank and rushing toward them.

The stone-thrower's crew turned and fled. Markos raced after them. Still reaching for the rope, the man sitting on the shoulders of his friend gave a screech and fell as his friend ran out from under him. Markos had lost his Scythian. He looked around wildly for the streaming white hair and saw only people running. The next stone-thrower stood idle, deserted, its ropes also shorn. Then the one beyond it suddenly let go a huge volley of stones.

He ducked down, although he was well out of their aim. From the shore behind him a roar rose, thousands of voices, hungry and furious, a bellowing like the wolves of hell, as wave after wave of beast-men surged up over the bank.

The hair on his whole body stood on end. The stone-thrower beside him was deserted; he climbed inside the framework of it. As he swung his leg over the huge footing beam, he turned and saw, looking inland through the back of the scaffold, a sea of round helmets marching toward him, their spears pricking the sky. The rebel army was finally waking up.

From some long-abandoned schoolbook the image leapt to Markos of the clashing rocks that crushed ships; he saw these two armies clashing together to crush him between them. He climbed up on the bracing between the crossbeams of the stone-thrower and scrambled into the dark space behind its hide cover.

The leather was stretched over the outside of the great timbers, and only on the front half; behind it he pulled himself onto
the crossbeams, holding on with his fingernails. The great tower
trembled. On either side, past the end of the stretched leather,
hordes of men pounded by, huge, bellowing, waving double-
bladed axes.

Ahead of him, through the scaffolding of the tower, he saw
the armor-shiny ranks of Roman soldiers pushing forward.
They had to get through the parked wagons, and that held them
up, broke up their ranks. They were on foot. Even Markos saw
they were not ready. Before they could set and lower their
spears the two rivers of bushy men with their axes struck.

A horn blew. He saw soldiers in red cloaks crumple backward and the Scythians trample over them. A moment later, the
soldiers were gone, buried under the flood of Scythians.

Trumpets sounded, behind him. Romans, he thought, glad-
hearted. Romans. He shifted along the beam to a place where
the leather was ripped, and he could see the shore. Another big
dromon was nosing into the beach, he could see only part of it,
loaded with horses, rearing and lashing out with their hoofs, like
waves of the sea turned into animals. A flood of other horsemen
bounded onto the shore, the horses' manes tossing, the limber
lashes of the riders' whips driving them on, the hoofs thrashing
up white water in plumes. Markos leaned back against the beam
and prayed to be invisible.

The horsemen thundered by, their trumpet sounded again,
and a moment after that, quiet fell. The uproar of the attacking
army faded away into the distance. Behind, where Markos could
see, only broken, bloodied bodies lay, in among overturned and
scattered wagons.

He clung to the crossbeam, afraid to move, but he could

hear that the roar and thunder of the fighting had gotten far away from him. Carefully he lowered himself down. A moment later, a hand fell on his arm from behind.

He spun around, gasping. Looming over him, his white-haired Scythian gave him an amused leer.

Markos gave a glad cry, but immediately the Scythian was pushing him forward, out of the shelter of the stone-thrower. Markos stiffened. The Scythian shoved him, good-natured, saying, "Boats. Boats." Markos stumbled out into the blazing early sunlight. Dazzled, he put his arm up. A moment later, axemen surrounded him and Raef.

He shrank behind his raised arms, but one of the axemen, big-bellied, hairy as an ox, grinned ear to ear, stood forward, and thrust his hand out.

"Raef Corbansson!"

Markos's Scythian gripped the outstretched hand and said something in that gibberish. Amazed, Markos saw they understood each other. They knew each other. They were talking like old friends. He let out his breath, relieved. He was going to get out of this alive. With a quick glance at the other, ugly, oversized axemen around him, he shouldered up beside his Scythian, his hands on his belt, trying to look as if he had never had a doubt.

⟶⊰⟵

Michael Lecapenus let his horse drop to a trot, and then drew rein; the battle was over. In the first shock they had won it. The whole of Delphinas's army was either dead, surrendered, or in flight, and the plan was to let those run so that some would get down to Phokas at Abydos and let him know what had happened here.

Basil had galloped up far ahead of them, in among the Varangians. He had sworn to be first at the charge and Michael believed he had fulfilled it. He himself was a good rider but he had never been able to keep up with Basil. He wiped his face with the bottom of his cloak, feeling mostly relief.

Nicephoros Ouranos rode up beside him. The rest of the Imperial officers had gone straggling after Basil, who would have a thousand orders for whoever caught up with him soonest. Nicephoros laid his hands on his saddlebows; his swarthy, bearded face was jubilant.

"That was easy enough."

Michael gave a little shake of his head. "Delphinas couldn't make the general of a troop of wall-guards."

Down there Basil had found the last of the fighting, a knot of Varangians surrounding some soldiers trying to defend something. At the Emperor's arrival the axemen hacked down the last rebel. "Phokas will be harder," Michael said. He had met Bardas Phokas once, and hated him, a pompous bully.

"We'll catch Phokas between us and the sea, with Romanus in Abydos, and an Imperial fleet off the coast. This is a major victory, Mica. The sun is shining on us again."

Michael grunted at him. He disliked it when Nicephoros called him by the boyhood name, as if they were still children in the gardens of the Great Palace, playing with wooden swords. "You're always inclined to be an optimist. We still have nobody. Phokas still has the tagmata. Every important commander in the Empire except you and me, Romanus Sclerus and Nicholas Kallinikos, either supports Phokas, or is staying out of it and waiting to see who wins. If Romanus should turn on us, and hand over Abydos to Phokas, or one of the admirals takes his fleet over, we'll be right back where we started, only worse."

He thought, If Delphinas's men had fired off the petroboloi just a little faster today, Basil could be rolling along the bottom of the Bosporus and we'd be looking for some mercy.

Nicephoros said, "Romanus is good."

"I hope so," said Michael. He liked Romanus.

Basil galloped up before them, his horse lathered and wild-eyed with excitement. But when the Emperor took off his black helmet his face was rigidly expressionless. Michael bowed down, deeply as being on a horse would let him.

"You were right, Nicephoros," Basil said. "They did set up the petroboloi on this side. It could have been a disaster. The victory is God's and the Virgin's, not ours." He tossed the helmet to one of the other men around him. Carefully he unslung the shield, with its painted icon, and hung it from his saddle-bow. A page ran up with a purple silk veil for it. "Still, giving all glory to God and the Holy Mother, I can't help but feel we did very well here."

His voice trembled a little. In spite of himself he was excited. His pale eyes sparkled with exhuberance. His calm a cool film over the fire inside.

Nicephoros said, "I think so, too, Sebastos," and Michael at the same time said, "I hope so, Sebastos."

Basil said, "God's is the glory." He gave Michael a hard look, as if Michael were doubting God. "We took Delphinas." He gestured behind him.

Two horsemen were leading a man on foot up the hill by a rope around his neck. The man on foot was half-naked. His head hung down. They had taken his boots off, so that he stumbled on the hard ground.

Nicephoros murmured, "So the daughters of Priam came before Agamemnon."

Michael sniffed. "That's a stretch." But he thought he would not like now to be Delphinas, who should never have let himself be taken alive.

Basil turned to him again. "I want to get this army back into the City before they start looking for loot. We need to reward them, quickly, very well."

Michael said, "Gold, and plenty of it."

Nicephoros said quietly, "Find out who put those petroboloi out of action."

Basil nodded. His hand lay gently on the top edge of the icon, wrapped up now and hanging on his saddlebows. His blue eyes looked out of a round, boyish face; he had always had a stare as if he could see through iron. He kept the hair of his head cropped short almost to the skull but his red beard hung down to his chest. The triumph still blazed in him but as ever his will ruled and now he was thinking over what to do next. "Get them down to the waterfront. Nicephoros can do the honors." Basil smiled suddenly. He knew how Nicephoros hated speaking, and he of course would be there, probably in with the guards, watching for every slip. "Then we're going back, so be ready."

"Sebastos," they both said, in unison, and bowed. Basil wheeled his horse and galloped off, trailing guards. Delphinas in his halter staggered along in his dust. It occurred to Michael that they could all be in Delphinas's shoes, or lack of shoes, in another month.

He tried to shrug off this foreboding. They had won a fine victory today, after all. Nicephoros, beside him, sat stiff in his saddle, his eyes glazed, his lips moving, obviously thinking up an oration. Michael avoided these moments, the speeches hard to do and easy to do wrong, praising everybody properly, in the right order, proud, but not too much, God's will be done after all, and the whole oration well decorated, the neat quip, the unexpected but utterly apt reference, wasted of course on a bunch of hairy Scythians.

Nicephoros turned toward him. "You'll translate, won't you? And leave out anything that goes off."

"Just tell them they're mighty warriors, and give them all the gold he's willing to hand over," Michael said. "And hope they're willing to stay for one more battle."

Nicephoros laughed. "After today?" He leaned out and gave Michael a punch in the arm. "You worry too much." He reined his horse around and followed Basil at an easy lope. Michael followed, hoping he was right.

CHAPTER FIVE

"They'll take us back over to the City by dark," Leif the Icelander said. He whacked Raef hard on the back again. "You'll like it there. I remember how you liked Chersonese."

"Yes. Chersonese," Raef said, thinking how that had ended. "When did you get here?"

"About two months ago. I left Kiev when we heard about what happened between you two and the Knyaz." Leif shrugged. "I didn't see there was anything we could do to help you, so Ulf and I just came on down here. The Emperor here took us right on. Blud's the commander, you remember him, that windbag. There's already a lot of Norse and Swedes here, not all of them came through Kiev incidentally. They call themselves Varangians down here, but they aren't all Varanger, if you follow me."

They were walking along the bank of the sea-neck toward Chrysopolis. The hot sun blazed down. On their right was the bank, overhanging the ditch where Raef had prowled around the night before, and on the left the flat ground that had been the enemy camp.

The place was blasted as if a storm had struck it. The hillsides looked much closer than he remembered. The tents were almost all stripped down and either gone or in shreds. Crowds of the Varangians were picking over the place, taking whatever they found. What they did not want made piles of broken gear on the dusty ground. Here and there a wagon stood, horses dozing in their traces, while people slung corpses into the back.

He shortened his gaze to Leif. "And of course when you left Kiev you and Ulf took all our money for safekeeping."

Leif said, "Aaah," looking vaguely off.

"When did Blud get here?"

"Just a week ago. They rode in from the land side. They're saying there are six thousand of them, but there's nowhere near that many. Still, it's enough, with the rest of us, and the local guard." He gave a throaty, satisfied chuckle. "This Emperor here put us all on boats and shipped us over with barely enough time for them to eat a good meal first. And it worked. They weren't expecting us. Easy killing, that's what I like."

Raef said, "I suppose you have some of that money left?"

Leif swallowed, and his smile got stiff at the corners. "Now, listen, Goose."

"Don't call me that."

"You know, we thought you were dead. In fact, that's the rumor, all over. You're dead. No sense leaving that money for Pavo, right?"

Raef turned and spat at the sound of the name. They were coming up to the gateway into the city. On his left the three crosses still stood, but the bodies were gone. He thought of Ruskas, his chest cold, and glanced at Markos, who walked along beside him, whistling, noticing nothing. Markos could have been the fourth body up there. Townspeople streamed back and forth over the bridge from the land into the city. Out there a wagon lumbered off, piled up with dead men.

They turned to go into the gate. Ahead of them went another wagon, this one loaded with chests and folded tents: loot. Raef looked around at Leif again, toward the one solid thing he knew.

"Pavo is dead, too. You took our money, and I want it

back." Raef scuffed his bare feet on the pavement of the gate-way. From its height he looked over his shoulder toward the battleground. The ground was chewed to dust and nothing grew on it. "Who else is here? Ulf?"

"Oh, yes. Ulf wants to be an officer. They want us to make companies, centuries, they call them. Bjorn the Christian came down with Blud. You remember Blud, from Kiev, the boyar who tried to kill Volodymyr once? He's our commander but I don't know how long that will last. Things are bad in Kiev, I hear. I've no wish to go back there." They had come to the archway of the gate, where the road narrowed between two stone walls.

The gate was yawning wide. The streams of people coming in and out were so thick they all slowed down, wove among each other, pushed by one another. The men wore brimless hats, what Raef already thought of as Greek hats, in bright colors. The women were wrapped in shawls. Along the curved stone wall sat two beggars in rags, jiggling their cups, and a half-naked man clawing himself with his fingernails and screaming, "Jesus! Je-sus!" At the gate itself a shrine was built into the wall, a pretty tiled niche beneath a rounded arch, with a painting of the Mother, her face a perfect oval inside the blue frame of her cloak. The hood of the cloak was cleverly figured into the arch. The icon was set a little low for Raef and seemed to be looking at his chin. Markos bent his knee before it and made his cross sign. The banners flying above the gate were blue, with strange figures, and flapped heavily in the wind off the strait.

Inside Chrysopolis most of the houses were well boarded up, although people came and went out the gateways. Big, with pitched tile roofs, the houses stood close together, flush with the streets, the streets narrow and uneven and paved, where they were, with slabs of rock. Just inside the gate three Greek soldiers on horseback fell in beside the Varanger and moved along with them, keeping them to the main way down to the harbor.

Raef said, "I'm certainly not taking orders from Blud. Dobrynya didn't come, hah?" On either side behind a covered row of archways there were boarded doors and windows. Maybe shops. He was hungry, and he began to look for a way to get food. These people here seemed all closed up, probably afraid of looting.

"No," Leif said, and elbowed him. "Dobrynya stayed with Volodymyr. Miss the honeyed bastard, do you?"

"I'll kill him if I ever see him again." Empty threat. A Greek horseman jogged along beside them, the shaft of the lance laid down across the horse's armored shoulder, the long point glinting. The horse was chunky, short-coupled, with heavy fringes on its hoofs, its neck arched almost round. Each step precise, muscular.

Ahead lay the harbor, blue between two curls of white rock, rows of buildings slightly pink in the sunlight. The long breakwater stretching out from the eastern side kept the inshore water still as a pond. All along the shallows, like shark's teeth, there were boats drawn up in rows. The broad paved ground before them was already packed with Varanger. Varangians. Raef stopped, not wanting to wait out in the sun. Markos said, "Boats," and pointed. Across the crowd a horseman turned toward them, not a Greek, but Blud himself, the Rus boyar, his long red hair flowing.

He wended his way through the gathered Varangians, leaning down to speak to men on either side of him, reach out to shake a hand. Markos stepped back toward Raef and spoke a string of Greek, including the word "boats," and Raef nodded.

"Yes. Soon. Aren't you thirsty?" He made a gesture for drinking. "Look for someplace we can eat." Markos's face sharpened, eager, as if he understood that. Leif was talking at the shout to Blud, waving his hands, and Blud made a broad gesture in answer.

Leif turned around, his chest out. "I told you Ulf wanted to be an officer? Well, they want me, now. I guess they liked how I handled the landing."

"Good for you." Markos was waving to him. Raef went along the back of the crowd, toward another of the covered walkways, where he saw a door opening.

Walking along at his elbow, Leif said, "He says to wait here, the Hertysomething is coming, wait until you hear some of these Greek titles. Hekatoniarch, and—"

"Hektatontarch," Markos said crisply, falling in beside them. He gave Leif a brief, sideways, condescending look. They went into the shade of an archway, where the ground was paved with red tiles, and a fat man in an apron was just stepping out of an iron-braced wooden door.

Raef sniffed; he could smell meat inside, cooking, and bread. Markos stepped in front of him, stuck his chest out, and rattled off a stream of important-sounding Greek. The fat man looked unimpressed. He wore a tunic shiny with grease, two big wooden spoons thrust into the belt. He crossed his arms over his chest, standing on his threshold, and his eyes flicked from Markos to Raef and Leif behind him. In dansker, he said, "Drink? Drink?"

"Drink," Raef said. He gestured to Leif. "He'll pay." He glanced off toward the waterfront and saw other people already coming this way. "Pay him," he said to Leif. "Whatever it is. This isn't going to last long. I'll take it from what you owe me."

Leif made a pleasant face and produced a coin. "Notice. This is gold. One of yours, even." He spoke to the Greek in Greek.

At the sign of the gold the fat man's whole face changed, and he nipped the coin out of Leif's hand and disappeared inside the doorway. A moment later two other men brought out a bench, and the fat man himself returned with a jug and a cup. By the time he had filled the cup there was a long line of men waiting at the door for their own.

Raef took the jug. Leif gave the fat man another piece of gold and yammered some more, and they moved the bench up close to the front of the archway, still in the shade, and sat down. They passed the cup in silence, Leif on one hand, Raef in the middle, Markos on the other.

A servant of the fat man's brought out a big dish full of some brown mush, studded with little green bits, and a pile of flatbread, and set it on a stool in front of them. Raef took some of the bread and used it to scoop some of the mush into his mouth. The servant lingered, his hand thrust out.

"Pay him." Raef nudged Leif with his elbow. "This is good."

Leif shrugged and dug more coins from his purse. "There's a limit to this. I remember how you used to play dice."

The archway now was crowded with Varangians, and out of the mass Bjorn the Christian appeared. Raef had fought beside him in Chersonese. He was Raef's age, dark-haired, with a silver cross around his neck; but he crossed himself differently than Markos. "Is that the Goose? By God, it is."

"Don't call me that."

His mouth full of food, Leif said to Bjorn, "He was on the bank when we landed. Who do you think did that damage to the tray-buckets?" He nodded at Raef. "You remember Bjorn."

Bjorn shook Raef's hand and sat down on the other end of the bench. "The last time I saw you your ears were pinned back and you were running hard. Where's your brother?"

Raef shook his head. They did not deserve to know what had happened with Conn, and he had no words to tell them anyway. He didn't much like the remark about his ears. He worked on feeding himself; the mush was made of beans and meat and onion, deliciously flavored with some kind of spice. Bjorn shrugged. "Well, though, I'm glad to see you, you're good luck." He gave Leif a wise look. "I always said that."

Leif's smile twisted. "Sometimes you said that. Sometimes you said it the other way."

Raef said, "I'm not going to be here very long, lucky or no. I'm taking my gold back and going home, wherever that is."

Leif glanced at Bjorn, and then turned earnestly back to Raef. "Son, son, listen, there's a lot to be done here. This Emperor, he's made some mistakes, but he's got a good head for war, and he likes to fight. We could all get rich. If I'm already an officer—"

Bjorn said, "Anyhow, you're supposed to be dead, and you're not. Let's drink to that."

Raef turned and took the cup from Markos. The Greek was staring out at the crowded waterfront. Leaning around Raef, Leif tried out some of his broken Greek, and Markos laughed and shook his head and said something. Leif turned to Raef. "I asked him how he came to be with you. He's not a fighter, is he?"

"He rowed on a ship with me," Raef said. He handed the

cup on to Bjorn. "That cross thing turned out handy for you, didn't it? Back in Kiev."

Bjorn said, "I rowed on a ship with you myself, several times, remember? And I told you the Christians would win. It's not my doing, don't walk on me about it."

Raef said nothing. He didn't believe very much of anything, and he saw no reason to change that, even if the kings were all Christ-lovers. He ate the last of the bread, his belly full for the first time he could remember, and of the best food he had eaten in months.

Bjorn said, "So that's how you got down here? Pulling an oar? That's a waste. You'd do well to throw in with us, they give us the best of everything, lots of drink, everybody's got a new shirt." He gave a pointed look at Raef's filthy tunic, torn and muddy, with most of the fancy stitching in shreds.

"Dobrynya gave you all new shirts." Raef nodded off across the waterfront. "What's going on here?"

He could see, above the crowd, that a little group of horsemen was riding in from the street. Some soldiers led the way, carrying banners. As they passed, a lot of the Varangians stood up, which surprised him.

Leif went out to the sunlight and shaded his eyes. "Oh. A couple of the generals. They're going to talk to us, I suppose. They do this a lot. We have to stand up. They'd like us to kneel." Leif chuckled. "But Michael there, he's a good friendly fellow, and he speaks dansker." He pointed, craning his neck from side to side to see over the heads of the other men. "That's Nicephoros Ouranos, we're getting the good treatment, he's another friend of the Emperor's, and a very good eye for a battleground."

Raef said, "What are they doing?" More and more of the

Varangians were standing, which seemed strange to him, when they had just won these men's battle for them. At the middle of the waterfront, the little crowd of Greek horsemen had drawn up between the Varangians and the boats. The horses were beautiful, with arched slender necks, legs fine and long as a spider's, their tails flying. Most of the Greeks formed a line facing the Varangians, with the banners flapping overhead, but two rode forward and began talking both at once. The Varangians hushed obediently to listen. Now most of them were on their feet, and even Raef had to stand to see.

"What's he saying?" He frowned. At first he couldn't untangle the two skeins of words, the two languages at the same time. The men behind the two speakers drew his gaze, behind the brilliant blue and red coats, the gilded hats: someone back there meant more than all the rest together, although he couldn't have said which or why.

Leif shrugged. "Nicephoros says we've captured the big head man here, Karlos Dolphins, something like that."

Markos said suddenly, in a withering voice, "Delphinas." He had stood up on the bench, and Bjorn had, too, Raef noticed.

Leif twitched his hand at him. "And we've taken hundreds of prisoners, and the Emperor, in token of his great love for us, is bestowing a lot of titles on us, and of course there will be plenty of gold."

Midway through his last words a roar went up from the crowd around the waterfront. Raef looked around him. All around him, every other man in the crowd had risen to his feet. Next, he thought, they would be standing in neat rows. He looked at the two speakers at the front of them all.

He had thought he recognized the voice: one of the two men speaking was the Greek from Chersonese. Raef could not remember his name—Michael something. Leif had said that name. The man on his right was brawny, dark, with a blue shirt that winked silver down the front and on the sleeves. He spoke, but in Greek, and Michael turned it into dansker. Now, fixing his interest on him, Raef could pick it out.

"We will give with full hands to the men who so well served the Emperor, in Christ's name. My lord Blud, I see you there."

There was more to this originally than Michael bothered with, the man in the blue shirt actually going on after Michael was done, with some very elaborate gestures. Blud rode his horse forward through the crowd. His face was red with excitement. Halfway there he dismounted from his horse, and walked up the rest of the way. Raef could barely see him for the crowd between them. He heard his voice, booming with stiff new Greek.

Michael greeted him in the smooth-flowing dansker Raef remembered from Chersonese, that was like the language that Raef spoke but not really.

"Well, hail, chief of the Varangians. This was a great victory, the first we hope of many to come. You charged straight into the teeth of the enemy. Tell me who served the Emperor and Our Lord Jesus Christ best of all."

The Varanger gave a shout, and stamped their feet on the ground. Leif himself bellowed. His fists shot up and shook in the air. Raef looked around for the bench, pushed Markos off, and sat back down again. Markos poked him, outraged, gabbled in Greek, and Raef shoved him. All this was reminding him of Chersonese, and Conn, and what he had lost.

He thought of Conn, lying still in the yellow cave under Kiev, and his heart clenched, a pain unbearable.

Blud was shouting names, calling out men to come forward and get some reward. Raef folded his arms on his chest. He had seen this before, in Chersonese, the magic of money. The whole crowd pressed forward, eager, and he had to stand up again to watch.

Blud said, "My lords, we're glad to win honor in your cause. You should know that Tryggve Haraldsson, here, killed six with his own hand."

Tryggve Haraldsson bending and stooping up, a big red-bearded man, who took many thanks from Michael and the magister Nicephoros in his blue coat, and who bowed down so deep his beard must have hit the ground. Put the gold in the dirt, Raef thought, and they will stoop far to get it. It would take all afternoon to give it out, and he began to think of going somewhere else. He yawned.

"Raef!"

He startled, all over. Just in front of him, fat bellowing Leif was turning to wheel his arm at him, so that everybody swung around to look. Leif's voice boomed out again. "Nothing good would have happened if Raef Corbansson here hadn't taken out those tray-buckets."

Across the way, the Greek Michael's head swiveled around, his gaze turning hard toward Leif. Blud said, "Yes, they'd have wiped out a few boats with those stone-throwers, if they'd gotten them into action. But we would still have won."

"Still," Leif bellowed, "it was Raef who took them down. Give him some gold!"

"I'm not one of you," Raef said. "I'm just on my way home, and I don't want anything but what's due me." He kicked Leif, trying to get him to be quiet.

The men in front were passing something around toward

him. Michael up there still peered sharply at him across the heads of the crowd, his brows curled. Raef avoided his stare. He hoped Michael had forgotten him. The other man, Nicephoros Ouranos, was passing out money by the handful, and all the Varanger were lining up to get some.

In a flurry of words and gestures, Nicephoros Ouranos handed on the whole duty to Blud, and went back with the rest of the Greeks, and on their nimble-legged horses they filed slowly away down the waterfront.

The man in front of Leif turned, and handed something round and heavy to Raef. He hardly noticed it, was watching what was going on up at the waterfront; he could see that as each man took his handful of gold, Blud and his men were herding him onto a boat at the wharf. As each boat was filled, the oarsmen rowed out onto the pond of the harbor. Several boats were already waiting there but none had yet started onto the sea. They would go when everybody was together. He said, "This is going to take a while."

Markos pointed, pushed Raef, said something in Greek, his uptilted face earnest, and pushed him again.

Leif said, "He says the Emperor was there. He says you should have bowed, at least."

"One of those two was the Emperor?" Raef said, startled.

"No—one of the others. Among the guards. He does that, Basil, he goes about plain as an ordinary man, to watch what goes on."

Raef snorted at him. "He sounds like an ordinary man to me." He looked down at the thing in his hand, a round of solid gold, an armband, chased with runes, and held it out to Markos. "Here."

Markos seized it, his face lighting. See, Raef thought, now

it's me he loves. Leif said, "Come on. How can I pay you back if you just give it away?"

"You will," Raef said. "But you've got to earn it yourself." He reached down for the cup, and looked for the jug again.

⸎

The Emperor Basil had never won a battle before. He was amazed at how good it felt.

He had been Emperor since he was two years old, a great weight over him, a vague but dazzling sense of intention. Yet it had meant nothing. He did nothing. Other men wielded the power in his place, in his name, at first because he was just a boy.

When he got too old to ignore, when he proved that unlike his younger brother Constantine, his co-Emperor, he would not be ignored, bought off with sweetmeats, women, ceremonies, toys, groveling, they began trying to replace him. Make him nothing.

One by one, he had outmanuvered them, the generals and courtiers, regents and stepfathers, his uncle, his own mother. Now, when he was thirty-two, the age when Alexander died, perhaps the age when Jesus died, Basil of the Makedonai had come down to his last rival.

He thought it was a sign from God, this victory at Chrysopolis. Surely it was a sign from God.

One month before this, when Bardas Phokas's vanguard invested the City on the Bosporus, everybody had thought it was the end, even his friends. He would finally lose Constantinople and the crown. Now, with no army, with every major army either against him or neutral, he had won this victory. It was God's will. He swelled, fierce with the righteousness of God.

The Imperial dromon was carrying him back across the Bosporus to the palace, leaving Chrysopolis while the Varangians were still loading onto their boats. There were hundreds of the northerners, if not thousands, and they were loud and drunk, and getting them across was going to take the rest of the day. In the stern of his dromon the Emperor stood looking back at them as they grew smaller in the distance. He was already thinking about Phokas, down at Abydos.

The dromon rowed quickly through the sea gate and out onto the open water. Outside the shelter of the harbor, a cutting wind swept along the Bosporus and he shrugged his cloak up. The grunting oarsmen in the deck below strained and heaved their oars through the choppy sea. Basil's retinue had followed him onto the rear deck, and a glance over his shoulder brought Michael quickly to him, Michael Lecapenos, his cousin, the perfect courtier and his oldest friend.

"Sebastos." Bending in his customary graceful bow. Straightening, he stood, his head bowed, his eyes lowered. He would say nothing more until Basil spoke first. Michael was a master of practice; the scribblers came to him for advice on court customs, the minute details of address, of precedence.

Basil put his hands on the railing. The figured tapestry of the ceremonial around him mostly was ridiculous to him but it kept the others busy and in order. Just sometimes it seemed to him justified.

He lifted his face again into the bright touch of the wind. The whole narrow sea sparkled around him, glistening with his triumph. He felt as if he might float off the ground in his buoyant delight. The oarsmen were struggling against the current and the City seemed to stand still in the distance behind them. The shore was black with men waiting for their boats.

"They're a rough bunch," he said.

"The Varangians, Sebastos."

"I don't think I'll see them soon in the Nineteen Couches."

Michael cast a quick look toward his pets, back on the shore behind them. Their yells came floating over the water. Michael loved these men, Basil knew, their rough animal spirit, their courage and their strength, the simplicity of their code of honor; he was responsible for the large numbers of them in the Guards, even before this last contingent arrived from Kiev. Michael, the perfect Roman gentleman, great-grandson of an Emperor, loved the rude Scythian.

Michael said, "We shall teach them civility, Sebastos."

"Don't unteach them how to fight. They were very good at that." A slave crept across the deck on his knees, holding out a cup of wine. The dromon was rocking in the chop and the slave braced himself with his free hand. Basil sipped the wine; the slave stayed to hold the cup for him. "But we should have planned ahead to take out the petroboloi."

Michael bowed again, wordless. Not his decision. They were moving slowly across the strait now, letting the strong Black Sea current take them past the mouth of the great harbor tucked along the City's eastern edge. The blue water of the Horn was flecked with sails, people out working even while the Empire hung in the balance at Chrysopolis. South in the Propontis more long white sails lay flat to the wind on the blue sea. Ahead the City jutted out into the narrows, a high point surrounded on three sides by deep water. On the southeastern side, its gray seawall, its brushy slopes, were topped with the white walls and tiled roofs of the Great Palace. Around the foot of the point the seawalls carried the cliff straight down into the water, massive cliffs of brick and stone, lashed along their footings by the endless white surf.

The dromon was swinging around to skirt the point and the feel of the wind changed; the sea rolled in longer swells. Ahead loomed the little pharos that marked the Imperial harbor. The oarsmen struggled with the tumultuous currents where the narrow Bosporus spilled into the Propontis. For a while they seemed to be moving backward. The sun was at its height, glaring on the bright water. Dimly, Basil heard cheering voices ahead of him.

He looked up; the dromon was edging into the harbor of the Bucoleon and it rocked under him, sliding off the rough water of the open sea onto the calm. Up there the hill along the side of the Bucoleon Palace was black with people, and they were all shouting his name.

He straightened, his elation abruptly dissipated, uncomfortably aware of himself in their eyes like an image in a curved glass. He felt the pressure of their attention all over him, making him somebody else. Vulnerable. He reminded himself that all the great work remained to be done. He could still fail. Ahead, over the narrowing strip of flat water between his dromon and the wharf, the landing was jammed with people waiting. He considered how many there would have been had he lost. Above him the long balcony of the Bucoleon Palace loomed out over the seawall, the doorways like eyes looking out toward Asia.

He said, "Michael. Bring me the icon."

The dromon eased alongside the pier, smooth as a door opening, and two boatmen leapt onto the pier to make the stern fast. Michael came up with the image of the Holy Mother in its purple silk wrapping and Basil took it carefully into his arms; he bent and kissed the top. Then, with his eyes straight ahead, so that he might not meet the gaze of ordinary men, he went up the step and onto the solid stone of the landing, and guards and boatmen backed out of the way and knelt and put their heads to the ground.

"Basileus!" the crowd chanted. They stood in rows along the back of the landing. "Basileus, Kosmokrator, Victor of the World!" In unison, they went down on their faces. Basil went in through them, heading for the stairs, Michael and Ouranos coming after, rising up to the Great Palace of Constantinople.

CHAPTER SIX

Raef gaped around at the immense chaos around him, the boiling and bellowing of the harbor, above it the greatest city he had ever seen, looming on its hilltops, covering the whole long promontory above the bay. A seawall, studded with towers, divided the water from the land on both sides of the narrow finger of the bay. Along the foot of the wall were moorings and wharfs; ships and boats and barges swarmed through the harbor, churning the water to a constant chop, so great a crowd that the fleet bringing the Varangians back seemed just a few more hulls.

Raef's boat reached a wharf, and tied up; Leif said, "We'll go ashore here, come on." He had to shout to be heard over the racket around them. Seagulls shrieked and people screamed from ship to ship, while beside their boat the men of two little cargo barges fought over the same mooring, thrashing at each other with oars. Three naked children, screeching and fighting, ran along the wharf, plunged into the water, and slithered back out again. Slaves splashed around in the shallows unloading the two barges even while the two crews fought to tie up.

Leif led him into one of the towers in the wall, which housed a stairway. The stair was narrow and people were coming down in a steady stream and they had to push along the wall to get by. At the top of the stair they came out on a broad street running above the harborside, the inner edge packed with open stalls, crowds of people moving along past them. Under the flapping awnings he saw slick silver piles of fish.

Beyond the harbor street, the hills rose. Roofs and walls stretched away up the slopes and down the shore as far as he could see. Some were huge, some little shacks, some ruined and some beautiful, all jumbled together, climbing so steeply up the slopes they seemed sometimes on top of one another. White walls, red roofs. The round golden domes of churches stood in collars of plumed trees. He smelled fish and smoke, and shit, and rotting seaweed. There were people everywhere, working on the water and walking along the street and sitting along the wall begging. Leif nudged him.

"Don't worry, boy. You'll get your head around it, it's not so big."

Markos was saying, "Raef. Raef."

Raef turned to him, startled; the Greek was holding out his hands, his eyes actually full of tears. Raef stupidly put his hands out and was engulfed, the young man kissing his cheek, pressing their faces together, saying things Raef was glad not to understand. Then he backed away. He pointed up the street.

Leif, looking on, a peculiar glint in his eye, said, "He says his house is down there, by the water, on this side from St. Mamas. That's where we're going, St. Mamas."

Raef said, "Good-bye, then." He put his hand out, and Markos took it and again the young sailor lunged at him, hugged him, made kissing sounds by his ears, and seemed about to burst in tears. Then he turned and went off. Raef stood watching him.

Leif said, "Had a good time with him, I guess."

Raef said, "Not really." He turned and looked up the hill again, all around him, at all these houses, these streets, winding cobbled pathways up and around, narrow, filthy, loud, wonderful. Up there, a row of tall white stones marched across the top of the hill; they looked more like trees than stones. A great arched bridge crossed the gap between two hillsides. At the southernmost end of the land, the slopes dipped and then rose again to a broad wedge of plain, where the bright blue sky framed a glistening dome, like the top third of the sun.

Leif said, "Come on, then. We're supposed to stay at St. Mamas and not get in trouble with all these Greeks. St. Mamas is a big old monastery, it was abandoned, in the bad times they had, and we've got it now."

"What kind of trouble?" Raef followed him through the fish market. The cobblestones were slippery with scales. Women with bright red faces screeched from the shade of the awnings, shining fish oozing out of their hands. A string of small children trailed after him and Leif. Half the Varangians had come into the City before them, and the street ahead of them was jammed with a mass of big men shouting in dansker.

"Well, this," Leif said. "Come on." He led the way skirting the back edge of the mob, which all seemed to be standing around one house. Before they had passed entirely by, three girls rushed up toward them.

None of them wore very much, one had hair of an impossible orange, and their faces were all covered with powder. They shrieked something, over and over. The redhead pulled open her thin tunic and thrust out her breasts, round and flowing, the nipples painted red. Another kicked up her leg, showing her thigh to the hip, and the third wheeled, bent over, and lifted her skirt, turning up her round white bottom, neatly divided down the middle into her dark bush and through the little purse beneath.

Leif said, "We have our own whores. Just keep on. They want too much anyway." They left the girls behind, who now burst into snarls.

"What were they saying?" Raef asked. "Po—pro ay—" He tried to remember the sounds.

"Porne' p'lutimos," Leif said. " 'Whore—not too expensive.' But they are. That's why we got in trouble. Come on." Most of the Varangians were behind them now, and the street seemed emptier. The sun was setting and dark shadows filled the steep lanes they passed on their left. They walked some way back along the bay, which was long and deep, and steadily narrowing. Raef knew he would find a river flowing into the small end of it. There was enough room in the harbor for hundreds of ships and Raef thought there could be hundreds of ships here right now.

They climbed away from the water. A scarred gray cat watched him from a roof. A man led past a donkey with two great jugs balanced on its back, cups dangling from its harness; the waterman's long tired shout was like a donkey's bray. On every corner a cobbler sat making shoes. An old woman hurried past them, wrapped in a black shawl and carrying a covered basket that streamed the aroma of fresh bread. The street wound up a slope, each step steeper, until the rise turned into a staircase. Just inside the door of a little shop near the crest, a man was shaving strips of meat from a huge roast hanging from the ceiling. Several bright-colored shirts hung drying below a window just above him.

Leif said, "We get in trouble because the Greeks are always trying to cheat, it seems to me. Everything's one price, but then suddenly it's another, and they're all cousins and got this particular thing special, but they're giving it to you cheap, because they like you so much. Buy it, and you find out a day later you could have gotten it for half the price. Whatever it was." His voice was suddenly tired. "They have everything here. Everything you can imagine, all the food, the drink, the ways of enjoying yourself, the women, everything. All the time. For a price. Makes you wonder."

They went down a second flight of steps, to another street, and followed that winding way between scattered houses and fields, fallow gardens and bare-branched winter orchards. Off to the left, beyond the naked heads of trees, the top of a high wall loomed, a square tower, and then, beyond and to the right, another tower. The street wound down the hill and leveled out. Another wall crossed it, and they went through an open, untended gate and were back on the harbor street again.

Here the bay was considerably narrower. They were well past the main harbor. Small boats floated on the blue surface, and lay hauled up on the shelving beach below the seawall. Ahead a bridge ran on stone arches across the water to the other side. They walked through a dense clump of houses, where women leaned on their windowsills, talking. Many shouted greetings as they passed.

"They booed when we rode in," Leif said. "It's a wonderful thing, victory."

Raef laughed. They walked onto the bridge; the water ran green and slow through only the middle four arches, although he could see fresh tidelines well up the side of the footings, green rags of weed on the stone piers, clumps of black shells. He could smell the old salt from here. Looking back over his right shoulder, he could see the City rise and spread outward beyond him like a great staircase.

Leif said, "That's St. Mamas."

Raef turned to look. Leif was pointing ahead of them, where the street was taking them. The beaten dirt and rocks of the path led through a gate, out toward open land, another wall, with a great sprawl of buildings inside it. Some of the buildings had no roofs. Leif's hand hooked inside Raef's arm. "And this is Maria Day-dokes, where we really live."

He pulled Raef around off the street, toward a half-ruined wall. They could have climbed over as easily but Leif went in through the gate. Climbing vines covered the crossbeam on the gateway and Raef had to duck to keep the tangled half-dead twigs out of his hair. Inside the gate, across a little trampled courtyard, was a squat sway-backed building with a tiled roof, and behind it the back of the old ruined wall, taller by half again, stone and brick, sprouting tufts of grass.

Raef followed Leif inside, ducking his head under the lintel of this door, too. The place was dark, and packed with other men. The air reeked of garlic and lemon. At Leif's appearance a general roar of greeting went up. Leif shouted back, clapped Raef on the shoulder, and pulled him off to a table in one corner. The other men there moved out of the way and let them sit down with their backs to the wall, the best places.

One of the others was Ulf, the lean, silent, redheaded Norseman who had been in the raid on Chersonese. He looked at Raef and said, "It is you. You're supposed to be dead."

Leif said, "He wants the money back."

"Does he," Ulf said, and smiled, and pushed the cup toward Raef. "Where's Raven?"

Raef said nothing, took the cup, and drank; it was raki, and strong, and he spent a long while with it so that he had no reason to answer Ulf. Leif said, "In any case, he's not here. Bjorn!"

He waved his arm across the packed drinking hall. "Might as well have the full set," he said. "You're staying on with us, then?"

"I haven't made my mind up," Raef said. The raki was

swelling his head, light and airy and expansive. He wanted to go out into the City, he wanted to see what there was here; at the same time he was suddenly very tired and getting drunk fast.

Ulf sat cracking his knuckles together, his face taut. After a while, he said, "Well, that could be good, I guess." Raef wondered what he meant. Ulf said, "Listen, there's a lot of gold here. A lot of power. The Greeks are soft."

Leif said, "Quiet down, wind-mouth."

Raef said, "You owe me money. You in particular. I don't care about the Greeks."

Someone else was coming through the mob toward them, big Blud, the Kievite princeling who thought he was a Viking. Raef had known him when he and Conn fought for Prince Volodymyr. His red hair was combed and curled like a woman's. He wore a gaudy blue cloak with a big pin fastening it at his shoulder, Greek style. His gaze was fixed on Raef. He said, "Volodymyr cannot know you are here."

Raef leaned back, his hands on the table. "Here, I don't think Volodymyr matters much."

A whoop went up from the surrounding men, and Blud's face flattened, his lips tight, but he made no other move, which convinced Raef he was right. Blud said, "Nobody matters in this company but me, oathbreaker."

"Who are you to call me an oathbreaker? I'm the Varanger, not you. I gave my free pledge to a prince and took it back when he dropped his end of it. But I've never knelt to anybody. That's the free part."

All around, men were pressing in close to hear. A ripple of comment ran through them. Blud lifted his head, insulted, more insulted because people were listening, and put his hand on the sword under his cloak. Raef leaned back; he had no weapon. Then Leif said quickly, "If it hadn't been for Raef, a lot of us would be lying at the bottom of that narrows, anyway. He's not in your company, Blud, leave off."

Blud's face relaxed. "All right. I'll overlook it." He puffed himself up as if that was a big thing.

Ulf said, "I'll drink to that."

Raef said, "I'll drink to anything right now," and emptied the cup. More raki appeared. He decided against going out into the City and for getting completely drunk.

Later, a man he had seen earlier that day, at the waterfront, came up to the other side of the table. Tryggve Haraldsson was Norse, like Ulf; he seemed all red beard and broad shoulders. In a voice that hissed between yellow mottled teeth he told Raef, "Listen, you. I've been here six years now, I was with the Emperor when we got our tails whacked in Bulgaria, and the real leader of this warband is me, not Blud, just remember that."

He snorted off. Raef glanced at Leif, who shrugged one shoulder. They were eating little bits of pepper stuffed with meat and cheese, like tiny savory pies. Drunk, repentant, Leif had given him a handful of money. "I don't have that much left, but you should have most of it." Raef made a pouch for it in his sleeve. He was thinking maybe he would stay here awhile.

Blud came back, sank down beside him on the bench, and whispered, "Whatever was between you and Volodymyr, I can deal with."

Raef was eating something else now, a sweet seed-filled fruit whose name he had forgotten. He thought, No, you can't. Unless you can bring back my cousin, no. But he said nothing.

Leif said, "This is Laissa." He had a girl, very young,

seated comfortably on his lap. Her hair was a mass of yellow curls and she had a lot of paint on her mouth. She did not look Greek. She did not look more than twelve years old.

She snuggled happily against Leif. "You won? Who's this?"

Leif was busily quarrying with his hand down the front of her clothes. "That's Raef. He already has a boyfriend."

Raef growled at him. He didn't want whores and Leif probably remembered that. Lamps shone on all the rafters now, and in niches on the walls. The place was jammed with Varangians.

"Laissa." Leif kissed her noisily with his tongue on the ear. "Go get us some more raki."

The girl slid off his lap. She was barefoot, naked under the thin shabby dress; her little breasts were still just buds, her body thin as a boy's.

Raef said, "Young, isn't she?"

Leif shrugged. "They start young here. The older ones are sour, and they can make you sick."

"Thanks for telling me that."

"Oh, you can count on me," Leif said. "Come stay in our hold. There will be empty beds."

"I'm clearly not going very far," Raef said. He smothered down a yawn. His head was swimming and he was considering lying down on the floor. "All right. Show me where I can sleep."

———⚬———

Leif took him through the gate and into the monastery, where he spent the rest of the night on a cot with a lumpy straw mattress in a big room with a hundred other lumpy beds. Drunk as he was he could not sleep at once, but thought of the teeming City, and the delicious food, and all the different kinds of people here.

Then he dreamed of the hawk, but when he woke, he could not remember anything save her reproachful red eye.

"If I have failed you," he said aloud, "leave me alone."

When he said this he was out in the back of the long mud-colored building, making water into a bush. Past the bush was a broken wall, in places knocked down to the basement course, and part of a tower: some old fortress fallen to pieces. Lichens and moss grew bright on the shady part of the wall. He looked back, over his shoulder, at the path that led through the gate and back past the taverna, over the bridge, into the City again, and he was moving that way even before he had his drawers closed.

The first thing he did was search out one of the street cobblers, and have him make him a pair of shoes. The cobbler did this with surprising speed, his hands deft with knife and awl, and many already cut pieces to hand in his wooden box. He had Raef stand on a piece of leather and ran a piece of chalk around the outsides of his feet, murmuring at the shapes that came of this. In the end Raef gave him some of the money, and the shoes fit very well.

He was learning more Greek; he knew how to say a few numbers. At a streetside grill he bought a slab of bread wrapped around some roasted meat and got a few more words.

He climbed up through the twisting lanes and staircases to the top of the hill, toward the row of white stone trees, which turned out to be a long straight street lined with pillars and paved with square blocks, worn smooth and glossy between the wheel ruts. Among the pillars people sat selling fruit and nuts, grilled meats, uncut cloth and cloth made into shirts and cloaks, strings of beads, jewels, little boxes full of wonderful tastes and smells. In the middle of the street, on a tall column, was a statue of someone in a crested helmet, pointing.

He wandered down the stone street looking at everything and soon came to another long straight paved street lined with pillars, this one along the ridge of the peninsula. This level ground led toward the tip of the promontory, high over the Bosporus, and he started that way. No one paid any heed to him in the steady coming and going of the crowd; he was just one of hundreds walking along.

The road climbed along the ridge, and then dipped down into a little valley, and curved to the west. Off on his right hand now was the broad white flank of a wall that seemed to stretch out even larger than the hill. It shut off his view of the sea, and the street was leading him down anyway into a narrower way, between high buildings, toward a towering pillared gate. Statues of horses topped the gate. The great golden dome of the church shone against the sky, beyond. He saw guards there, spears. He turned and went the other way.

Ahead of him, coming toward him, he saw Blud, riding his dark gray horse, his hair and beard combed slickly down, several of his Rus warriors around him. Blud did not notice Raef at all; the Kievite's eyes were fixed on that golden dome in the distance.

Raef went along the street awhile, looking around at everything, until he realized the whole rest of the crowd was stopping on the side of the street, among the rows of white columns, and turning to face the road.

He stood, looking around, and then suddenly all the people

were getting down on their knees. The old man beside him tugged at his tunic, trying to get him to kneel also, and he backed off, into the cover of a pillar.

There was a procession coming down the street, girls in white gowns and veiled headdresses, then other girls, carrying silver chimes and drums and flutes, and then four burly men carrying a big box on poles. Through the window in the side of the box, he saw a woman sitting inside.

She was looking out the window, and for a moment he thought she looked straight at him. A veil covered the bottom of her face, but her eyes were huge, dark, deep, and beautiful. For a moment she looked toward him, and in her eyes he saw a desperate, aimless longing, a shimmering desire. She looked forward again after a moment. He went along awhile, keeping up with her, watching her through the window but she never turned toward him again.

He stopped. The procession took her on out of his sight. Around him people were getting off their knees and going on as before, some calling out wares to sell, and others hurrying around, back and forth, and a few just leaning against the columns, watching the crowd go by. Raef was hungry. He went down toward the harbor to find something to eat.

CHAPTER SEVEN

The Great Palace—where Septimius Severus had lived, where Constantine, Justinian, Theodosius, Heraclius, the first Basil, Nicephoros Phokas, and John, the heroes of the past, had lived— covered the southeastern part of the promontory overlooking the sea. It was not one building but many, churches and halls, meeting chambers and dining chambers and courtyards, all linked with paths and adorned with gardens and plantings of trees, kept perfect by hundreds of servants. The oldest part of the palace was the Daphne Palace, on the opposite side of the grounds from the great domed basilica of the Holy Wisdom. It was not a single building either, but several set around a courtyard, too small now for the Imperial government.

In one of these rooms, away from the bustle of the court, the Emperor Basil had caused a big table to be set up, and covered with sand, and on it he and his closest men laid out the fields of battles. On this table now were the Bosporus and Chrysopolis. They were starting to change it to model Abydos, at the far end of the narrow seas, on the lip of the Mediterranean, where Bardas Phokas was laying siege to the city and proclaiming himself Emperor.

Nicephoros Ouranos laid his chart down on the corner of the table opposite Basil and bent over the sand. A crew of slaves waited behind him while he traced lines on the surface. Basil watched from the other side. In a corner of the raised edge that kept the sand in place was a pile of the little lead markers they used as soldiers, and he fingered one of them, watching

Nicephoros smooth the hills of Chrysopolis into the low ground around Abydos.

"The Varangians, now." Basil turned toward Michael Lecapenus, standing against the side wall with the others. "How trustworthy are they?"

Michael lifted his head, steady-eyed. "The men who've done long service here, yes. Tryggve Haraldsson, for instance. There's an Icelander named Leif who is very competent. They have their honor, and they've sworn pledges. Some, I'd say, though, are less honorable than others."

Nicephoros traced lines in the sand and put down some tiny white blocks for buildings where Abydos was, even before they had shaped the flow of the sea-neck there. He held his beard back with one hand to keep it out of the sand while he worked. Basil's gaze went again to the white city; now he was thinking about Bardas Phokas, his enemy, and his siege of Abydos.

They were related, somehow, second cousins. Bardas had been at court, when Basil was a little boy and Bardas's uncle was Emperor, Basil's stepfather, the gruff old Nicephoros Phokas, whom his mother had married after his father died. This current Phokas had been a grown man then, one of a crowd of soldiers who hung around the Emperor, and Basil had never known him well.

He knew well of him. The Phocaides produced great generals like a stud farm for strategists. Bardas was one of them. He had beaten Bulgars, Saracens, and other Romans, calm, fierce, forceful. Victor in a dozen wars.

Until Chrysopolis, Basil had never won a battle. He had lost a few, disastrously.

Phokas was an Achilles, far-known for his many single

combats. Basil had never fought anyone hand to hand to the death.

So the sand table. On the sand table he practiced, and when he made mistakes he didn't lose armies. He saw the land down there, where he and Phokas would meet, and tried to see what Phokas would see. What Phokas would do. Trying to think ahead of him, trying to get in front of him.

Trying to see larger than a single battle at Abydos.

Phokas could simply wait until they met on the battlefield, where God would decide. Basil himself had no intention of waiting. Even while Nicephoros Ouranos looked at his chart, and leaned over the sand, shaping the jagged coast by Abydos, Basil moved over to line up the enemy soldiers in front of it.

"You've put the bargain to those men in Chrysopolis?" Over a thousand of Delphinas's army had surrendered, and were still camped outside the wall there.

Nicephoros straightened, the chart in his hand. "They've all sworn allegiance to you. I promised them they would not have to walk in the triumph and we'd keep up their pay."

Basil said, "Are they going to be of any use? They didn't do much against the Varangians."

"The Varangians surprised them. They're not tagmata, but they'll serve. Most of them still have their arms and gear."

"I don't want them in the City. For that matter I don't want them in Chrysopolis." He juggled a little marker, his eyes on Nicephoros's chart, where he recognized the red stripe of the long land road down from Chrysopolis to Abydos. "My brother can lead an army for once. We'll send him down to Abydos with them."

From the men around him there rose, not so much a

protest, but a kind of general exhalation of alarm. Nicephoros was watching him owlishly. Basil said, "They'll think they're the Spartans, with an Emperor leading them."

"His Imperial Majesty isn't a soldier," Nicephoros said.

Under his breath, Michael Lecapenus muttered, "He'll get lost."

Basil laughed. He nodded at Nicephoros. "You go with them, Nicephoros. You'll be the actual commander. Take your century." Nicephoros's Ouranian Guard, although only eighty men, were the finest troops in the city, given the Varangians' uncertain loyalty. "You should leave within a few weeks. My brother will march slowly, so you can secure the ground as you go."

"Sebastos."

He turned to Leo Agyros, another of the men standing by the wall. "What do the astrologers say?"

"Sebastos." Leo came forward, slender, his hair pale as wax, his eyes hollow from reading old books. "There are several very advantageous times to fight, and some very bad ones also. The planets are moving rapidly in and out of conjunction, and there are some critical cusps, particularly lunar cusps. I am drawing up a chart. I'll bring it in tomorrow."

They talked awhile of that. Michael Lecapenus was staring down at the sand table; Nicephoros directed the slaves as they laid down the blue silk that formed the water in the model. Basil drew back from them. In his mind questing after his enemy. Bardas Phokas had been scheming to become Emperor since his uncle wore the crown. It was his life's work, and he was getting older, running out of time. He would not wait. He knew all the chances, all the openings possible, he would use every advantage. Basil turned to Leo.

"Read the stars also for Phokas."

"Sebastos."

To Michael, he said, "With Nicephoros gone I want some of the Varangians up here for a guard." He would keep them constantly under his eyes. If he found good men he could shape them into a company, a reliable core.

Michael said, "I'd suggest Tryggve Haraldsson to command. Not Blud Sveneldsson."

That was the Kievite. "What's wrong with Blud Sveneldsson?" He struggled a little with the outlandish name.

"He's a prince of the Rus, with his own castle there, he's got ideas of his own worth, and I think Vladimir sent him to us to get him out of the way. He was up here just today, trying to get in to see you, he said, without a summons or even any previous request. But the gate was closed."

Basil gathered up another handful of markers. He wished sometimes he could make real soldiers out of lead, and not have to deal with living people. God would decide the battle to come, of course, but he had noticed God favored men with crack armies. He crossed himself with the hand holding the lead soldiers. "There has to be some way to make sure of them."

"Sebastos."

———⚬———

Raef walked along the street beside the seawall, eating a handful of sticky, sweet-skinned fruit with long slim pits. A harsh wind was blowing, and heavy-bellied dark clouds rolled over the northeastern sky. The plume-branched trees that grew here bent to the wind and their long arms swung like mill vanes. The fishing boats were coming in early, the quays jammed with bright-painted prows, rows of men struggling to get their catch in. He walked past a man sitting on top of the seawall, packing his nets back into a barrel. A cat lay in the lee of the wall, licking its paw.

He raised his eyes, looking across the bay to the far side, just as busy, just as crowded. Then one of the men behind him gave a yell, and rushed up to him: it was Markos.

He had just come in from fishing, he was filthy with fish scales and guts and blood and he had a net over his shoulder, but he was beaming at Raef. He said, with a grin, "Pull. Now!" and waved his arm, and Raef laughed and followed him.

Markos dropped in quickly beside him, chattering away in Greek. From his gestures and the few familiar words, Raef gathered he had just caught every fish in the sea, the net so full they had strained to bring it in and only God had kept it from bursting apart. They went up along the harbor, past another church. The snow was light, and melted as soon as it struck the ground. The winding way led down again toward the water, where the bay pinched in very narrow. Markos's house was on the shore, in a walled compound with its own wharf.

Markos led him through the arched front door into a covered courtyard, roaring and shouting in Greek, and from the houses on either side of the compound women came out, wiping their hands, carrying children, pulling on their shawls. By the wharf a few men turned around. Markos shouted again, and one of the women threw her hands up, and dashed forward. She bowed down before Raef as if he were an idol, and then flung her arms around him sobbing.

Raef held her off a little; he could make out from her gabble of words that she was Markos's mother, that he had saved her only son. Finally he got her to stand away from him, and by then, they were all around him.

Markos said names, and the two other men smiled broadly at him and bowed. The older one, bald and short, was clearly Markos's father. He took Raef's hand and wrung it, smiling, while the mother wept some more and patted him. His sisters came up around her, two little girls, and one almost as old as he was, with big dark eyes; Raef looked at her and wanted to keep on looking at her for a while.

Then the crowd drew back to let another old woman approach him, sobbing. She, too, was wrapped in black shawls. She fell on him like a hewn tree. Raef caught her and held her up. She kept saying Ruskas's name, and Markos was babbling on, and he realized she was Ruskas's widow.

At this, he made her sit down, unknotted the corner of his sleeve, and emptied the money onto her lap. It was all the money he had gotten from Leif, including several pieces of gold.

A cry went up from the packed onlookers. Most of the family had gathered around them now. Markos's mother put her hands to her mouth, and Ruskas's widow, her face crinkled with bewilderment, bent and picked up the money, and let it run through her fingers, a shower of silver and gold.

Raef licked his lips, trying to get some words together to explain this. Markos was shouting at him, and he understood most of that: "What are you doing? What are you doing? You saved me. We owe you everything."

"You save me," Raef said, and to the widow, "Ruskas save me."

Markos said, "No, you idiot—oh."

Then they were all hanging on him, Ruskas's widow clutching his hand, wailing, more in grief again than in happiness over the money. She said Ruskas's name, over and over, and sobbed on Raef's hand, and kissed it. "I love you, I love you," she said. He thought she meant Ruskas; her pain over Ruskas made his heart hurt. The family brought out bread and cheese and meat, and more of the delicious sticky fruits with the long pits. He sat among them, trying to talk to them in Greek. He could catch a lot of words but how they connected escaped him. Markos's pretty sister smiled at him, lowered her eyes, and then looked up at him again through her long lashes, and he felt the quick clutch in his groin, the fire in his gut. His face grew hot. In the middle of her family she could do this all she wished.

They passed around a jug of raki; the more he drank, the faster he could speak Greek, although fewer people understood him. Markos's father talked to him for a long time, very intently, sometimes pounding on his knee for emphasis, about body and will and nature, and whether there were two of them. After a while Raef realized he was talking about Jesus, or perhaps the Father God, or, since two was a constant word, both of them.

He got away from there before dark, although they all begged and cajoled him and offered him more food and raki. He went up again to the harbor street in the softly falling snow. The snow melted as soon as it hit the ground but the cobbles were wet and slippery. Three turnings up from Markos's house he came on the street that led to the St. Mamas bridge. In the drifting whiteness some women who had been selling fruit and nuts there were packing up their wares.

He crossed the bridge over the black water and came to the taverna. The door stood open in spite of the snow and the light of lanterns spilled yellow into the blue darkness. Several

Varangians were scattered around the big room, one of them Ulf. On a stool near the door sat the tavern-keeper's wife, a barrel-shaped woman with beautiful eyes and a soft round chin in an aging face. She wore the front of her hair curled in a stiff arch over her brow. She gave him a looking over as he went by. A few of the Varangians said greetings to him and he waved. Ulf was sitting at the table in the corner, where they had all sat the night before, and Raef slid down onto the bench, his back to the wall.

The girl Laissa came up. "Are you hungry? What do you want?" Whoever she was, she was not the daughter of the woman on the stool: her hair was pale as flax.

"Where's Leif?"

"I don't belong to Leif," she said, and leaned her hip against his arm, giving him a look down the front of her dress. He put his hand on her side and pushed her away.

"Go home to your mama, girl. Grow up."

Her face turned bright red; to his surprise, he saw tears in her eyes, and she flounced away, her chin up in the air. Ulf laughed.

"She hasn't got a mama. Probably wishes she did." He gestured toward the woman on the stool. "What I heard, she was a street brat, an orphan, before old Maria took her in. They think she's from somewhere else. That name's not Greek. They think maybe her parents died on the pilgrimage."

Raef grunted in his chest. "She still doesn't have to be a whore." But he was ashamed of mistreating her. She was coming back, carrying an ewer and a cup, her eyelashes stuck together with tears. She dropped the cup on the table and slammed the ewer down next to it and marched off. A moment later she was climbing into the lap of another of the Varangians. Raef reached for the ewer and filled the cup. He had no money anymore, and he had to drink while he could.

—◦—

Around dark, Leif came back with a crowd of other men. The woman Maria got off her stool and went into the back of the taverna, and she and Laissa and the tavern-keeper himself, a fat bald man named Gregorios, began to bring out platters of beans and lentils and onions. Maria and Gregorios were married and kissed each other loudly whenever they passed each other. The Varangians cheered whenever they saw them and Maria flirted her skirt at them and laughed. All around the taverna lamps glowed. Leif sat down with Ulf and Raef and they ate. Red-headed Tryggve came in, to a general hail of greetings. The air was getting close and loud.

Then around the door there was a bustle of importance, two men came in with lamps, and somebody in a big helmet followed, stood in front of them all, and shouted, in mispronounced dansker, "Hail, the victors of Chrysopolis!"

The Varangians all howled back, congratulating themselves with a drunken joyous lust. Several other Greeks had come in behind the big helmet and they stood under the light up there making ceremonial noises. Raef put his back to the wall behind him; he did not want to be part of these men. But then, through the crowd, he saw Michael, the Greek from Chersonese, coming straight toward him.

A few men spoke to Michael, as he walked by, and the Greek gave them smooth smiles, and a few words, and his hand to shake, without breaking stride. He came up to the front of the table and glanced at Leif and Ulf, who both slid down out of the way to the next table.

Michael sat down opposite Raef. "So," he said, not smiling now. Not especially friendly. "Raef Corbansson, once again."

Raef said, "What is it, magister?" He remembered the other word, which Leif had mangled, on the waterfront at Chrysopolis. "Hetaireiarch?" Which meant, he knew, Michael was the real general of this band, whatever the Varangians said.

Michael waved off the mushed syllables. In spite of his gray hair he was not old: somewhere in his thirties. He said, "Do you remember me?"

Raef said, "Enough. Not all the names."

"Michael Lecapenus," said the Greek. "And a variety of other things, two of which you mentioned. What matters to you now is that I am a friend of the Emperor's, God give him many years, and he expects you to be one of these Varangians who will appear before the Imperial Family tomorrow, after the triumph."

Raef sat still a moment, taking this in. He thought a great pit yawned before him, full of flames and delights. After a moment, he said, "I'm not part of this army. I just happened to get caught in between you and the bunch at Chrysopolis. The last dealings I had with you, you stole a whole city out from under me. Why do I want to appear, as you say, before these Imperial Family people?"

Michael's fingers tapped on the table. His eyes narrowed a little. "Listen to me. You gave the Empire great service at Chrysopolis. Come and be presented to the Emperors, see some of the palace, let them reward you, and then go. Your friend Leif here"—he shot a glance at Leif, who slipped farther away down the bench—"has orders concerning the triumph. You go with him. I will be with you all the way, to escort you in." His gaze flickered over Raef's clothes. "Try to wear something clean."

Raef sat silent for another moment. He remembered the wall where the long straight street curved down into the dark chasm between buildings; that was the palace, behind that wall, he thought, nearby that golden dome, and here was a chance to see it. Michael's tone rankled with him. He reminded himself he was the son of a king, however awful the means, of a mother greater than kings. He said, "I'll wear my freshest leaves and skins. Magister."

Michael did not move. Above his elegantly trimmed beard his features showed no expression. He seemed to be thinking over his words. Finally, he said, "I remember the problems you and your brother gave Vladimir. That proud and free kind of thing may awe some barefoot barbarian prince, but here, we judge men by civilized standards. You don't even have words for those standards, and I don't expect them of you. But I'm sure even you can show some discipline and follow a few orders."

Raef lifted his eyebrows. "The Varangians won the battle at Chrysopolis. You should be bowing to them."

Michael shook his head. Abruptly he was getting to his feet. "I knew when I saw you here you were going to be trouble." He walked away across the taverna; some of the Varangians called to him and he waved, casual, as easy around them as he probably was up in the palace. At the front of the room, he joined the other Greeks, his back to Raef.

Raef turned, and his eyes met Leif's. The Icelander said, "Don't worry. We'll get to see the palace, like he says. They'll likely feed us, and they'll certainly give us more gold."

"That's all you think about," Raef said.

"What else is there?" Leif asked.

—◦—

In the eighth hour of the night, trailing three yawning guards, Basil rode out through the City. Wrapped in his black cloak he took his horse from the Hippodrome out down the Mese, with its white columns, to the Golden Gate, that looked out on the Propontis. Then he followed the road that ran along inside the enormous double wall that the Emperor Theodosius had built, centuries before, stretching from the Propontis to the Horn, the wall a hundred armies had attacked, and which had never been conquered. At the far end he rode back through the harbor toward the palace.

The streets were almost empty. Those few people he saw shrank back out of his way and were gone when he passed. He rode by the crowded stinking houses where the poor slept, the broad walls of the powerful, the shops and stalls selling every possible thing now closed up for the night, the orchards where they grew apples and pears, the fields of cows that gave milk. Constantinople was overrun with cats and he saw many of them, darting across the street ahead of him and slithering over walls. He met the night watch, who prostrated themselves on a corner. He heard the bells of the churches ring the ninth hour. In the harbor the boats lay at anchor in the murmurous little waves. A late moon rose, thin as a claw.

He had ridden his city since his boyhood. He knew every street, every tree, every wall and house. He saw every stone that had been moved, every new leaf unfurled. He knew the people were afraid of him, but he loved them. He loved their hearts. In the past they had risen up in mobs to defend themselves and their faith and their law. They had battled for the holy images, they had driven out some Emperors and put others on the throne. It was the mob in the Hippodrome, after John Tzimisces's coup, demanding to see him and Constantine, that had kept them alive. He still remembered standing there in the doorway, looking at the butchered body of the old Emperor, the previous usurper, and telling himself he would be next.

The City sustained him. Without it he would have gone down long before. Holding it, loving it, ruling it, he was always Emperor no matter who said what elsewhere. All these people, selling and buying, sewing and nursing and cooking, fishing and making jewelry and pottery and weaving silk, the thousands of them now and gone back through the centuries to the first Constantine who brought them here, all those hands moving, all those hearts and souls, they sustained him. He only impersonated them. They were the City. And the City was the Empire. And the Empire was the World.

CHAPTER EIGHT

The Emperor Constantine, splendid in his golden breastplate, stood proudly in the center of the Imperial dressing chamber, inviting the admiration of his household. He loved being looked at. He was blond and tall, sleekly groomed like a great race-horse, every gesture practiced and assured. The three eunuchs responsible for his jewels, his clothes, and his shoes stood respectfully with their heads turned slightly to one side, eyes downcast, waiting to be called on, and his wife was silent, but his three daughters babbled with compliments, with adoration, his golden reflection gleaming in their eyes.

The Emperor Basil, wearing the same clothes he had worn and slept in for the past three days, watched from a couch by the wall. They could not start the triumph until the fourth hour, deemed most auspicious by the priests. Soon enough, they would leave, to assemble by the Golden Gate for the parade into the City, but until then Basil had nothing to do.

The Empress Helena sat opposite him, pretending not to see him. They hated each other. Basil disliked women in general but Helena he especially loathed. Once, in his childhood, he and Constantine had been betrothed to Bulgarian princesses; when they told him this, the news had made him physically sick. That prospect, fortunately, had disappeared with John Tzimisces's Bulgarian alliance. He watched Constantine strut around the hall to the applause of the little Porphyrogenitae and thought of drowning them all, like a litter of kittens.

He had since then refused to marry. Constantine had

married, when they came of age, because so many of the
ceremonies required an Empress, representative of the Holy
Mother, Protectress of Constantinople. One of them had to
be sacrificed, therefore, and Constantine had been entirely
willing. He loved pleasure, and women for him were a pleasure.

Helena had seemed meek and obedient at the time, and she
was well educated and well bred; even Basil recognized that
she was beautiful. The three little girls were beautiful, although
Eudoxia, the eldest, was losing it under a layer of fat. She had
pocky skin, also, and a sour temper. Her mother had begun sug-
gesting husbands for her, but Basil declined them all. He meant
never to let any of the girls marry. Anyone they married, any
son they bore, would just become another rival. He thought
now Helena had finally begun to realize that.

He could put Eudoxia into a monastery. He could order Helena into a monastery, too, now that the little girls were getting
old enough to perform her functions.

The snippy one, Zoë, the middle girl, who was nine, came
dancing toward him, her face glowing. She was a small, delicate imitation of her mother. "Uncle Emperor," she said, in a
light, malicious voice, "Uncle Emperor, why aren't you beautiful, too?"

He stared at her, saying nothing, and she danced off
again. Constantine said, "It was my brother who won the victory we are currently celebrating. Let's remember that." His
perfect, condescending smile appeared, lips firmly closed
over his bad teeth.

Helena said, "It was Basil's hairy Scythians." She gave him
a single, fierce, furious glance. Her eyes were huge and dark.
She wore a long tunic covered with rubies and pearls; her

women waited behind her with her cloak, her crown. She hid her face for a moment behind a raised hand sheathed in gold rings. "Basil brought savages out of the woods to kill Romans."

Basil said, "They did a very fine job of it, too. I have several more Romans I'd like them to kill."

"And in a few days," Constantine said smoothly, "I shall go out, leading Romans, my dear wife, and recover the Asian side by spring. The hunting is so much better there and I shall be in the perfect position to enjoy it. Helena, my dear, I believe the horn is sounding." He nodded to one of the eunuchs, who bowed and went off to deliver this command. The other two stepped forward, precisely in unison, tall, slender, hairless, expressionless, dressed almost as richly as Constantine, one holding the Emperor's long red cloak with its emerald and diamond clasps, the other his golden helmet, chased like the breastplate with emblems of Christ and Troy and Alexander, its frothy red plume tipped with gold dust.

The girls lined up behind him, and Helena rose, shimmering red, with her emblems picked out in pearls down the front of the robe. Her women moved in around her, pulling her skirt straight, adjusting her shoes, her hair, and then putting on her crown. Without a glance at Basil, they all moved off, their servants around them, as if they traveled in some gilded ball of air and light, separate from everybody else in the world.

Basil stayed where he was. He would enter the parade later, and had less to do; he had only to get himself to the Golden Gate by the fourth hour. He was thinking of Phokas, down at Abydos. That army was bigger than the one at Chrysopolis, and Phokas would not allow himself to be surprised, as Delphinas had been. On the other hand, Phokas dared not lift the siege, not even to go meet Constantine's march toward him, for fear of looking as if he were retreating. His army would melt away if he retreated.

Outside, a church bell rang, and Basil crossed himself. The emptiness and silence of the hall soothed him like a cool balm. He leaned back, his eyes almost closed, imagining the lay of the land around Abydos, imagining his army attacking.

The perfect stillness cracked. A door opened at the far end of the hall. No one came through; they would wait for him. But it meant he had to go now. He straightened up. "I'm coming." His helmet sat on the floor by the couch and he scooped it up in one hand and tramped on out the door.

The triumph began gathering in a field outside the great wall that edged the city, and with the Greeks shouting them into lines the Varangians led off. In a crowd they walked in through the elaborate double gate, there, and up the paved white road called the Mese.

Michael Lecapenus and several other Greeks in helmets rode ahead, with somebody carrying a big white banner with blue runes on it. Raef walked next to Leif. Crowds always made him uneasy and he was beginning to regret this.

Behind them the rest of the Varangians tramped along, and somewhere back there was the Emperor himself.

At first they passed fields, and little clumps of houses, where the people stood cheering on their own doorsteps. The road had been swept, and scattered with fresh sawdust, which gave up a scent of roses. On either side were rows of columns, garlands looped between them, and wreaths of silk.

They climbed higher, into the City. Now crowds jammed both sides, and wherever the street widened out at all the whole space was packed. Children ran along beside them, screeching. As they passed, a number of people unfurled a great banner covered with runes and spread it out. The double row of columns turned outward, neatly forming the base of a broad square, and the parade started across to the other side. The thundering of the cheers made it impossible to hear the officers up there anyway. Every column crawled with onlookers. Raucous boys scrambled over the great bronze ox in the center of the square, screaming and waving pennants. Farther on, on a wooden platform, to the blasting of horns, painted wooden angels swayed on the ends of cords, carrying a crown.

With Leif on one side and Tryggve on the other he followed the Greek officers up and along the white stone backbone of the City, past little boys clinging to the leafy heads of the columns, and people crushed into the spaces between to scream and wave their arms at them. Ahead the great buildings of the palace loomed. Now the huge floating banner was turning smartly to the right, and through another archway. Above this archway was a tiny wagon pulled by four huge metal horses, and they walked beneath it out onto the crunching sand of an enormous racetrack.

All around the long oval were slopes layered for people to sit on, and they were packed. The screaming of the crowd met him like a wall of noise, intense, deafening, a single voice emanating from a vast expansive swarm. He was not ready for this and the wash of sound was like a blast that wiped his mind clean. Slowly he came back to himself. He cast his eyes quickly over the vast mountain of faces. He could not guess how many people there were. He thought he probably didn't know a number that big. He thought, It's true, then, this is the heart of the world.

They walked down the golden sand of the racetrack, with the whole parade following after. A row of columns ran along the center of the track. One was covered with odd figures, snakes, and a hawk, and another was sheathed in bright bronze that showed the Varangians, passing, as a streaming blob of motion across its surface. Around the sharp curve at the southmost end, a wall of two tiers of columns rose over them, cutting the sky into squares. Raef, looking up, saw in the spaces between the columns hundreds of people watching, some living, some statues.

Midway up the long side, Michael Lecapenus swung down from his horse, was leading them up the steps toward a tall square tower built into the slope of the arena. On the top was a silken purple canopy that flowed up and down in the wind; along the foot of it was a platform about ten feet high. Walking along beside them, calling directions, Michael got them all up the side steps onto this platform, standing in line again, facing the racetrack.

Now Raef could see everything at once, the whole great long open arena, filled with people, each a patch of color, each moving, shouting, looking on while the parade passed along beneath them, as if everything that had happened in Chrysopolis was for them alone.

He thought all of Hedeby would fit inside this oval. He remembered what Michael Lecapenus had said, that dansker had no words for the ways of Constantinople, and realized it was true. His gaze drifted down the line of monuments along the center strip, not pillars, more like the standing stones that stood on heights in Denmark and England, messages raised to gods. One was a dark green twisted column, with snakeheads at the top. He lowered his gaze to the parade.

The last of the Varangians were wandering along in a shambling pack, keeping no rank or order, gawking around at everything. The crowd now and again broke into jeers and screeches, and fierce yells in unison, as if they practiced, like musicians, at all striking the same note. They stamped their feet together, and clapped their hands. Great patches of them swung their arms back and forth, or rose and fell as one, making a game out of sitting there. Swaying and shifting across the broad stretch of the rising tiered seats they gave off a feeling of warm, comfortable pleasure in their own size. He thought, This is some kind of rite, like the water blessing.

A troop of horsemen followed the Varangians, trotting neatly in ten rows of eight riders each, their officers jogging along midway among them. The officers had red crests on their helmets and the ordinary riders black. The mob gave them one of their practiced cheers, in one voice, the same words.

"Ouranian! Ouranian!"

Raef shook himself; the great mob made him jumpy, he could not think. The crowd suddenly gave up a thunderous yell, and a shiver went down his spine. Down before them walked row on row of men in gaudy armor, and then four white horses in gold harness drew along a box on wheels, white and gold.

In the box stood a man in a helmet with a huge red plume. His armor shone like sunlight. His long red cloak rippled out behind him like a wing. He waved his sword over his head, one hand on the reins of his horses, and the crowd shrieked and pounded their feet on the ground and banged their hands together. The horses leapt and reared, their tasseled harnesses swaying.

Raef thought, That is the Emperor. He felt the excitement of the crowd as if they had picked him up and carried him away with them. His hands were locked together behind his back. His mind felt thick. He was breaking into a sweat.

After the Emperor, there came some more soldiers marching in neat rows, and then, all alone, a man with a rope around his neck, and no shoes.

He was trudging along, his head down. Raef remembered him from Chrysopolis, the general who had lost that battle, Delphinas. The crowd booed and hissed at him. He ignored them, dragging his feet along, his shoulders slumped.

Then, abruptly, the crowd grew still, not silent, there were too many for that, but hushed. Raef looked down the racetrack, where two men in black robes were walking into sight around the corner—monks, he thought. They walked one at each edge of the track, and each carried a picture in his arms, face out. After them, down the center of the course, rode a man all in black, carrying another picture. The mane of his black horse tossed, and it pulled impatient at the bit, its ankles slim as a girl's. The rider controlled it effortlessly, cradling the picture in his arm like a beloved. After him two more men walked into sight, placed like the first two on either side, so the four made a square around the rider in the middle.

All the people knelt down before these images, sinking down before and rising up after the great square had passed. Raef decided they were holy pictures. The rider looked neither right nor left, sat straight as a lance in his saddle, holding his horse to a flat walk. The painting in his arms was of a woman, cloaked in blue, with a child in her arms. Raef knew her, the Holy Mother, sacred even to him.

Then there was another troop of soldiers, and at last everybody circled off and the racetrack was empty, the sand rumpled and pocked from so many feet. The crowd settled down. Raef could see, looking nearby, that people were selling food and drink up and down the tiers, walking along with their goods in baskets before them. Down below him three men were opening up greasy-looking packages, and all around them people were turning and reaching. He smelled garlic and mushed lentils. He thought, These are all Markos. Two little boys clambered up onto the platform where the Varangians stood, and crouched there, staring at them.

The crowd gave a low, spreading growl of interest. The captive general Delphinas was walking out alone onto the racetrack below. Several armed guards came after him, and behind them, two men carrying a long pole. The people in the seats stirred to attention. A chorus of long jeering catcalls swelled and faded away. Delphinas strode up in front of the Varangians, but his gaze was aimed higher than they were. Raef twisted his head and looked up at the high square boxy tower behind him, under the fluttering purple silk.

So close under the tower, he could see nothing on top, but Delphinas could; he began to shout, directing his words up there, a defiant yell, with more spirit than he had shown walking into the place. Then, by chance, he saw the men with the pole, coming along behind him.

He staggered away. His hands went up. All his courage vanished. He wheeled toward the tower again, and cried out something in a piercing voice, a plea, this time. As the crowd began to laugh, he wheeled and ran.

The crowd whooped. Bits of food and garbage, shoes, dead flowers, rained down out of the tiered seats. Delphinas tried to escape between two of the standing stones in the center of the track, but the guards chased him down. He dodged them, turned back, raced the other way. When he eluded another guard, the crowd gave him a cheer. Then the guards dragged him down. They spread-eagled him on his face on the ground, screaming now, struggling, and the two men with the pole set about working the tip of it up between his legs into his body.

The crowd watched this with a lazy attention. The cries of the drink sellers sounded from all over the great arena. Eventually the two men with the pole began to use a small hammer to tap the pole deeper. Delphinas screamed, but he could not move; the pole held him fast. They had gotten a couple of feet of the pole into him and they were still pushing it deeper.

Leif said, "I saw a man get the bloodred eagle once."

"What was that like?"

"Not as boring as this." Leif laughed at his own joke. They were hoisting the pole up on end, with Delphinas stuck on the top like a spitted fish, the butt of the pole sliding into a hole in the ground.

Raef said, "He deserves it, the way he handled his army." He thought of Ruskas. Ruskas had been dead when he was hung up. He wondered how long it would take Delphinas to die, up there on the pole, what it felt like, and stirred his whole length, looking away.

Delphinas was still alive through the races that followed, his arms twitching, and his head, as the horses flew by raising dust in clouds, the whips cracking, the boxes of their carts tee-

tering on one big wheel at the impaled man's feet as they hurtled into the tight corner there. In the third race, the two carts
collided at that corner, and one of the horses got up with a broken leg and had to be killed. The crowd moaned over that. The
vast voice, the huge sensation of the mob, wore on Raef and he
began to think of going.

Then Michael Lecapenus was tapping him on the shoulder.
With Leif, Blud, Tryggve, and two other Varangians he followed
the Greek out through a door at the back of the platform.

CHAPTER NINE

They went down a spiraling staircase into a hallway, where another officer joined them, a very tall man dressed in an embroidered coat, carrying a short stick with a gold knob at each end. Michael turned and gave them all a sweeping, critical look, shrugged one shoulder in resignation, and led them away into the palace.

They went the length of the hall, past walls made of dark veined stone, polished smooth as glass, over a wide floor inlaid with images. Raef slowed, looking down at the floor. He saw fish down there. With the other men crowding past him he scanned the floor and saw that there were pictures all along it, artfully made of tiny chips of colored stone. A child holding a rabbit. A big clawed fanged tawny animal attacking a deer, in gouts and pools of blood. He thought the tawny animal was a lion. He had never seen one but he had heard stories of them, and he knew they had manes, like this one's. The image looked real and yet not real. Its eyes were shaped like human eyes, and the mane around its neck was a wild fringe of curlicues. Yet it almost seemed to move, its body coiled, its claws raking the deer's neck.

He had fallen behind the others and he walked on fast to catch up. They went out through a double door covered with figured metal onto a colonnaded porch. On either side of them now were several other great stone buildings, some roofed with domes, and some with peaks, like vast stone tents. Among the clustered buildings, there were gardens, and pavements, benches, ponds, rows of little tamed trees in pots, the whole place swarming with servants, working, going somewhere, carrying baskets and trays.

Michael was talking; looking around at all this, Raef was not paying much heed to him, and the Greek reached out and pulled on his arm to get his attention. "Listen. This is important. There are several people to be presented ahead of us, but in a few moments, we will come into the Imperial dinner chamber. You will stand in a single row behind me. The Emperor will call each of you forward separately. You will come forward up beside me, where the Emperor will present you with a gift, which will be substantial. A servant will present the gift, not the Emperor himself, of course. You will bow"—his bright eyes looking straight at Raef—"and kneel to accept the gift. After that you will touch your forehead to the floor, rise, and move back into line." He was still a moment, looking at each of them, but still, mostly at Raef. "The Emperor will speak only to me, not to you, and if for some reason you speak, you are not to speak to him, but only to me. Better you don't say anything. When you've all been presented you'll be dismissed, we will go into another room, where more gifts will await you, and we will discuss certain titles to be given you if you take long service with us."

Tryggve and the other two veteran guardsmen had obviously heard this before and looked bored. Blud was composing himself up straight as a flagstaff, putting his best face on, as if he entered into glory. His red beard glistened with oil. He smelled fragrant. Leif said, "That sounds good to me." He gave Raef a puzzled look. Michael and the other officer turned and led them through a doorway, into a broad, sunlit room.

The walls were all made of polished green stone, trimmed with gold at the corners and ceiling. Gold the brackets for the lamps, the pots for flowers. Heavy soft cloths lay here and there on the white stone floor. When Raef walked across one he felt the swirling patterns even through the soles of his new shoes. Soft music played but although he looked all around he saw no musicians. He guessed they were behind one of the hangings on the walls—he remembered the hangings in Volodymyr's palace at Kiev; these were bigger even than those. Detailed, colorful, sparkling in the light of the lamps, they showed scenes of deer and boars and horses, men on horses with spears killing deer and boars, chariots, lions, a great double curve of pillars, like the end of the racetrack outside. He smelled a delicious aroma of roasted meat, of bread, of something else, spicy, sweet.

Somewhere ahead of them a man was speaking in very odd Greek, halfway singing. When he stopped there was a little patter of applause. Raef drifted closer to the hanging with the lions. The claws, he saw, were golden thread in stitches too small for him to see. It delighted his eyes to look on this. He had seen nothing so beautiful before, even in Chersonese.

After a few more moments of doing nothing, they went down the hall. At the far end, in front of broad windows, on low couches, around some tables, were several people, many of them lying down.

Michael, in the lead, said something softly in Greek. The other officer walking beside him nodded and whispered back, and Raef caught enough to understand: "You're right, he's not here." Raef saw they were relieved about that. He wondered who they were glad not to see.

The two Greek officers lined up before the people on their couches, bowing very deeply, first, and then kneeling down, their heads bent to the floor. Michael managed to do this gracefully but the other man just looked like a slave. As the Varangians moved into line behind them, Raef looked up overhead, at the beautifully painted ceiling, blue and gold, from which lamps hung like stars. He stopped, when Blud in front of him stopped, and Leif behind him who was also gawking around walked into him. Raef knocked him backward. He wished suddenly he could take his new shoes off and work his toes into the soft floorcloth. He tore his gaze from the magnificent room to the people opposite them.

The man sprawled on the middle couch was probably the Emperor, tall and slender, fair-haired, in clothes crusted with jewels. Michael had stood again, at a word from the man on the couch, and was talking in Greek, with gestures; Raef could see he was going over the battle. The Emperor leaned elegantly on his arm. His skin shone as if polished. Jewels studded his ears, his throat, his chest, his hands. Listening to Michael he turned and looked at the Varangians and smiled, without meeting anybody's eyes, as if someone had pulled a string in the back of his head.

Raef was disappointed. This man just seemed vain and silly. He remembered the man in the parade, his radiance of power, and thought, It was just the armor, or the crowd. He thought, I am not bowing to him, I don't care what he gives me. Several other men sat and stood around the Emperor, silent, gorgeously dressed, clipped and trimmed like pet animals. Raef looked at the women.

They were sitting on the right side, on several couches, a dozen of them, in long draped gowns, with fancy cuffs and gold-bordered cloaks. They were giggling together. Two were little girls, pretty as wildflowers, with creamy white skin and blue-black hair, and there was an older girl, plain, fat, lavished out with gold necklace and rings in her ears. The other people standing around were obviously servants, but the center of them all was a woman he recognized at once: the woman he had seen carried in a box-chair on the great street.

All he had seen of her then was her eyes. What he remembered was the flash of longing and bottomless desire. Now he saw her without the veil. She had a wide red mouth, thick black hair under a jeweled hat, from which on either side hung thin pendants of white jewels that framed her face. Her eyes held him, even not looking at him, large and dark and direct, made larger and darker with paint. She lay on a low couch, propped on cushions, a girl beside her with a mass of flowers in her arms, and none of the flowers was as beautiful as she was.

Michael Lecapenus called Blud up to get his present, and the women all murmured and laughed and talked. As much by their looks as the words he overheard, Raef realized they were making fun of Blud, with his long beard and heavy boots. The black-haired woman laughed and said, "Rooooossss!" Blud didn't hear, or didn't care, knelt, banged his head on the floor, stepped back glowing, a gold brooch in his hand. Beside Raef, Leif muttered something under his breath; he didn't like this either.

Michael called Tryggve up, and the women cooed. They preferred his looks, in detail, as if they were choosing one horse over another. On all fours he had a horse look to him. Now he was upright, already sliding the fat gold ring up his arm. Michael said Raef's name.

He walked forward, and the women burst into cackles, at his slouch, his braided white hair, other words he could not catch. He stopped still, his knees locked, his back stiff. His skin felt rough under their examination. He felt like a slave, exposed for sale. He could feel the tiny prickling of all the crystals they wore. His temper, already warm, caught fire. He turned and stared into the beautiful eyes of the black-haired woman and said, as best he could, the Greek he had heard from the whores in the street, "Porne' p'lutimos?"

He didn't get it exactly right, but they understood it. His voice hit their talk like a dash of cold water; the pretty faces all froze, and the room fell into a sudden, momentary silence.

Then the black-haired woman reared up on her couch and let out a shrill, furious string of Greek, and pointed at him, and Michael Lecapenus was turning and heading for Raef, and Raef wheeled and made for the door, the woman still screaming, and Michael trying to catch up with him. Raef went through the doors, and outside again, in the open, he stopped and let Michael catch up to him.

Michael did not stop walking as he reached him. "I'm getting you out of here before anything worse happens." In stride, he took Raef by the arm and tried to get him walking forward. "Give her a moment and she'll be in there like Salome, demanding your head on a tray."

Raef resisted him, his feet planted. "I didn't get my gift," he said.

Michael wheeled around, his face dark with rage. "You are an idiot even for a letterless backcountry oar-pulling Scythian. Order, decorum, civility, doesn't any of that mean anything to you? How do you think the world works? By idiots like you doing just as they please? Come on." This time Raef let him pull him on across the pavement; he was in trouble, again, and he knew Michael was keeping a lot worse from happening to him than merely being thrown out.

The sun was going down. Servants were going around

lighting torches on the wall and columns, one every few yards. The open ground spread out like a field of fallen stars. Ahead was the big metal gateway into the hall with the wonderful marble floor, and then someone came up from one side, and spoke Michael's name.

Michael stopped, and whatever the other man said sent a look of panic across his face. He swore under his breath. He turned to Raef. "Come with me. And be quiet, for once."

Then they were going back, up the pavement. Before they reached the long elegant hall the man who had come for them turned right onto a walk trimmed with little bushes, and they followed. They passed through a colonnade, and went around a corner and in through a doorway into a well-lit room, full of men.

Raef went through the doorway after Michael, and was in the blaze of lights before he saw how many other men were standing around. None of them were Varangian. They wore the same kind of splendid clothes and glittering jewels as the Emperor. He knew now why the centurion had tried to salute his tunic that night in the enemy camp. He still wore that tunic, but if they recognized it now beneath the layers of grime they would know it wasn't his.

The room was smaller than the dining hall, the walls pierced with several windows. A few of the Greeks there turned and stared at him and a little laughter rose. Uneasy, he followed on Michael's heels; the other men bowed and muttered greetings, and Michael spoke, smooth, assured. Raef felt gooseflesh all over his skin from the people looking at him.

Half the room belonged to a big boxed-in table covered with sand. Raef went up to it, something to look at that did not look back. The sand was shaped and formed into hills, with little green trees, and a forked strip of blue down the middle.

He put his hand against the miniature country. Michael said, "Don't touch it. What do you think?"

Raef drew his hand back. "Better than birch bark," he said, and then someone else came into the room.

He turned. In a single stroke all the rest of the men in the room had fallen down onto knees and elbows and laid their heads to the floor. Like the last tree left in a forest, Raef looked across their bent backs at the man who had just come in.

He was shorter than Raef, with hair cut so close its color was indistinguishable, a round face, round pale eyes, a thick red-brown beard. He wore a shabby black coat, with no insignia of rank, only a massive carnelian on his shoulder pinning the coat closed. The force of his stare nearly drove Raef a step backward. For an instant, he thought he was looking at Conn.

Not Conn. But another hero. In spite of the clothes he knew at once this was the Emperor, the real Emperor, and the other was a decorated phantom.

He thought, They'll kill me, this time, but he stood where he was. He would not bend his knees, not for anybody, and he would not look away. He fixed his gaze on the other man's eyes, resisting him; it seemed for an instant all that mattered in the world was this resisting.

The round pale eyes never wavered. "Stand." The Emperor walked into the room, through the flock of upturned backs, coming toward Raef. Behind them, the other men rose to their feet in whispers of fine cloth. Nobody else spoke.

"What chimera is this?" The Emperor's voice was deep

and mild, almost musical. He walked in a circle around Raef, looking him up and down. "Thin as a string. His hair could make pelican nests. And ears like a deer, I think they're actually pointed." The other men began to laugh; Michael Lecapenus was translating quickly into dansker. In spite of himself Raef lowered his eyes, humiliated, put his hand up to his ear, which felt hot. The slow, cool Greek voice went on. "Muscled like an ox. Feet like a camel's. You, Scythian, it was you who took down the petroboloi at Chrysopolis?"

Raef startled, having forgotten that. He raised his head and stared at Basil, only a few feet from him, the hard, intelligent pale blue eyes watching, always, poking at him.

"Oh, yes. For that," Basil said, "I will pardon you from my sister's anger, and your own impudence. You saved my army. I'm grateful to you. You smell like a goat. Michael, get him wine." The Emperor turned abruptly and walked away.

"Sebastos," Michael said. His Imperial Majesty. Raef turned, putting his back to the rest of the room, the other men. His body felt hammered, as if a wave had broken over him.

The sand table lay before him and he lowered his eyes to it. He recognized it for the land around them here. There were the hills, on his left hand side, the water running narrow through a little sea to a greater. Close by his hand on the wooden rim a delicately made domed building of white stone marked Constantinople.

At the far end of it, on some flat sand below the water's edge, was a cluster of white blocks and some little footed markers. Some of them looked like horses, and some had flags. Behind him, Michael said, "I think you are probably too stupid to appreciate how lucky you are."

"Where's the wine?" Raef said.

Silently Michael handed him a cup. Raef turned to take it, and saw the Emperor standing among several of the others, all the other men bent and curved in deference to him. He thought again of Conn. It was just something in the way they both had stood so upright, that they seemed alike; Conn had run hot, but this man was cold, cold. The wine was red, and strong, and he drank another swallow, and then another.

Michael said, "The last time I heard of you, you were in Kiev. How did you happen to be on the shore there at Chrysopolis?"

Raef turned his eyes back on the beautiful little country before him, admiring how it was made; shining blue cloth formed the water, the trees were looped green sprigs of wire. He said, "I rowed down the river. Got another ship in Chersonese. That ship capsized in the strait, there."

"Then why did you fight on our side?"

He looked up from the table to Michael, but he knew the Emperor had come up right behind him. "They made me angry." His back felt hot.

Michael grimaced. Raef saw this was not the right answer. The Greek's eyes shifted away from him, and he spoke in his own gravelly speech to the man standing behind Raef.

Then he turned to Raef again, and said, "So you are not one of the Varangians."

"No," Raef said.

"But you have many friends among them. They admire you."

"I have friends," Raef said, frowning.

"Then, perhaps, you would be open to the prospect of working for us, say, giving us a sense of their true feelings about us, and such information."

Raef said, "You mean spy."

"If you want to call it that. We would reward you very well."

"I'm not a spy." He held his arms by his sides, feeling hot all over, and his fists clenched.

Michael shrugged, as if he had anticipated this, and spoke to the Emperor, who said something in a mild voice. Michael's gaze swiveled back to Raef.

"What if we put you in a cell, until such time as you decided you were a spy?"

Raef was stiff with anger. He wanted to hit Michael; he wanted to hit them all, just for hearing this. He knew that way would get him killed. He said, "I wouldn't be much good to you in a cell, would I. Or dead, either, much. I'm going now. Unless he didn't mean it, about the per—the petrobolee?"

He circled around Michael and started toward the door; the big man in the blue coat stepped at once into his way, and the black-helmeted guard behind him. Raef gathered himself, his guts contracting against his spine. Then the Emperor spoke, and Michael said tautly, "Get out, before he thinks it over."

Raef went toward the door. Someone behind him called out sharply, and the dark man in the blue coat and the guard stepped to either side. He walked between them out the door, into the cool darkness.

He strode along at a fast walk, back toward the long hall that led out. After a few moments he heard steps running after him. He said, without turning his head or slowing down, "You again. Are you my keeper?" He felt steadier, calm again.

"Well, think of me as your guardian angel," Michael said.

Raef went out through the colonnade and toward the main walkway. A stream of people carrying dirty dishes was coming out of the big hall on his left, and backed off to allow him and Michael, at his heels, to go by. They came to the tall metal doors, figured with people standing on clouds, and went into the hall with the wonderful floor.

Raef slowed, to study the floor. The torchlight on either side shone down on the pictures. Down there under his feet two men were standing with lances and breastplates and helmets, talking. A man on a horse with a tossing head. Tall plume-leafed trees like the ones he had seen all day in the City. A goat, chewing grass.

They came out onto the broad porch of the Chalke gate, massive in the deepening night, the sky beyond the looming pillars the darker for the torches blazing all around. Michael said, "Well, you are a lucky man. He hates Helena. He says he wishes he had been there to see you humiliate her. But he certainly did make you look like a fool, and he gave you the chance to serve the Empire, and you refused him, which is not common."

Raef said, "I don't serve anybody."

"Which is why nothing you do will come to anything," Michael said. "He's the Emperor. Are you too ignorant even to understand what that means? What a chance you turned down?"

"He owes me something, too. He was man enough to admit it. About being"—he tossed off the title with his hand, not saying it, some poison in it—"that's just an accident, like being King. His father was."

"Yes, that's where you're wrong, you bumpkin." Michael was angry, and he moved, shifting into Raef's path; he wasn't going to let Raef go until he said this. "Basil's father was the Emperor, that's right. But he died when Basil was four, and his brother, dear Constantine, who is probably just as pleased with seeing Helena insulted, by the way—anyway, Constantine was two."

"He's Emperor, too?" Raef remembered the jeweled doll-like man on his couch.

"Yes. Co-Emperor. It's a good arrangement. Constantine does the ceremonial things, which are very lengthy, sometimes. He likes to drive chariots, too, as you saw today in the Hippodrome. But they were only little boys, when their father died. Their mother had to protect them somehow, so she married Nicephoros, who became Emperor." Michael gave him a quick frowning look. "Not our friend Nicephoros Ouranos. She married Nicephoros Phokas, the uncle of Bardos Phokas, whom we're fighting now. It gets complicated sometimes. Anyway, Theophano made Nicephoros the Emperor, to protect the boys. Otherwise, they'd have been killed. Or blinded and tonsured and gelded and put into monasteries. Instead they stayed Emperors, living in the palace, named in the services. But at any time, Nicephoros could dispose of them, and he always let them know it."

Raef said, "Here I thought our Kings were hard."

"Your little tin-plate Kings," Michael said, with a sniff. "I'm talking about the Emperor of Rome. Listen. To you, I can see, this is all very amazing, as it must seem to somebody who was impressed by Chersonese." The Greek poked Raef in the chest with his finger. "There's more to this than you know. I can still remember how bad things used to be, and it wasn't that long ago, and it was very bad. My father told me, 'Boy, it's gone. The Empire is finished. God has turned His face away and delivered us up to the Hagarites.' After we lost Marash—I was a little child— I remember people packing up to leave the City forever."

His lean face was intense, as if at prayer. He said, again, low, "We thought we were done." His voice changed, lightened. "But then things started moving our way. Nicephoros Phokas took Crete and drove the pirates out. That saved Thessaloniki. He got Aleppo back. Unfortunately, he was an old and ugly man and Theophano tired of him. He had a nephew, John Tzimisces. One of his favorite generals. Apparently also one of Theophano's favorite generals. John was . . . well, good with women. You probably have an apt word. Anyway, Theophano took him to bed, and with her help and maybe because she told him to, he murdered Nicephoros and became Emperor."

Raef said, "Everybody is Emperor."

"Only one is the Megalos Basileos. Only one matters. Although it's not exactly . . . John Tzimisces was a great general, though, and he took back Damascus from the Arabs, and Antioch, and even threatened Jerusalem. We could have had Jerusalem back. Then he died."

He shrugged. Raef said, "Theophano again?"

"Maybe. Although she was in exile by this time. Now, when John died Basil was old enough to take over the throne himself. But nobody wanted to give it to him. He had to dislodge older, more experienced men, men with power, titles, armies, and clients and money. I know of at least three who seemed at first more likely to be Emperor than Basil. He beat them all. Now—now—"

His face blazed. He was staring away toward the City. "Now he can take it all. If he defeats Bardas Phokas, he will surely be Megalos Basileos, Autokratos, Kyrios."

"As you said, it isn't exactly a promise of long life and glory."

"Basil will change that. Basil believes in the Empire. Not

the poor shattered corrupted sorry place it sometimes seems is all it is, but the true Empire. Rome when it was everything, and everybody was Roman, or wanted to be." Michael's lips pressed tight together, holding back a sudden depth of feeling. "He makes the rest of us believe it, too. We can rule the world again. Right this time."

"All the world that matters," Raef said. In his mind, briefly, he saw a round gold ring, suspended above the ocean.

Michael faced him, cool again, his handsome face composed. "That's why you should have been glad to help him. If you can't do that, at least, rejoice you left tonight with all your parts. My advice is, either join the Guards and learn to bend your stubborn neck, or get out of Constantinople. Soon." Michael backed up a step and, to Raef's amazement, dropped him a deep, elegant bow. Then he walked off, back through the Chalke into the palace grounds.

CHAPTER TEN

Raef walked down into the City along the great main street. Night had fallen but torches set in brackets on the pillars lit the street almost like day. People thronged along it, and some of the shops were still open. A steady traffic of the rolling horse-drawn boxes minced along, their wheels bouncing in the ruts worn into the paving. Bells began to ring; he saw people coming out of a church. A procession of monks plodded along ahead of him and he moved out to go past them down the middle of the street. A beggar squatting at the foot of a column held out a cupped hand to him. He passed two old men going along with brooms, sweeping the pavement. A crowd of ragged boys ran by, shouting to one another, and darted into the dark side street. Lights glinted in the shadows on either side, and music drifted to his ears.

Raef was thinking about the palace, with its splendors, and the great number of people there. He wanted to see all of it, and without Michael Lecapenus following him everywhere. Yet he thought he had already gotten himself into trouble, and unless he was careful he might wind up sitting on a sharp stick on the racetrack.

What Michael had said returned to him, back at the gate, the passionate way he had said it, like a god story. He understood Michael a lot better now, if not so much the Emperor.

At least he knew now what the right answer would have been, back when Michael asked him why he fought on their side.

Where the street divided, he made his way along the eastern side, past the pillars like gleaming white trees, each one carrying a lit torch, so the street was a bright trace through the dark. In among the columns here and there were figures of people, a boy with a horse, half-size, and three women with their arms around each other's shoulders. Even in the darkness beyond, he could see how thick the houses grew along the slope down to the harbor.

He had the same feeling he had gotten during the day, that with so many people here nobody picked him out of the crowd; he was invisible. But just as he thought this, behind him, somebody hissed, "Goose!"

He turned, startled. The girl Laissa hurried out from behind a column and came up to him.

"Help me," she said, first in Greek, and then in her sloppy dansker, and looked back over her shoulder.

"What's wrong?"

"Someone has been chasing me," she said. "Just walk with me back to the taverna." She gave him a slanted look. "I'll make you happy you did."

Raef snorted at her. He thought she had been waiting for him; she was somebody's spy. They went on along the street awhile, and turned along a side street, beyond the reach of the torchlights.

She said, "So, what happened?" which confirmed it.

"What?" he said.

"We—I heard you were taken under guard."

The street was steep underfoot, an old wall curving around on one side; he could see the gleam of the water in the distance, between buildings. He said, finally, "I saw the Emperor. The real one."

She caught her breath. "Basil. You saw him? What was he like?"

"Not like the other one," he said. They came out onto the harbor street. There were fewer people outside here. He twisted once and looked up, and saw the lit columns way above him, shining against the dark.

"He's one of us," she said. "Not like Constantine, and the dynatoi. Basil is one of us."

That startled him; he said, "What do you mean by that?" He could think of no one less like her than Basil.

"Isn't he? They say he is—simple, and plain-speaking, like one of us. He loves God, and the icons and the Empire." She glanced around them, as if somebody might be listening to them, and her voice sank. "Anyhow, he comes from ploughboys and innkeepers, like us."

She used the Greek words; he knew innkeeper, and he said, "What is ploughboy?"

"Someone who works all the time with his hands and eats lentils and obeys. Listen." Her face shone. She loved telling gossip. "Basil's father was Emperor, and his grandfather and great-grandfather, but somewhere back there, one of them wasn't Emperor. That was the first Basil, and he was a ploughboy. So I guess there's reason for this one to be a ploughboy, too."

"How did this ploughboy get to be Emperor?"

"Oh, that. The first Basil was big and strong, and he came to Constantinople to seek his fortune, and the then Emperor saw him lift up an ox in the Hippodrome. That was Michael. The Emperor. Michael the Drunkard. He was, you know"—she bunched up her face and jiggled her head—"a little prone to vice." She gave Raef a long look, and Raef shook his head, not understanding; she was using a lot of Greek words.

Laissa said, heavily, "Prone—supine. Get it?"

"Oh," Raef said, wondering if he did, and wanting her to go on with it.

"So this Basil was the Emperor's favorite. At first Michael would do anything for him. He adopted him, and then crowned him co-Emperor. Then Basil lost favor, and the old Emperor wanted to call it quits. Basil found out." She drew one finger across her throat. "Basil. Murdered. The Emperor." She watched Raef closely for his response.

"Clearing the way," Raef said. "I've heard of that before."

"So that's where this Basil comes from. A murdering peasant. And his mother was the daughter of an innkeeper."

"Theophano," he said.

"So he's one of us."

They went through the little cluster of houses on the street that led to the eight-arched bridge. The torches on the bridge shone in patches on the water. A fish plopped out there and the splash rippled the lights, one after the other.

Her steps slowed; even from this side they could hear the shouts and laughter coming from the taverna across the bridge. "Umm . . . so, you weren't taken. Nothing happened?" She stopped at the stone apron leading up onto the bridge. "We could do it here," she said. She reached for his crotch.

"Never mind," he said, pushing her hand away.

She said, in Greek, "What, is it true, you like boys?"

He fumbled through that a moment, figuring it out, and said, trying to use Greek, "No. Like woman. So no like whore."

Laissa wheeled on him and smacked him across the face. Without pausing she ran off across the bridge and raced into the taverna. Raef laughed and walked up after her over the water.

"Goose!" Leif yelled, from inside the taverna. "Is that you?

Come in here and tell us what happened! We thought you were finished. You should have heard that woman scream. I thought they were going to drag you in and slit your throat, right there." Raef went into the taverna, to the lights and the buoyant cheers of the Varangians.

—⋅⋝≡—

Laissa didn't see why she shouldn't let the men put their hands down her clothes, if they gave her coppers, and it didn't hurt. It felt good sometimes. When they put their pokers up between her legs, it did hurt, and so she preferred to do what they called "the Greek thing." This she did mostly around the taverna, where she could run to Maria if anything bad happened.

Maria said to her, "Well, you're no better than you need to be, God knows," and crossed herself. Then she crossed Laissa, too, for good measure. She was as good as a mother, and Laissa loved her. The girl hauled in the water, and set the fire in the oven, and Maria showed her how to chop herbs and onions, and how to make broth, all the while singing hymns with her. Laissa loved to hear Maria laugh, a loud heart-deep guffaw that trailed off into amused little chuckles.

She knew that Maria and Gregorios did what she did, anyway; she had seen them.

But later she heard Gregorios say, "She's a whore. After all we've done for her."

"What else does she have, the poor little thing?" Maria said. "But you leave her alone."

"That little stick. When I have you? My darling one."

Laissa's heart quaked. There was something she was

missing here. She went back out to find Leif, who would pet her.

It was midday. Leif sat with his friends in the corner, playing dice. Her steps slowed; Raef was with them. Her gaze lingered on him, the mean words he had said coming back into her mind. His bony face looked sad more than mean. His hair hung down his back in long white braids. She went around the table there, to Leif's side, and leaned against him, her arm on the fat man's shoulders.

Leif was reaching for a little pile of coppers in the middle of the table, the dice in his other hand. Raef sat on his other side, and then the black-haired Bjorn, his eyes following the money away.

He said, "Well, that's it for me. I'm soaked. When are we fighting again?"

Raef said, "This place takes money, for sure." Laissa could see he was purposefully ignoring her. He nudged Leif. "Give me a couple of those coppers."

"What," Leif said, tossing the dice from hand to hand. "So you can dice? Not with me, lucky boy. If you needed money, you should have stayed around at the palace last night and kept your mouth shut."

On the far side of the table, Tryggve grunted his humorless laugh. Laissa noticed he had a big new gold ring on his upper arm. He had treated her roughly once and she did not like him. She knew Blud hated him, too, and she listened for something bad to tell him about Tryggve.

"We have to fight this Bardas Phokas next," Tryggve said. "Down across the inside sea."

Bjorn said, "Make them pay us something before then. You keep saying you're the captain of us."

Laissa put that in the back of her head to tell Blud. Tryggve said, "Oh, there's ways." He turned the jug over his cup, but nothing came out. He held the jug across the table to Laissa. "Run fill this up, kitten."

She hesitated, not wanting to leave them, but Leif gave her a little shove, and she took the jug and ran to the big barrels along the back wall, one wine, one raki. When she came back, another man was coming in the door.

This was a Greek, short, with curly black hair; he looked around in the dim light, saw the men at the table, and reached them just before she reached them.

"Raef," he said, "I've got something for you."

Leif repeated this in dansker, and the other men hooted, as if it meant something bad. Raef slid back against the wall, his face kinking. He said, in Greek, "Hello, Markos. What goes?"

Markos was looking around at the other Varangians, wary. He smiled at Leif as if he knew him. To Raef, he said, "I need somebody to help me row a cargo over to Chrysopolis and another back. I'll split the take."

Leif translated this, but Laissa saw that Raef had understood it even in Greek, because he straightened up right away, interested. She remembered that he had said he needed money. The other men all hooted again, less lewdly. "Hard work, sounds like," Tryggve said. "Although you're good on the water."

Raef said, "It beats banging your head on the floor." He pushed Leif ahead of him out of the way, slid off the bench, and went over to Markos. He used his strange little stock of Greek. "Good. I go. Now?"

"Today," Markos said. "When the tide ebbs." He ruffled his fingers in the air from one side to the other.

"Tide," Raef said. "Good. Good."

"I come here for you," Markos said, speaking each word very slowly and loudly.

"Good," Raef said.

He went back to the table, and Markos went swiftly out again. Laissa hung back. She had that little bit from Tryggve to tell Blud, who might give her some money, or at least a sweet. The men were all joking at Raef for doing this low work, but in their midst Raef looked happier. She went out to find Blud.

⊸⊸

Markos said, "Well, your Greek is a lot better now."

Raef nodded at him. Markos could tell he understood much more than he spoke. They were in Chrysopolis, waiting for the tide to change so they could make the run back to the Horn. Markos looked around the dark taverna where they had come to drink. The trip across the Bosporus had been rough and frightening, but faster than he was used to: they had been able to sail most of the way, and he had realized quickly that he should give Raef the tiller. The blue water, spanked to white ruffles in the wind, was crowded with boats and they had come close sometimes and once a wake from the ferry had nearly swamped them. Nonetheless the crossing had been very fast.

He said, "You're a good waterman, you know."

Raef smiled at him. Markos nodded, enjoying this friendliness. "You know Irene?"

"Ruskas woman."

"Yes. My auntie. She comes to me, anyway, and says, Now it's up to you, Markos!" He laughed, cupping his hands around the wine. "Up to me to find work for the boats and get crews and all. So everybody else now is staring at me. That's why I went looking for you." He fingered the stamped piece of metal that hung around his neck. He had not cleared Raef's work with the Eparch, which could be a problem.

He said, "But you know, when I was so close to death, back there, it changed me. I'm going to be an upright man now. Not that I wasn't before."

Raef gave him a quick, amused look. He said something in his own tongue, and then, "What you do not right?"

"Oh, nothing much," Markos said. That was likely the real trouble. He said, "You know that gold ring you gave me?"

Raef nodded; he glanced at Markos's arms, but the ring of course was safe under a floor tile in Markos's room. Markos leaned toward him a little.

"I'm holding on to that. Irene is too old to do business anyway. I say, let the crone keep the money you gave her. You and me, we can go in together. I can use that ring to buy another long-haul boat." This was not going to be easy to get past the Eparch but he knew the perfect answer. "You can marry my sister." As part of the family he would be eligible for the guild.

Raef gave off a little ripple of alarm. He said, "Long-haul boat," and Markos explained trading with Chersonese and Sinope and down to Lampsacus, the bigger the boat the better. Raef was not meeting his eyes, and his forehead was creased. Markos said, "My sister is a very pretty girl, and obedient, and she can cook as well as my mother."

Raef said, "Pretty, yes." He got up abruptly. "Make water." He went off toward the door, and as soon as he was out of sight a stranger came up to Markos.

"You're going back to the City today?"

"On the tide," Markos said, startled at the direct talk. "Who are you?"

"Never mind that. Take this." The man laid a folded paper in front of him. On top of it he put a gold nomisma. "Keep that."

Markos understood at once. He reached for the nomisma, an old one, the two faces worn almost smooth. His heart was pounding suddenly. He glanced around for Raef and did not see him. Swiftly he took the paper and put it into his purse.

"Give it to Theodore," said the stranger. "He'll give you another nomisma."

"How do I—"

"He'll find you." The man turned and vanished.

Markos gulped. He needed to ask more questions. Maybe wheedle some more money out of this. But now Raef was coming back. He straightened himself, the nomisma also in his purse, and drew his face calm. Raef gave him a sharp look but said nothing.

They set out again for the City with a cargo of wine. At the end of the breakwater the rough sea took them, and now with the wind foul for the Horn they had to row. Seagulls floated around them. The little boat fought the current, lurching and bucking against the hard chop. They were rowing as hard as Markos could go and still getting nowhere. The raki he had drunk made his muscles soft, and he groaned at the pace Raef set. He leaned into each stroke, his teeth clenched, giving himself to the rhythm.

"What this?" Raef asked.

Markos lifted his head, startled. They were far out in the middle of the strait; they were pulling well after all. To the north half a mile away the ferry was wallowing past, heavy with passengers. From the south, a big dromon with gold trim on its bow was rowing across their course.

"The Eparch," he said. "Ship the oars."

They pulled in the oars, and Markos stood up, holding up the stamped oval tag around his neck. "I'm legal," he shouted. "I'm legal." The letter in his purse suddenly seemed on fire.

The big dromon came alongside, its freeboard looming above the littler boat. A man in a dark dalmatic leaned over the rail. "Where are you going?"

"Just to the City." Markos waved the tag at him. His voice squeaked. "This is wine, here, I'm legal for that. I have a buyer—Gyrtas Brothers."

"Go on," said the Eparch's man, and Markos sat down, rubber-legged with relief. The dromon turned off. Raef sat watching her go, her oars running out in their long banks.

"What's that?" He turned to watch the dromon slide away.

"Makes sure we aren't smuggling," Markos said. "Come on, let's go." He reached for his oar, eager for the reason not to talk.

Dolphins rolled by them, as they struggled on, a good sign, smooth gray backs rising briefly from the water, a ruffled spray of breath. Finally they crept into the Horn, where the waves smoothed out. Markos's arms ached. Gratefully he picked out his own wharf, way down on the City side.

On the harbor street a procession of monks filed along, carrying icons. Raef watched them. Markos said, "They're dressing the Great Church for tomorrow. It's the churching of Our Lady. We wouldn't even have been able to go, tomorrow, because of the Holy Day."

Raef said, "Churching," in the way that meant he did not understand.

Markos shrugged. "It's a woman's thing." They were coming to his wharf and with the work done he was starting to feel better. The sun was still in the sky. He thanked God for the idea of bringing Raef. The trip had gone very well and God was with him. His cousin Elias was coming out to catch the hawser and the boy bellowed over his shoulder for the others, to help unload the boat.

Markos stepped up onto the wharf. Raef came after him, stretching his long arms over his head. His nose was sunburnt. Markos was forming words to bring up again his idea about buying a boat together, but before he could Raef thrust out his palm to him.

"Unh." Markos reached for his purse. The nomisma belonged with the letter and he left it in there. Raef had nothing to do with that anyway. The rest was a little puddle of silvers and coppers. Scrupulously he divided these, and dumped four coins into Raef's palm.

The big Scythian gave him a blank look. Markos said, "Well, I paid for the drink. And the tolls."

Raef's face settled. He said nothing, but Markos with a shrinking belly realized he knew somehow about the letter, about the nomisma. He swallowed. But the tall man was already turning away, going straight through the compound, toward the street.

Markos shouted, "Don't forget what I said—about doing something together!" He licked his lips. Raef was already gone.

But then Theodore didn't give him another whole nomisma anyway, only a few more silvers. So it didn't really matter.

⸻

The crown and the vestments were so heavy that the Empress Helena could not rise to her feet without help. She stood perfectly straight within the column of holy ornament, her arms cocked, elbows at her sides, her forearms level, in each hand a turtledove, bound by feet and wings in gold bands to keep it still. She took each step as if it were itself a holy mystery, her weight firm on the front foot before she lifted the back foot from the floor. Her eyes aimed always, unblinking, straight ahead, at the great silver templon of the church, hung with icons, glittering with candles, and the shadowy golden gleam of the sanctuary beyond.

On either side the people were packed in so tightly they seemed one solid thing, made of eyes and mouths. They spoke along with the chanters, the old, beloved hymn.

Virgin Theotokos, Hope of all Christians! Protect, preserve, and save those who hope in You.

We the faithful saw the figure in the shadow of the law and in the Scriptures.

Every male child that opened the womb was Holy to God.

Therefore we honor the firstborn Son of the Unbegotten Father.

The firstborn Son of the Unwedded Mother, O Virgin Theotokos, Good Help of the world!

Behind her the three Porphyrogenitae, her daughters, sang with the rest, then, in strict order, the court women. After them, like the tail of the dragon, followed rank on rank of well-born women, choosing to be churched on the Virgin's day, a great rapturous female train. Out of their wombs the promise: the world will never die.

She reached the templon and stood in front of the icon of the Virgin just right of the Royal Door. A priest came from either side and with a hand on each elbow helped her to kneel down. There she made her prayers, for her children, for her husband the Emperor Constantine, for the City itself. She did not offer any prayer for Basil. Around her they did, their voices rising with the memorized exhortations: "Many years to him! Many years!"

She thought, Mother of God, make it not so. Few days to him, and wretched. What had happened at the reception with the Varangian still burned in her mind. With the aid of the priests again she rose to receive communion. The patriarch himself served this holiest mass, of course, his gorgeous robes stitched with sacred words and symbols, trailed by his acolytes in their sleek bonds of silk. She opened her mouth for the golden spoon and took between her lips the Body and Blood that joined her to the Savior of All, the true Emperor.

No one had avenged her. They had laughed at her.

The patriarch chanted, "O Pure Virgin Mother! That which was fulfilled in You is beyond the understanding of angels and mortal men—"

Throughout the great hollow of the sacred place the response followed: "Holy! Holy! Holy!"

She bowed her head; yet, as usual, it rankled on her that they fixed first and mostly on the Son, and not the Mother who bore Him and nursed Him, not even on this day of her praises, her purification, her apotheosis.

Incense floated through the church. The patriarch brought her a lit candle, and bowed down and adored her. Virgin Mother, Conceived Without Sin, Blessed Among Women.

Huge, those words, on every lip in the vast basilica. She turned to face them. The long sweep of women behind her moved to either side, perfectly as a dance, leaving her the broad lane between them to the far door. The basilica soared above them, as if into another world, tiers of columns on either side, and over all, floating like a cloud of heaven, the light-flooded dome. Christ Pantocrator watched from that dome. Slowly, again, the candle in both hands before her, she started down the aisle again, each step exact, slow, perfect.

As she passed the people on either side sank down on their knees, many weeping. Now and then one flung herself in ecstasy out onto the aisle itself. From the door the guards came hastily up to drag them off before Helena reached them.

Then, halfway down the aisle, her candle winked and went out.

The folk near enough to see her let out a wail of distress. The procession wavered. Beyond, voices rose, uncertain. In a moment everyone would know. Helena swung her arm around with the dead candle, back behind her.

Behind her, among her daughters, with their own candles, Eudoxia sobbed. But Zoë said, "I have it, Mama Augusta!" She felt her hand touched, and brought it forth again, the candle burning again in her grip.

A gasp went up from the crowd, triumphant. Helena smiled, holding the candle steady; that was a sign, too, she thought.

"Maiden Mary! Enlighten my soul which is grievously darkened by the passions of this life."

She paced out onto the porch of the basilica, where a dais had been raised for her. The priest took her candle and fixed it on a frame before the image of the Virgin Theotokos. Carefully they helped her onto the dais and to the throne there. She settled herself onto the cushion. Here she would sit the rest of the morning, giving out blessings and gifts and receiving them.

Her children put their candles into the hands of the priests, and sat behind her. As they settled themselves, she said, to Zoë, "You shall be Empress, child. You are chosen."

The little girl kissed her hand. Eudoxia turned fretfully away. On the far end, Theodora looked around quizzically. Helena turned forward again, toward the first row of courtiers, kneeling down to adore her.

Constantine said, "My dear, Basil talks like that to everybody. He's that way. When we were little he used to say the most filthy things, words he learned from the stablehands, to bother my poor mother. My poor mother." He shook his head.

Helena whirled toward him. "It wasn't Basil who called me a whore, sir. It was a grunting barefoot hairy Scythian. Basil did nothing to avenge me. Nor did you."

She stalked away across the balcony. Where the sun shone, the air was warm and sweet, and Constantine had come out here to enjoy it and play draughts. She paced along the railing, the sea breaking on the rocks far below. A seagull glided by on its black-tipped wings. From here, she looked out over the Propontis and the mouth of the Bosporus, a knot of waters, the omphalos of the world.

"My dear," Constantine said, "I don't know why you're still fuming about this. You remind me of someone in a play, who remembers the smallest slight for years so that the last act works." He laughed.

She went back to his side. The eunuch playing with him was his chamberlain and devoted to him. Therefore she could ignore him. She said, "Constantine, Basil leaves you no power. He decides everything without you. He decided to attack Kalokyros Delphinas, and then he decided to impale him in front of the whole City."

"I wouldn't have done that," Constantine said, half to himself.

"No." She knelt suddenly beside him, her hands on his knees. "Darling, he's evil. For the sake of Rome, you must stand up to him. Rome needs you, Constantine."

Her handsome husband leaned back and patted her face. "Basil does the work. That's best for everybody. Dear, we have all we want. Imagine anything, a fruit, a gown, a jewel, a palace, we will have it, at once. And everybody adores us. Putting up with Basil seems a small price."

She stormed away from him, her cheeks hot. No one had witnessed that except the eunuch, who would say nothing. The two heads bent over the checkers game again. Suddenly she hated Constantine as much as she hated Basil. He had no understanding; he skipped over this like a stone across the water. He wanted only to have his stupid games, his horses, his stuffed quails and ceremonies.

She went off the balcony, and through the hall of the Bucoleon, toward the women's quarter at the center of the palace. They all treated her as if she meant nothing. Worse, they intended that for her children, the same diminished, insulted future. And it was true, if she did nothing to prevent it.

In the women's hall the servants were busy with their looms, and she went on to her privy chamber and shut the door. Sinking down on the couch she squeezed her hands together against the intolerable pressure of her rage.

"Mama Augusta?" from the door.

"Stay away," she said, almost breathless.

The door swayed gently closed again. She got up, and walked once around the room. Everything in it was as she had required, the gold walls that set off her skin so well, the silk hangings of

Aphrodite and the Wedding at Cana, the gilded scrollwork on the couch and desk and stool, the floor daily strewn with fresh rose petals. It was still a cage. I have no worth, she thought. I am nothing.

As she went by the door she pulled it firmly closed and latched it. She didn't even want to see Zoë, her dearest.

Yet it was for Zoë's sake she had to act.

Almost against her will her pacing took her by the chest at the foot of her couch. She looked all around her, furtive as a weasel. A touch at the base of the chest let a shallow drawer spring out. In it, one sheet of paper.

"Helena, queen of my heart—" So it began.

She should have burned it when it came. Constantine was her husband. Love notes to her from other men did not amuse him, especially other men who were trying to seize his throne. But Constantine had failed her. Had failed Rome.

She read carefully through the rest of the letter, whose writer cast himself at her feet, promised her eternal love, and offered the name of one who could carry a message, if she chose ever to give hope to his despairing soul.

She had already used this messenger several times. Between her and this letter-writer now there was a certain understanding. She read the letter over again, confirming this in her heart, and then took the letter to the nearest brazier and burnt it to a white ash. There was no more time for words. Now was the time to act. She paced around her room, composing herself.

CHAPTER ELEVEN

Michael Lecapenus came out to St. Mamas to distribute more gifts of gold and money to the Varangians, and afterward Blud rode back with him toward the palace. He admired the Greek's horse, finely made as a deer, its hide polished like silk.

"He's a good horse." Michael leaned forward and patted his mount's sleek neck. "He was supposed to be a racehorse but he took a disliking to chariots."

Blud said, "I'd like to do that sometime." He was trying to find a way to steer their talk to him.

"It's very hard," Michael said. "Much harder than riding a horse." He glanced at Blud's horse, a hand shorter than his, its rough winter hide matted on its neck; Blud felt himself warming with embarrassment. Michael said, "We should see you Varangians are properly mounted. After we beat Phokas. The best studs are in Anatolia, and right now he controls it."

"When will we fight Phokas?"

"We don't know yet. But we will choose the time. You should be ready."

They were riding along the harbor street, toward the way up to the Mese, through crowds of women in shawls and men with red and gray hats, surging around the shopping stalls. Blud saw his chance, and said, "You know, you ought to make me commander over everybody here, and not just those from Kiev. And St. Mamas is too far away. You should post me and my men nearer the palace. That would make things easier, when the time comes to move."

Michael gave him a wide-eyed stare. He did nothing that Blud could see but his horse turned across Blud's path and stopped, and so Blud had to stop. "We must consider the interests of people who have been here longer than you have, my lord Blud. Many serve the Empire."

Blud said, "You mean Tryggve Haraldsson." He knew Tryggve was behind this latest gift-giving.

Michael said, "I've worked much with Tryggve, who speaks passable Greek, for one thing."

Blud said, thick-throated, "My men will follow only me."

Michael bowed his head. "You are the true commander of the Rus."

Blud was silent a moment. He suspected Michael knew Volodymyr in Kiev hated him and would give him no help. Ahead, the street widened and forked, the right branch climbing up to the great pillared main street. A fountain flowed in the broad common, and there was a crowd of people around it, taking water, and just talking. It was hard to argue with Michael with so many nearby to listen.

He said, "Get me a chance to see the Emperor about this. I should be commander of the whole army. It's bad for warriors not to know who their leader is."

Michael turned to him, smiling. "Why, their leader is the Emperor, of course." He reached out and shook Blud's hand, and was going, going on up the street, sloughing off Blud and his demands as if he were old skin.

I should learn better Greek, Blud thought. He watched Michael Lecapenus ride up the street toward the Mese, his red cloak weaving in among the bright clothes of all the other people in the street. Or he should go back to Rus.

His mood sank. In a leaden temper, he rode back along the harbor street. He needed the Emperor's favor to go back to Rus, where, while he was gone, Volodymyr was building up his power, eliminating any threat, any rival, making everything his. Volodymyr wanted to be more than merely Knyaz. He wanted to be on the steppe what the Emperor was here. But if Blud left now, without the Emperor's goodwill—without something—he would have no more weight with Volodymyr than a thistledown.

When he set out to come here, he had imagined himself drinking with the Emperor, sharing stories, advice, and counsel, fighting side by side, maybe saving the Emperor's life, or something, certainly getting his admiration, gratitude, even a princess for a bride, as Volodymyr had done. Now he was finding it hard just to get into the palace. He was always having to talk through somebody else, and when he did finally come face-to-face with the Emperor, it wasn't even the right one.

"Sir." A man with bulbous eyes and no chin rode up beside him on a rawboned horse, leaned toward him, and asked him something in Greek.

Blud grunted. "I don't speak that much Greek, and I'm not from here."

"Oh, no," said the other. "Your Greek is very good, very good, sir. But I can tell you're Rus, aren't you? Then let me thank you. They tell me that you Rus won the fight at Chrysopolis. Let me buy you a drink." He smiled, a broad-lipped mouth over no chin. "My name is Theodore." He held out his hand.

Blud's gloom lifted slightly. Here was somebody at least who thought his Greek was good enough. They stopped in a taverna, on the harbor street, a great cavernous room where the man at the pipes greeted Theodore by name. They drank in a corner, sitting on a bench at the end of a long table. The servant brought them tall cans of raki, not too watered, either.

Theodore was curious about the Rus, and asked many questions, speaking clearly and slowly, so that Blud could keep up, and repeating when he had to, helping Blud find words. When he heard that the Rus were all quartered in St. Mamas, his eyebrows flew up. With his receding chin and pop eyes he looked like a frog.

"You saved the City for them. Yet they keep you over there in the back woods. Don't they trust you?"

Blud gave a disbelieving laugh. He lounged back on his bench, his head buzzing. "They'd better trust us, we're all they've got."

"You're from Kiev? I've never been so far away. It seems like the end of the world to me. You must be a great man there."

Blud gave a shrug, considering how to explain. Of course this Theodore would never know. He said, "The Knyaz is not as well-born as I, I tell you."

Theodore was smiling at him, admiring, his eyes warm. "I knew you for a prince, from the moment I saw you. Your bearing, your pride."

He sent for more raki, and a dish of bread and beans and meat. Blud looked around at the rest of the taverna: sailors, mostly, and local people, nobody he knew, of course. Or who knew him. He fumbled for a few words, and said, "You see me better than these people then—they would put a low Norse adventurer over me."

Theodore leaned his arms on the tabletop, and spoke in a

confidential voice. "Are you surprised? You seem one who sees below the surface. You must know how this is going."

Blud said, "Below the surface," not really understanding. But he knew what surprised meant. He shrugged, not wanting to be that stupid. "It's obvious. Isn't it?"

The man with no chin leaned even closer. He spoke in words Blud only halfway understood. "My master is Alexander, striding the battlefield; Hector, scattering all before him. When he shouts, whole cities cower. One blow from him lays any man down. Against him you have these . . . boys, Basil and Constantine."

Blud grunted. He was struggling with the gist of this, but the contempt for the Emperors came through to him. As drunk as he was, that gave him a start of alarm. He knew he was going onto dangerous ground. He said, "We are Basil's men, the Rus."

"Let me show you something." Theodore held out his hand.

Blud said, "I've seen them." On the Greek's palm was a gold basileus, very new. What they called a nomisma. But looking closer he saw it was different from the others he'd seen. He took one from his purse to compare them. The coin from his purse had two men on its face. Theodore's coin showed only one.

The man with no chin turned the gold piece in his palm. His voice was low, quiet, clear. "This is my lord the Emperor Bardas Phokas, many years to him. Let this suggest what might be yours, when Phokas wins. Which must happen. You can see that. Why not be on the right side?" He laid the coin in Blud's hand. "Think on it."

Blud sucked in his breath, his gaze fixed on the gold coin in his hand, fighting through the haze of the raki to make sense of this. When he looked around Theodore was gone. He turned his gaze back to the coin, excited. Nobody had to know but him about this. But he saw the possibilities already. This could be the answer to everything.

—⚬—

Raef said, "I've never gotten on with horses." He put his hand out to Tryggve's brown mare; she sniffed cautiously at his palm. They were in the little hippodrome at St. Mamas, much smaller than the big one in the City, and the Varangians were out running their horses. A lot of St. Mamas had once been much bigger, and had some half-ruined buildings over it. Nobody took care of the racetrack here anymore and it was growing back to grass and weeds.

"You're a sailor," Tryggve said. "Your legs bend the wrong way. What an ass he is."

He was looking down the dirt stretch of the track, patchy with clumps of grass. In the middle of it, Blud and some of his men were trying to hitch their horses to an old box-cart Blud had found, like the ones in the Greek races. They had gone through the stables of the monastery and found pieces of harness that they augmented with lengths of rope.

They had gotten the four horses harnessed up and standing side by side, and now they were trying to bring up the cart behind them. The half-savage steppe horses heard the rumble of the cart coming and began to snort, to rear, lunging away. Blud shouted, and the cart stopped.

Tryggve shouted, "You're no Greek, Blud!"

From around the racetrack there rose a stir of laughter; a lot of other people were watching this.

Blud cast an angry glance up the track, and then around him in general. He spoke to his men, who were untangling the harness. They got the horses straight again, and two of the Rus bounded up onto the backs of the outer two horses.

They brought the cart up once more. With men on their backs, the outer horses held, but the inside horses began to leap, and rear, and one half climbed over the other. Red-faced, Blud strode up and down yelling at his men. The two on the outside horses held their mounts still and the men on the ground attached the harness traces to the tree of the chariot. By main strength they got the two middle horses straightened out again.

Blud yelled, "Out of the way!" and climbed into the open box.

Tryggve said, "Oh, this will be interesting."

Blud was arguing with the two mounted men; he wanted them to dismount, and finally one did, bringing back his reins to Blud, and the reins of the next horse. Blud took them, and both horses suddenly bolted down the track toward Raef and Tryggve.

Blud gave an astonished yell. The rest of the team, dragged along, galloped raggedly beside them, the remaining rider trying to keep the left-hand horses straight. The car bounced behind them. One wheel stuck in loose sand and the whole box slewed around, tilting up on the other wheel. Blud clutched the rail with one hand to keep his feet.

"Let's get out of here," Raef said.

"No," Tryggve said. "I'm betting they don't get even this far."

Half the track lay between them and Blud. Clinging to the cart with one hand, the Rus prince was hauling back on the reins with the other, yelling to the horses to stop. Th rider on the outside wheeler was wrestling with his mount, which bucked and kicked and veered out of line. The other three horses were running flat out, and not in any particular direction. The chariot swung wildly from side to side. The inside wheeler horse swerved suddenly off course. A trace had broken. The horse swung around across the infield, and the other trace snapped and the horse burst free.

The chariot swung, and a wheel spun off, careening down the track, past the remaining horses, bouncing and bumping along, while the chariot, behind it, sat down on its axle end and dragged to a stop, the horses pitching and screaming ahead of it.

Blud still stood in the back of the cart, his hands gripping the reins. The rider jumped down, trying to calm his mount. One of the remaining horses kicked back, and its hoofs crashed through the thin wood of the front of the car. Lowering its head the horse set itself steadily to kicking apart the rest of it. The other horse stood still, its ears flopping. The loose wheel, still spinning, hit a rock and flew through the air into the weeds.

Tryggve laughed.

"You owe me, for once." He turned, his hand out to Raef.

"I didn't bet," Raef said.

⚬

"I'm paying," Leif said. "This is what I spent most of your money on, anyway."

They walked in through a gateway, crowded with other people going in, and stopped at a little house with a window, to pay money. Leif gave the man in the house five coppers for each of them.

"This gets you the best of everything," he said.

"This better be good," Raef said. "The bathhouse at Novgorod didn't cost anything, as I remember. Not even for the whipping."

"You just wait."

They went on through an open court, with high stone walls, but no roof, where several people were running and wrestling on the grass. Most of them were naked. Leif said, "Usually I skip this part."

"What are they doing?"

Leif shrugged. They went on into another big room, this one lined with cupboards, and here Leif began to take his clothes off.

Raef stared at him. Leif said, "Go on, this is what you do. See?" He nodded across the room. A slender young man in a silver-gray tunic was coming toward them. Silently he gave each of them a thin soft coat that opened down the front. Leif bundled his own tunic, his drawers and leggings and shoes and hat into one of the cupboards. He carried his belly like a shield boss in front of him; Raef thought he was noticeably fatter since he had been in Constantinople. He wrapped himself in the thin coat, waiting with visible and satisfied patience for Raef.

Raef took off his clothes and put the coat on, and followed him into the next room.

The top half of this room was filled with billowing steam. Below it was a blue pond of water, all the sides covered with white tiles; the tiles ran up over the floor around the pool, which was awash with water, and then up the sides of the room. Along the top of the room was a row of windows, so the whole place was filled with dim light, filtering through the steam. On all four walls were benches of wood, with men sitting on them in the thin coats, or naked. The floor was hot. Leif led the way to the nearest open bench.

Immediately another slender boy was coming up to them, with a bowl in his hands; he began to pour water over them. Raef sat on the bench, astonished. The heat of the room loosened his muscles and the drenching waves of water soaked him all the way through. His skin tingled. The boy had put down the bowl, and taken up a wooden blade, and made a sign at him.

Leif said, "Stand up, he says, and he'll scrape you."

"Scrape me," Raef said.

Leif said something in Greek and the boy turned to him, and began to run the wooden blade over Leif's back, skimming off the dampness down to the clean skin, like cleaning the hull of a ship. Raef sat on the bench, wrapped in the sodden coat, water dripping from his eyelashes, beginning to enjoy himself. He got glimpses of the other men around him, talking, being scraped, being drenched. A lot of them were Rus; he could tell this even though they were naked, by their long fair hair and square-cut beards. The Greeks were darker, smaller, and not as loud. In the billowing steam, the most visible part of anybody was his legs. A man in a green hat was walking around, a tray suspended from his neck, holding some little glasses filled with amber water.

"Raef!"

That was Bjorn the Christian, walking up from the other side of the tiled pool. The little silver cross around his neck hung on his chest. He wore his bath coat wrapped around his middle like a skirt, a brown leather purse stuck into the waist. "I never thought I'd see you here." He sat down on the bench between Raef and Leif. "Watch out for these peddlers. They'll cheat you. Give them half what they ask for."

Raef said, "How can they see you to steal anything?"

Bjorn beckoned over the drink-seller, and made a big show of getting them all a cup of the amber drink, which he paid for with a flourish and several coppers from his purse.

"Plenty more where that came from," he said, tossing his purse up into the air and catching it. He looked from one to the other. "So. What can I talk to you about?"

Raef sipped the drink, another full, rich taste, like drinking an apple, sweet as honey. Leif said, "Personally, I prefer the raki. When are we going to fight again?"

Bjorn said, "That, I don't know."

"You don't know anything," Leif said.

Bjorn's eyebrows arched. "If you knew what I knew—" He tossed the purse up into the air again and caught it.

Raef snorted at him. "You'll tell us everything you know just to make us listen." He waved off the boy waiting to scrape him. Taking off the coat, he went to the pool and lowered himself into the warm water. The steam clouds above his head glowed and sprang momentary rainbows in the light through the upper windows. He swam lazily around on his back. The water was warm enough to make him sleepy. A few moments later he heard a shout and a roar from Leif.

The floating steam hid everything; he swam toward Leif's voice, found the Icelander standing on the side of the pool, and saw that Bjorn was gone. Leif was yelling at somebody in the doorway, in a crowd of yellow-headed men, and waving his arms, and then abruptly somebody turned and swung a fist at him.

At once they were all fighting. Raef stroked over to the edge of the pool. A body flew almost over his head and splashed into the water behind him. In front of him was a thicket of stamping, hairy legs. He hauled himself up out of the pool and plunged past two grunting men braced together on the slippery tiles, their arms intertwined. Naked men loomed and vanished through the billowing steam around him. A slithering back glanced into him from behind and he slid across the wet tile into the doorway.

This room was cooler, and clearer, with rows of waist-high benches all through it. As Raef came into the room, half the benches had men lying on them, with other men bending over them, but then the fight erupted through the place, and the men on the benches burst up and joined in. Leif was right in front of him, staggering backward, his arms wheeling. The man who had just hit him swung around, off balance, and Raef tripped him face-first onto the floor.

He grabbed Leif by the arm. "Let's get out of here."

"Hell, no," Leif shouted. "I haven't got my rubdown yet."

The man on the floor was getting up; he saw Raef and drove straight at him, and Raef dodged and kneed him in the head. Somewhere outside a horn sounded. Leif looked around, and all around the room, the fighting stopped and men bounded for the doors. Raef said, "Come on."

Men were scrambling out the doors. He pushed his way back into the room with the pool, which was brighter lit, anyway, and in the direction of his clothes. Leif followed him, still complaining about losing his rubdown. Even the pool chamber was rapidly emptying, its steam in a wild churning.

Raef started down toward the next room, where his clothes were. Leif grabbed his arm. "Look. Just stay put. There's nothing going on here, see?" He spread his arms. "Wait a moment, we can finish up." Then something caught his eye. He swore under his breath. Raef turned around to see. In the pool, floating toward them out from under the obscuring layer of steam, was a body, and it was Bjorn the Christian, facedown.

—⧗—

"What happened to the body?" Tryggve asked.

Leif leaned on the table, his face long. He and Bjorn had known each other a long time. "Apparently that's part of the deal with the Greeks. You die here, they bury you." He shrugged. "He was a Christian, he won't mind."

Tryggve said, "This is not going to make them very happy, up there in the palace. They're always on us about fighting."

Raef sat back, his arms folded over his chest. He had pulled Bjorn out of the pool and his hands still stung, as if he had grasped nettles.

Leif said, "Come on. What's the real question here? Did somebody murder Bjorn? And do we have a wergeld to collect?"

Ulf tossed the dice from hand to hand. "Come on, he was drunk, you said. Maybe he just took a hard shot to the head and fell in the water and drowned." He was refusing to dice with Raef, who had no more money left anyway.

Raef said, "He did drown." The whole fight seemed to him to have begun and ended with Bjorn, as if it existed only to cover killing him.

Tryggve said, "Where was Blud when this was going on?"

"Hold on," Leif said. "You can't make everything into this feud you've got on with Blud."

"He was no kin of mine, in any case," Ulf said. "And I wouldn't follow Blud out of camp at night to piss."

Raef said nothing. He remembered almost all the fighters as being Rus. He thought somebody had murdered Bjorn, and he thought he knew why: Basil had bought himself a spy who couldn't keep his mouth shut. The question wasn't really who had killed him. The question was what Bjorn had found out, and about whom.

CHAPTER TWELVE

Tryggve said, "I've seen this. Don't run. Whatever happens. Stay right here."

"Run," Raef said, startled. He looked around at the great hall. It was one of the largest buildings he had ever seen and yet it seemed light and airy as a tent. With the high ceiling, the towering walls and columns, the sunlight coming in through windows all along the top of the walls, it seemed made for somebody much bigger than he was. The rows of columns on either side were sheathed in gold and the floor again was of tiny tiles formed into patterns and shapes, people and animals, natural as if they lived. The polished stone of the columns on either side drew his eyes, smoky green and gray, streaked with white, flecked with gold. Again he remembered what Michael Lecapenus had said, You don't even have words for this.

He was standing just behind Leif, in one of several long lines of Varangians filling the central hall. Three rows ahead of him was an empty stretch of floor, about ten feet deep, separated from the rest of the room by a silken screen that stretched from floor to ceiling, so sheer everything beyond it was visible through a golden haze.

Beyond the screen, across the empty stretch, the whole floor stepped up six feet into the air to a broad, deep platform, on which stood two thrones, both empty. The two thrones were tall, with high backs and heavy arms and swagged tops of fringed silk, every surface inlaid with jewels, so he had no idea what they were made of. Each had a plump cushion to sit on.

On one cushion there was an open book. Beside each of the thrones a great brass lion stood, heavy-maned, with one paw raised. The teeth were made of something white, maybe real teeth. It was beautiful but he saw no reason to run.

The hall was rapidly filling with other men. On his left he saw the Ouranian Guard, which rumor said was moving over to Chrysopolis in a few days, crisp rows of black-crested helmets. Their chief officer was the Emperor's friend Nicephoros Ouranos and he stood in the middle of them, his red helmet bright against their darkness.

Beyond them were other men, and apparently these were the reason for whatever they were doing here. Leif had called it a great reception, had talked him into coming, which was not hard, since the Greeks were paying them two silvers apiece for their presence. And he wanted to see the palace again. He was glad he had come.

Those new men were moving up to the front of the hall. His memory jolted him. All four of them wore white cloths wound around their heads, long robes, dark cloaks over one shoulder, and one especially reminded him of someone he had known in Kiev. The sheer golden screen rose out of the way, and they moved into the open space between the soldiers and the thrones on their platform.

One spoke, his voice tiny in the giant room, but clear.

"Emperor of Rome, in the name of God Almighty, Ruler of All, we bring the greetings and reverences of the great lord Samsam Al-Dawla, amir of Baghdad."

The four men bowed, and lowered themselves to their knees. And the two brass lions by the throne turned their great maned heads, and began to roar.

Raef's jaw dropped. He forgot about the man he had just

recognized. The lion in front of him turned its head again and more thunderous roars resounded through the hall, tremendous animal growls. Someone behind Raef screamed. Lights flashed in the space over the thrones. Several sharp bangs sounded, like rocks exploding in a campfire. All around him people were falling to their knees, doubling over, covering their heads with their hands. Raef stood utterly still, his gaze fixed on the thrones.

They were rising upward into the air. Where a moment before there had been only the open book on one throne now a man sat on the other. He glistened from head to foot in the light, all diamonds. His headdress was like a sun rising.

The roaring of the lions crashed through the hall. More explosions banged out. Raef's ears rang. He imagined suddenly the thrones marching forward and crushing them all. The great jeweled chairs rose through drifting clouds of smoke; he smelled something rank, like bad eggs. Abruptly the man on the throne was shimmering red, from head to foot rubies.

He thought abruptly, This was what Volodymyr had been trying to do, back in Kiev, that time. Now he saw how feeble that really was. Yet the memory steadied him. He had thought the Greeks had drowned their magic, but they had not.

The roaring of the lions faded, and an ordinary Greek came out at the foot of the throne and accepted the Baghdadi men to the Imperial court in a long windy speech full of strange words. After that the Varangians all marched out of the hall again, got their silvers, and went home.

—⚬—

Back in the taverna, thinking about the roaring brass lions, he began to wonder where this magic came from, and why they used it only for such things as this. Why it seemed to spring from Constantine, and yet Constantine was an empty figure, a name and a suit of armor.

Gregorios himself brought him a cup of raki; Raef owed him money and he hovered around, scowling, after he set the cup down. With a flourish, Raef paid him everything he owed. This was a kind of magic, changing the gruff tavern-keeper into a smiling, bowing servant. Nursing the cup, Raef wondered how Constantine could command anything, much less the power to make a metal lion roar. Someone else could be evoking it.

But it came into his mind it was not magic, that the Greeks could do such things without magic. He thought, That is not possible. He thought, It is possible, because they are doing it.

A deep alarm stirred in his gut. He understood nothing of this. Michael was right, he didn't know the words.

"My young friend," said the man standing in front of him, smiling.

"Rashid," he said, surprised, and stood up. "That was you. I thought I recognized you." He moved down on the bench so that the Baghdadi man could sit down.

"Yes, cowering in the Emperor's shadow." Rashid gathered his long robes and sat carefully on the bench. "But you, Raef, you are talked of in the Great Palace, I have heard much of you." He did not ask about Conn. His dansker, always tinged with sclava sounds, seemed a little rusty.

Raef said, "They don't like me, up there."

"On the contrary, Nicephoros Ouranos told me that without your help they might never have gotten ashore at Chrysopolis."

Raef shrugged that off. He said, "Today, in the palace . . ." He shook his head. "The thrones, the lions. What was that?"

Rashid tucked his hands together over his belly. "They are

the masters of it. I've seen it before—the last time there were diamond-studded birds singing in ruby trees. Basil is more martial. Hence the lions. They do it with pumps, under the platform."

"Pumps," Raef said, uncertain, and a little disappointed. "Still, it's amazing." He wondered what kind of pump flashed lights. He thought suddenly Rashid was just guessing—putting something he knew into the space he didn't understand.

Rashid said, "They want you to be awed. Did you get the message I left for you in Chersonese?"

"I got what you left," Raef said. "I didn't know it was exactly a message. Why are you here?"

"Well." Rashid shrugged. "I came here with Yahya, to try to sway the Emperor to give my lord in Baghdad more money. We have an army now, if we can pay them—" He slapped the table. "No use convincing you. Unless you have his ear?"

"Not at all. I told you, they hate me. Are you so sure he will be Emperor much longer?"

Rashid gave him a steady look, his eyes wide. "Oh, yes," he said. "He has been true Emperor all along. Everybody has known this. The stars show it. It's in his looks. His fate. He wears the purple boots and he will until he dies. What is your place in this?"

Raef had not noticed the purple boots. He said, "I just want to get out of here."

"Oh. I see. And making good progress, too." Rashid waved over Gregorios, and asked for a drink in Greek. He drank, not raki or wine, but the infusion of apples Raef had tasted at the baths.

Rashid said, "You should know this also about Basil. He will never stop fighting. He must have everything. His power is boundless, or nothing. If you disobey him, even in the smallest thing, he will crush you."

"He's not giving me orders. I'm not really in his army."

"You're not listening to me," Rashid said. "But you never did, and you seem none the worse for it. I take this as a personal chastisement. You like Constantinople."

"Yes," Raef said. Rashid always thought he knew everything. "Why does your king need money? I thought Baghdad was as fine as Constantinople. I've never seen a place with so much money."

Rashid made a face, his hands fussing, his eyes elsewhere. "The ways of luck. Which is said so much more elegantly in Arabic. Even Greek." He smiled. "I'm glad to see you again, Raef. May your luck stay good, and you find your way home. Good-bye."

"Good-bye," Raef said, and started to put out his hand and remembered. He smiled. Rashid left. Raef sank back against the wall, thinking again of the brass lions, roaring.

━━⚬━━

Nicephoros said, "I suppose I should learn some of their language."

Michael reined his horse in to let his friend go ahead of him onto the bridge to St. Mamas. A crowd of people passed by, going to the markets in the City. It had snowed overnight, but the sky was bright blue now. At the end of the bridge he caught up with Nicephoros again.

"Certainly, learn some dansker. It's very useful, sometimes. But it's hard. You can't always say things properly. This is the taverna."

They rode around the side of the broken stone wall to tie their horses. Half a dozen men, all Varangian, were sitting around the yard in the sun, and a few called out and raised their hands. Michael lifted his hand in answer. Michael could see Nicephoros's face settle at this lack of discipline: nobody stood up, and certainly nobody saluted.

"Do they all come in here?" Nicephoros said.

"Not all. Many of the officers. The old hands all eat here."

"We should drill them. Give them a sense of discipline."

Michael laughed, thinking it very unlikely the Varangians would drill: like herding cats, he thought. He waved Nicephoros ahead of him into the dark smelly interior of the building. Here more men sat around on benches, dozing and drinking. In one corner Tryggve Haraldsson was playing dice with another man he had seen before, but whose name he did not know.

It was Tryggve they were looking for, and Michael was rather glad to see Raef Corbansson wasn't there. Michael went over to them, Nicephoros now on his heels. Tryggve stood up, but he stretched out his arm, and Michael shook his hand.

Tryggve spoke Greek, and Michael spoke to him in Greek. "I'm pleased to see you here, Tryggve. I am to present you to the Domestikos of the Numeroi Nicephoros Ouranos." Nicephoros had a flurry of other titles, none of which would mean anything to Tryggve. Michael turned and bowed to Nicephoros, so that Tryggve would see the proper degree of respect due. "My lord Nicephoros, this is Tryggve Haraldsson."

Tryggve bowed. The other Varangian, still seated on the bench, was watching them quizzically, his face creased, not understanding. In dansker, he said, "What's going on?"

"Tell me your name," Michael said to him, "so I may present you to the Domestikos."

"Domestikos." The other man recognized that, at least, and he got to his feet. He looked at Nicephoros with intense interest. "I want to be a hecktark, like him and Leif." He looked back at Michael. "I'm Ulf Hakonsson."

Michael exchanged his name with Nicephoros, and Ulf actually made an awkward little bow, very stiff. They all sat down around the table. Michael said to Tryggve, "Where are your friends?"

"At the bath. Trying to find out who killed Bjorn."

Michael said, startled, "Somebody killed Bjorn?"

Tryggve said, "Now, I shouldn't have said that. Raef is trying to find out who killed Bjorn. Leif is just having a bath. I think Bjorn drowned, all on his own." He turned, and said to Ulf, "What do you think happened to Bjorn?"

Ulf said, "Got slugged in the fight and fell in the pool and drowned. Is that why they're here?"

Tryggve faced Michael again and switched back into Greek. He spoke it well enough, although he often grumbled over the endings of words. "Raef is the only one who thinks Bjorn was killed. But he's mad, Raef, he's Irish, they're all mad, one way or another. It was just an accident. We had a little fight. Actually that was just an argument."

"I thought he was a Dane," Michael said. "Like you."

"I'm from Westfold," Tryggve said. He put his hands on the table before him. "Raef's father was the Irish wizard Corban Loosestrife, who kept a ship in his pocket, and spoke to animals. He's gone now, sailed back into the west."

Michael blinked at this revelation of unexpected depth to Raef Corbansson. He said, "To Ireland."

Tryggve smiled and exchanged glances with Ulf, who was still frowning; Tryggve said, in dansker, "I'm telling them about Corban." To Michael, again, in Greek, he said, "No, no. There are lands to the west you have never heard of. All the Irish know this. There Corban Loosestrife is the King."

Nicephoros said, "Where does the truth stop in this and the fable start?"

Tryggve bobbed his head to Nicephoros. "It's all fable, Magister. Domestikos. But you can tell us what's important. When are we fighting next?"

Nicephoros said, "I'm not sure of that yet. The weather is still a problem. Tell me—you've been here awhile, Tryggve."

"Six years," Tryggve said. "Longer than anybody still in the company."

"Why?"

Tryggve smiled, his lips fish-thin in his wiry beard. "I like the work. I like the Empire."

"Who is your master?"

"I serve the Emperor," Tryggve said.

"Which Emperor?"

At that, the smile widened. The man's gray-green eyes glittered, amused; Michael saw he knew this catechism. "The man in the Great Palace. Whoever rules from the Magnaura, I serve."

Michael smiled, and Nicephoros nodded, satisfied. If the Varangian had described some passionate personal attachment to Basil they would have known he was lying.

Nicephoros said, "Now to my business with you. I am leaving on a mission for the Emperor and my century is leaving with me. In the name of His Imperial Majesty, I order you to form a new Palace Guard—you and eighty other men you choose. Choose them well. You will be recompensed properly. Michael Lecapenus here will be your superior officer."

"Do they have to speak Greek?"

"No. Better if they don't."

"Not Raef Corbansson," Michael said.

Tryggve laughed outright. He said, "No wizards' sons?"

"If he refuses the obeisance again I think Basil will kill him."

"I know who to bring." Tryggve slapped Ulf on the arm.

"What," Ulf said blankly.

"Leif will come, too." Tryggve nodded to Nicephoros. "I'll have people begging to join up. We're your men."

"I'll expect you to report to the palace in two days."

Tryggve nodded again, and bowed, almost banging his nose on the table. "Yes, sir."

—⚬—

Crossing the bridge again, going back into the City, Nicephoros said, "He seems satisfactory."

Michael nodded. "Oh, yes, Tryggve is dependable. He's very shrewd, he understands exactly how to get what he wants, which is lots of gold." But he frowned, looking back over his shoulder at thc taverna.

Nicephoros said, "What's the matter?"

"This murder."

"Oh, they must kill each other all the time."

"Yes, but this one, Bjorn, he was ours."

"What."

"He was supposed to be keeping his ears open for me."

Nicephoros was silent for awhile; they came down off the bridge and went through the gate in the wall. "Maybe it was an accident."

"The world is an accident," Michael said. "Murders are on purpose."

Nicephoros bit his teeth together. They turned onto the harbor street. The corner of the city wall was just behind them and he could see the first of the great towers looming above the trees.

This was getting harsh, he thought. They needed the Varangians more than the Varangians needed them. But there were good reasons for keeping them outside the city walls. Now somebody in that army had secrets he was willing to kill for. Everything seemed to be fraying at the edges. He said, "I'm glad I'm going on campaign. All I have to deal with is Constantine."

"My prayers will be with you," Michael said.

⟿

Blud was still seething when he reached the taverna on the harborfront, raging first at Tryggve, then at the stupid Greeks, choosing the lowborn Norse sword-hack over him. The taverna was dark, which he was glad for. He felt everybody knew his humiliation. He went to the pipes and paid for a can of raki and drank it in a single draught.

That can only stirred his temper higher; his anger narrowed down to the Greeks, Michael Lecapenus, and the unreachable Emperor particularly. He turned back to the pipe for a second can, and there found Theodore, the frog-faced man, smiling at him.

"Well, well," Theodore said. "I'm so glad to see you. Come have a drink with me."

They went into the back of the taverna, where a few tables

stood around a brazier. The tables had little lamps on them but only one was lit. Theodore sat at a table with an unlit lamp and Blud took the shadowy seat opposite him.

Theodore folded his hands together on the table. "I was glad to get your message, I haven't seen you in a while. I hope you are prospering." He had to repeat the word slowly, twice, until Blud understood it.

Blud burst out, "Prosper! I cannot prosper when I am ignored."

Theodore said quietly, "You can prosper where you are valued, my lord Blud." He took a folded paper from inside his coat, and held it out before Blud. "I carry this for another who longs for the reign of the true Emperor. Of the highest rank."

Blud sniffed; the paper gave off a luxuriant scent, like a fine woman. The paper itself looked rich as silk. At least he wasn't the only one. In good company. But his throat was dry. Now that he had come to the edge he was afraid to go over.

Theodore tucked the letter back inside his coat. He said, "It's all over the City that the false brat Basil has formed another guard." His bulging froggy eyes were guileless. "You would not perhaps be in that guard."

Blud's temper stabbed him again, and his neck felt hot; he said, "No. I have bigger plans." With his anger to push him he leapt. "I've thought about what you said."

"Have you," Theodore said swiftly. He glanced quickly around them. "And you've decided?"

"I have a price," Blud said.

"Naturally."

Blud put his purse on the table and fingered out the nomisma with Phokas's face on it. "I want five thousand more of these. Then I can pay off my men."

Theodore laid his hands flat on the table. "I can deliver that. And you promise the Varangians?"

"Yes," Blud said. He slid the nomisma back into his purse. He wouldn't have to tell any of the other Rus about this; they would follow him anywhere. Enough of them, anyway. In the back of his mind, he was thinking he really didn't even have to give them any of the gold.

Theodore's eyes shone. He said, "May God bless you, sir. You will save Constantinople."

Blud said, "Just get that gold." With so much he could buy Kiev out from under Volodymyr.

"I'll send to you for our next meeting," Theodore said. "I have to see this is gotten off." He patted his coat over the envelope, and slipped from the table into the darkness.

Blud sat still, rigid; it was done now. He thought, I'll show them they can't pass me over, but in the back of his mind there was a flicker of dread. He had to be careful. The Greeks were wary, watchful, sneaky. He had gotten rid of one spy but today Raef Corbansson had been all over the bath asking questions. Blud wished he could get his hands around Raef Corbansson's scrawny neck. While he was brooding about Raef's nosiness it came to him there was a better, neater way to deal with him. He gathered up his purse with the nomisma, and throwing his empty can into the tub at the back of the taverna he went out and rode his horse back to the bath. There, he sent a man to bring Raef Corbansson to him.

—⚬—

Blud had left the taverna Maria Theodokos to Tryggve and his band, but he kept a hall in a court of the nearby public bath, on the City side of the bridge, inside the City wall. He sent to Raef to meet him there in the afternoon, when most of the City was taking its rest.

Leif said, "Are you sure you want to do this?"

Raef said, "I want to find out what he says about Bjorn."

"He'll lie."

"Lies are interesting." Raef went out of the taverna and across the bridge into the City.

Blud Sveneldsson held court on the outside of the long building that housed the bath, a gray wall enclosing three sides of a small grassy field, maybe one of the exercise yards. Nobody ran around or tumbled on it now. Raef went in past several Rus standing around the wide front opening. Their axes were stacked against the end of the wall. Inside the court, Blud was sitting on a stone bench in a corner, a drinking cup in his hand. He wore his shining red-gold beard down over his chest like a breastplate.

When Raef came up, Blud said, without greeting, "Sit down, have a drink." He snapped his fingers, and a Greek boy came in with a ewer. Raef glanced over his shoulder at the men up at the open front of the court, who were looking elsewhere.

Blud cleared his throat, and started talking again. "Well, Goose, you've seen Constantinople now. Rich, hah?"

Raef said, "I've never seen any place like it. There's enough gold in the palace to buy Denmark."

"Denmark, England, and Norway all," Blud said, nodding. It occurred to Raef that Blud had never been anywhere but Rus. The big red-bearded captain said, "Even a little of it would make a man a king, back in his home country."

"Where are you going with this?" Raef said.

Blud glanced around, looked intently into Raef's eyes, and

spoke just above a whisper. "We could raid this place. Forget their war, it's no matter of ours. We're already inside the walls. They can't fight us off. Steal everything we can lift and go back to Kiev. The old Varanger will follow you. My men will follow me. In Kiev, you help me overthrow Volodymyr, who murdered your brother, and I will give you ships to go north, with all the gold you can carry. You could be King of Denmark."

Raef sat still a moment, his gaze on Blud's broad, intent face. His back tingled. There was only one reason why Blud would propose something like this to him, and he began to wonder how far he would get before Blud tried to kill him, no matter what he said. He said, "No."

"Ah, come along. You're a Viking. Aren't you?"

"No."

"Why?"

Raef smiled at him, tensing, beginning to get to his feet. "Because you killed a friend of mine, and I don't like you." He rose.

Blud said sharply, "This is your last chance, Goose. Don't be a fool."

Raef glanced over his shoulder at the men by the door; his mouth was dry and his legs felt shaky, but he managed a harsh voice. "Order them off, or I'll take you with me."

Blud smiled at him, stiffly, like a wolf snarling. "Oh, I won't kill you myself, Goose. I'll have the Emperor do that. Run. Make it interesting."

Raef wheeled toward the door, and went out between the guards untouched. He knew he was doing exactly what Blud wanted. His bones felt like wires. His head was seething with anger and fear. He circled the bath to the street and went back down the slope toward the St. Mamas bridge, but as he got closer, his steps slowed. A great cold foreboding was clenching his guts. The taverna was the first place anybody seeking him would look. At the open gate where the street went out the wall and through the little village to the bridge, he stopped. He could make himself go no farther. He turned and went back up the street, into the City.

⸺❦⸺

"Does this Guard have to live in the palace?" Leif said.

"No, I don't think so." Tryggve was keeping track of his new guardsmen by tying knots on a string. He coiled it up and slid it into his purse. "They still expect us to sleep at St. Mamas, as far as I know, except when we're standing guard, three watches, all day, all night."

"I hate guard duty."

Tryggve said, "There will be more to it than that. It means we don't have to listen to Blud anymore, first of all."

"That's an advantage," Leif said. "Not that I listened much to him anyway. I hope the pay's good."

"It's good enough. The best is, when the fighting starts we'll be right around the Emperor, in front of everybody for the best loot."

Leif was thinking the fighting would be hardest there, too. He glanced down the table, where Laissa was hanging over the edge, her eyes on him. In the thin yellow dress her fine skin glowed. Under the grime and her sins, she still was a pretty little girl. He reached out and pulled her into his lap. She giggled. She acted more as if he were her father than a lover and he had stopped touching her much. He had told the other men not to touch her; they preferred anyway the compliant women in the village on the other side of the bridge, who would lie down for them. She said, "What's this?"

She held out her hand with a gold basileus on it. Leif said, "Ah, once I had many of those."

Tryggve, frowning, plucked it off her palm.

"Hey."

Tryggve studied the coin, his eyes sharp, and then showed it to Leif. "Then there's always the problem which Emperor we're talking about." He turned to Laissa. "Where did you get this?"

Leif took the coin between his thumb and forefinger and held it into the light. He stared at it for a moment before he saw what was wrong with it. It was new, the edges still sharp, but instead of the two heads of the Emperors, there was only one.

"I got it from Raef," Laissa said, her eyes round. "Raef Corbansson."

CHAPTER THIRTEEN

Usually Basil declined the great banquets Helena and Constantine enjoyed so much, but there had been no way to avoid this one, which was in honor of Constantine who was marching out in the morning against Phokas. Still Basil showed no grace about it. He did not lie down on his couch, as his brother and the rest of the Imperial Family did, but sat there hunched over his knees, eating and tossing the leftovers back onto the table. Helena made sniggering remarks about him all through the meal, which he ignored. Constantine lay there smiling and enjoying the music, the dancing, and the other entertainments. All around them, the servants moved in a constant wheeling, bringing and taking dishes, holding cloths and cups and ewers, messages and gifts.

As always Michael waited behind Basil, against the back wall, with Nicephoros on one side and Leo and John Barbos on the other. He was thinking that at least Basil could sit down. He had spent his life, he thought, standing behind Emperors eating. On the far side of the room several other patricians and nobles stood in rows, honored with a presence before the Imperial Family, waiting hours for a single glance. Most of them would have sent a message, or a gift, but Constantine would accept very few. Basil, none at all.

Helena, who loved excess and display, had planned this banquet, and the dinner was endless. There were fowls, roasted and grilled, fish in various sauces, seven different kinds of meat, stuffed fruits, bread in the shape of chariots and shields, ices, nut cakes, fruit carved to look like flowers, endless wine. At the center of everything were the Emperors and the Empress and the little Porphyrogenitae; everything whirled around them, like Ptolemy's angels. Constantine, splendid in his gold-trimmed gown, his jeweled crown, reclined like a great lion on his couch. Now, after a course of figs, he was letting a servant wash his hands, drying carefully between the fingers.

Beyond him Helena reclined with her elbow on a green embroidered pillow, surrounded by her women and her children; Zoë was already asleep on the next couch. She had been playing draughts with Eudoxia and the pieces were scattered on the floor. Eudoxia was staring grumpily into her mirror. Little Theodora was pinching her food into mushy shapes. In front of them all passed an endless stream of jugglers and panegyrists and poets. The servants were bringing in the next course, which looked like something else sugared.

Nobody ate, of course, but the Imperial Family; everybody else just watched.

Michael went to fill the Emperor's cup again. Basil nodded at the current performer, a tall eunuch reciting from the *Iliad* and noting an astonishing string of parallels between the Greeks' war on Troy and Constantine's march against Phokas.

"How much more of this shit is there?"

Michael said, "I don't know, Sebastos."

He saw, dismayed, that Basil had reached his intended audience. Two couches down, the Empress leaned forward, and her voice carried through the eunuch's mellow entoning. "What's this, Basil, you can't even sit here to honor your brother who is going out to do battle against Phokas? Are you afraid he'll actually succeed?"

"Now, now," Constantine said. He looked down at his

hands, covered with rings. "We must be one against the enemy." The eunuch was plowing along with his recital, his cheeks red.

"The enemy," Helena said. She was sitting straight up. The wine flushed her face and her eyes were black as coals and burning with anger and her voice was very loud. She glared at Basil. "God and the Blessed Virgin save us from the real enemy."

Basil wheeled toward her. Michael murmured, "Sebastos, this is an opportunity to get up and walk out."

Basil paid no attention to him. He said, "She is drunken, Constantine, she needs to go somewhere and rest." His voice rang like iron. The eunuch faltered and stopped; a hush had fallen over the rest of the room, where nobody moved, and everybody watched this happening.

"Now, now," Constantine said. His smile looked rigid.

Helena said, "What we need is a real general. With real Roman legions, not fur-bearing Scythians." She thrust her head forward; Michael could almost see a forked tongue darting between her lips. "Maybe Phokas ought to win."

"It must be easier for him to believe that he's Emperor," Basil said, in the dead silence, "since he's slept with the Augusta. But it's a false logic, since a lot of other men have too, and not all of them are Emperor."

Helena flushed even deeper; Michael remembered the rumor that she and Phokas had been lovers, years ago. That of course made it worse. He said, "Sebastos."

Constantine said, "Why can't everybody just relax and listen to the poems?"

Helena raised her voice. "Basil hates poems, he hates music, he hates beauty, he's as coarse and ugly and evil as his Scythians, he's the wolf cub, who drove off his own mother—"

At the mention of Theophano Michael rolled his eyes up to

the ceiling. Before him, Basil lunged onto his feet, shouting, "Get her out of here. Constantine—"

Helena was not moving. She blazed with indignant fury. She stood straight upright before her couch, her great eyes direct, her voice clear. "May the Blessed Mother desert you—as you deserted your mother—"

Constantine got up, one hand out, keeping Basil back. "Helena, dear—" Michael moved a little, trying to get unobtrusively into Basil's way. Helena shouted past him, her voice carrying to every ear in the big room.

"She begged you to save her, didn't she—she begged you to let her stay—"

Basil's voice roared over hers. "No constant woman was ever born, none but whores and murderesses!"

Constantine at last had his wife by the arm and was moving her by force out the side door. Around the hall the eunuchs were hurrying the rest of the crowd swiftly away. Nicephoros came up beside Michael, grim-faced.

On the threshold Helena wheeled again, and shouted again.

"I will not take such humiliation. While my husband is gone from the City, so shall I be. I shall retire to the seclusion of the monastery of St. Anthony. And you—you—"

"I will be here," Basil said, "until the last stone falls. You crawl into a hole somewhere, with a monk for company. I understand they love being on the bottom."

She yelled, but left, Constantine pushing her. The room was fast emptying of all but Basil and his four men and a few pages.

Basil wheeled toward Michael. "I don't go anywhere. You don't tell me to go anywhere."

Michael bowed down. "Sebastos."

Basil crossed himself. He muttered, "Except the Holy Mother of God, born without sin," and Michael knew he was still thinking of his rant against women. He looked around to give someone an order, and chose John Barbos. "Make sure she stays in that monastery." John bowed.

Except for them the hall was empty. The last of the guests and servants had fled. Basil sat down again at the table. "Here, come and eat this." He waved his hand at the litter of food on the table and Michael and the others came around to feed themselves.

Through a mouthful of bread, Basil went on, "While they are gone, no receptions. No ceremonies. I will hear necessary people in the war room, sign papers there, eat there, everything. Leo, what do the astrologers say?"

"I need to talk to you about that," Leo Agyros said, and came up, opening his charts. "Phokas's birth charts are confusing. One is clearly a fake, but I'm not sure which."

"I'll miss you," Michael said to Nicephoros, while Basil looked at pictures of stars. He had found a whole pigeon breast and was picking succulent strips of meat from it. The pigeon had been fed on berries and the meat was rich and sweet and tender and blue. "Have some."

Nicephoros tossed aside the core of an apple. "You won't have time to miss me, Michael." He ate some of the pigeon. "Ummm. Very good. I'm going to miss decent food."

"You're jesting. Constantine will travel with a full kitchen."

Leo was saying, "I shall cast both horoscopes, but I'm sure one of these is a false trail."

"Do it. I need a date." Basil was standing, stretching his arms, restless. A page had brought him a basin to wash his hands. Another waited with linen, his eyes properly lowered. Hastily

Michael finished the pigeon. He glanced at Nicephoros. "Who started that fight?"

"Basil," Nicephoros said. "To get out of more panegyrics. But she was magnificent, wasn't she? A veritable Hera."

Michael said, "A hair-raising virago, more like." He thought Helena had begun it.

"Nonetheless, a magnificent woman."

Michael gave him a suspicious look, remembering some other rumors he had heard, these about Nicephoros and Helena. Nicephoros smiled at him. "Not that you'd notice. Michael Lecapenus the voluntary eunuch."

"The better to serve," Michael said. He turned toward John Barbos. "Where is this monastery? Saint Anthony."

The tall eunuch shrugged. "Somewhere in Thrace?"

"I think Saint Paul meant serving God," Nicephoros said.

"God. Rome." Basil was leaving. Michael followed him, picking up a cup of wine as he went. "I don't see much difference." Nicephoros was right: with only three of them, they were going to work very hard for a while. He went down the hall toward the door, after the Emperor.

—⊷—

Basil could not sleep; he walked up and down on the balcony of the Bucoleon, looking out into the darkness over the sea. Thinking, unwillingly, of his mother.

Begged him, she had not. She had never begged. She had ordered him. When the patriarch Polyeuctes told John Tzimisces he could not have both her and the throne, and John moved with no hesitation to put her away, and Constantine wailed for her, she came to her elder son, there in the Triklinios in front of every-body, and demanded, "Basil, you are the Emperor. Tell him I am to stay."

He said nothing. Only two days before he had seen her in a much smaller, more private space, standing by his stepfather's hacked and headless body. The blood had gushed out and splat-tered her shoes. She was standing in her husband's blood. Be-side her was her lover with the knife. Behind her the bed where she had wallowed with each. He remembered her face calm as the rising moon above the slaughter of an Emperor.

"Basil, I am your mother. Tell him."

And when he still said nothing, her voice rose. "Tell him! You ungrateful little toad of a boy! You tiger-hearted villain! Tell him!"

He was silent. John Tzimisces, looking on, said, "You may choose to go with her."

Into exile. To a monastery. Even then, he had known what that meant: the tonsure, probable gelding, eventual blinding, a long, dull life in the dark. Constantine was sobbing, somewhere, in his tutor's arms. Basil stared at his mother and said nothing. She spit in his face, there in front of the whole court.

He had been eleven years old then. He remembered think-ing, One less person to tell me what to do. When she spat on him, John Tzimisces laughed, and turned away. They all laughed. They had thought, then, that he didn't matter, as long as they gave him horses and money, and let him miss the ceremonies.

He had never seen his mother again. Free of her, he made his own court, his own friends, his own plans. He had met Michael that same day, another misfit, the last Lecapenus.

Now, twenty years later, John Tzimisces was dead; most of

the people who had laughed, that day, were dead, and he stood by the balcony looking across the sleek black expanse of the Propontis toward Abydos and his last rival.

His mother had been the first and even now she troubled his sleep. He crushed her back into the depths of his memory. He worked not to remember her. He paced along the balcony over the sea, looking south, and willed that cold black stillness into his mind. Yet he could not blot her out entirely; she was always there, somewhere, that last ember he could not quench.

He walked along the balcony, looking down toward Abydos, the salt wind blowing across his face, longing for the battle to come.

———

"No, no." Helena took the little green pot away from Zoë before she could open it. "No, not that, child. That makes your eyes bigger but too much is bad." She made sure the lid was tight and put the jar into the sandalwood box. Her maids were folding her clothes into the big chest, not many, not enough to arouse anybody's suspicions.

"Oh, Mama Augusta, I wish you wouldn't leave." Zoë pushed the cosmetics tray aside. She leaned both elbows on the little table before them. "I miss you so much."

"I have to, dear." She patted her hand.

Eudoxia said, "Uncle Basil was horrible, wasn't he, Mama?"

"Yes he was. He is always horrible. Now, while I'm gone, you are to make sure you all go to Mass, morning and evening, and say prayers for me."

"Yes, Mama," they all said. Theodora looked wide-eyed at her. "Will you be gone long?"

"I hope not," she said. She put her second favorite earrings into the sandalwood box and closed it.

"Shouldn't you take someone?" Zoë asked, leaning on her knee.

"She's going to a monastery," Eudoxia said, scornfully. "There you wear habits all day long, and pray." She picked at one of the red marks on her face.

Helena gave a thin laugh. She loathed the woolen habits, always sought a dispensation whenever she had to stay in a religious house, intended to wear nothing but silk the rest of her life. Surely, she thought, where she was really going there would be a court of women to attend her. Eager to attend her. Empress of Rome.

She said, "You will be good. Mind the nurses. Go to Mass. Attend your lessons. Eudoxia, stop, that only makes it worse. Make a special devotion to St. Lazarus." They would stay in the gynacaeum, adored and petted and even more spoiled than usual. "Give me a kiss."

They lined up to kiss her. The eunuch was standing in the door; the boat was waiting for her. She hugged her children, nodded to the servant to bring her chest, and went down to take her fortunes in her hands. And incidentally, she thought, to save Rome.

⸻

For joining Tryggve's Palace Guard Leif got a new tunic and a cloak, a fancy gold pin to fasten his cloak, and a long-handled axe, but he had to stand holding the axe for hours outside doors. To ease his boredom he worked on his understanding of Greek by listening in on everything he could.

With Constantine and Helena gone, and the little princesses down in the women's halls, half the palace complex went unused. Tryggve's men patrolled that, also, but mostly they stood guard over the rooms where the Emperor went. For a while, Leif was posted outside the door to Basil's war room, where the Emperor also heard petitioners.

Leif realized right away that nobody spoke to the Emperor except his closest friends—three men, since Nicephoros Ouranos was gone. The petitioner, after suitable greetings, talked his problem over with one of the friends, who asked questions, or not, as he chose. Meanwhile the Emperor, seeming to pay no attention at all, played his endless game on the sand table. After the petitioner left, Basil said what he thought, and to Leif's amazement, he had been listening to everything and knew exactly what to do.

So after half an hour's courtly conversation between the Baghdadi wanderer Rashid ibn Samudi, whom Leif had seen at Kiev, and the lanky eunuch John Barbos, the Emperor said, "Give him some money for his amir. Not much. They did let Bardas Sklerus hide out there for a while. Give them enough to keep them fighting. That way, they aren't fighting us. The real Caliph now is the one in Egypt anyway."

"There are a lot of caliphs," John said. He had the gelding's fluty voice. "There's one in Spain, too."

"The more the better. Make them common as counts."

Leif was there when Blud came up, sneering down his nose, his hair and beard shining like strands of silk, bands of gold around his upper arms and gold chains lying on his chest. "Holding up the walls, are you? You just stand back when a real warrior comes in."

Leif did not stand back. He said, "Where do you think you're going?"

"I have to see the Emperor," Blud said. "Right now."

Noticing him, Michael Lecapenus had come over to the doorway. Leif drew back to his side of the door and looked in another direction but he kept his ear cocked.

Michael said, "What is it? You know you should speak to the parakoimomenos first, you can't just walk in here."

Blud said, "I have to see the Emperor. Directly. About a plot against him."

Leif twitched, startled. Michael thought it was serious, too, because he took Blud immediately into the room. Leif let out his breath in a whoosh. He remembered the funny nomisma. Bjorn floating facedown in the bath. Now Blud with a fish story. None of this made sense to him. He leaned against the wall, his ear aimed into the room, listening.

—§—

"Do you believe that?" Basil asked, when Blud Sveneldsson had gone.

Michael's face was white. He made pets of the Varangians, but also, Basil thought, he had known some of this beforehand and not understood. Or not understood it in the way Blud had just suggested.

"Tell me. Do you believe what he just said?"

Michael said, slowly, "That Raef Corbansson went to Blud and proposed they sack the City and sell it to Phokas?" He waggled his head from side to side. "I believe it of any of them. It's their country way. It's one reason we try to keep them outside in

St. Mamas. But they are pledged to us." He lifted his gaze to Basil's. "Something is going on, that I know."

"Either I don't trust a masterless wanderer, or I don't trust the commander of my army," Basil said. "None of this looks good." He glanced toward the door again. "What else haven't you told me about?"

"Well," Michael said, "actually, there's this." He held a gold coin, so newly struck the edges glinted sharp as knives.

Basil took the coin, and Michael stepped back, knowing what was coming. But the Emperor for a moment said nothing. He turned the coin over, and he fell into what Michael thought of as Basil's darkness. His face turned expressionless, his eyes unblinking, his body rigid as stone. He said, in a voice like ice, "Where did this come from?"

"Tryggve gave it to me," Michael said. He took another quiet step backward. "Just before Blud came in. It's the only one I've seen."

"Where did he get it?"

"He said a whore gave it to him. He said she said she got it from Raef Corbansson."

Basil lifted his head, and let out a yell. Michael shrank down a little, but he was relieved at this howling; the darkness was much worse. The Emperor wheeled around, shouting a volley of stableboy curses. He strode down the table to the nearest brazier and cast the gold coin into it. Staring down at it, as if with his eyes alone he could melt the image of Phokas on it, he said, "I am Emperor. I. I. No one declines me and accepts Phokas!"

Michael said, "One of our spies is dead, also. The last person he talked to seems to have been Raef Corbansson."

Basil said a long, terrible oath. "Where is he now?"

"Sebastos, I . . . can't find him."

"What?"

"I'm sure he's in the City somewhere, but he's not been at the taverna or at St. Mamas."

"He seems pretty hard to overlook to me," Basil said. He was furious; his eyes pierced Michael's. "All that hair. Find him." He clenched his fist. "I'll see his face on the floor before me, dead or alive, I don't care."

"Sebastos."

———

Michael did not sleep. They could not find the Varangian but it was the Phokas nomisma that held his mind. The puzzles in it drew him on. Where it had come from. What it was meant for. That there was only one made no sense. Phokas's agents would need many, he thought, if they were buying a mob, or bribing open a gate. Yet this was the only one. If there were more, certainly he would see them: big money like that got noticed. How had Raef Corbansson gotten hold of it?

The money was surely from Phokas, a bribe of some kind. The Varangian had fought against Phokas at Chrysopolis. He had turned down service with the Emperor. He seemed unlikely to have farmed himself out to somebody he didn't know. And why would he have given a gold nomisma to a whore? He was inexplicable as the single coin.

There had to be more coming. This had been used to impress somebody—Raef, perhaps—but to be useful there had to be more money on the way. It had to be coming from outside the City because to make a large number of coins would take a mint, and no mint in Constantinople itself could do this without being immediately caught. The Eparch's inspections were rigorous. All the business in Constantinople passed through the office of the governor of the City. In the morning Michael went back to the war room and fished the half-melted nomisma out of the cold brazier. Later in the day, after he had seen his share of the petitioners, he went to the Eparch and got his help, putting all his deputies on watch for that smuggled cargo, so heavy for its size, coming from the west.

—⁑—

Markos could not find Raef, so he had gotten his two oldest cousins to row this time. He had only a small cargo anyway, just an excuse, really. It was a beautiful sunny early spring day, with a spanking northwest wind, and so they could put up the sail. Markos sat at the helm, and guided them down the Horn through the usual mess of barges and people fishing, and they got across the strait easily enough.

It was on the way back that everything went crazy.

The rowing was harder, much harder than he remembered ever before, and he took turns with his cousins, who were only boys, and struggled against the wind and the wild current and the tide. Then the Eparch's dromon hailed them.

Markos stood up, waving his seal, expecting the usual easy off here. But they grappled his boat, they held him fast to the side of the dromon, beneath the gilded curlicues of the gunwale, and put down a ladder. A deputy climbed down and went through Markos's boat from one end to the other, making the crew all stand, and turning over the benches. They were looking for something in particular, he saw, panicked, praying they did not search him.

At last the Eparch's deputy climbed up the ladder again, and they released the grapples. As the big dromon was pulling away, his cousin Elias turned to him. "What was that about, anyway?"

"I don't know," Markos said, sitting down in the stern. The dromon was rowing purposefully down on the next boat. "Row. We're drifting."

The two boys sat obediently to the oars. He reached down into his purse, took hold of the folded paper there, and without taking his hand from the purse ripped the letter to bits. From now on, he thought, he would be an honest man. Straight and pious, forevermore. Carefully he let the bits of paper go over the side, a few at a time, all the way back to the Horn.

CHAPTER FOURTEEN

Raef spent the night under a haystack near the western end of the city wall. The watch came by seldom, and the hay kept him warm; he could burrow into the darkness, stretch out, listen to the birds, and think all this over.

He wanted to dream of the hawk, to get her counsel, but she never came when he wanted her.

He had one copper left. Desperate, he went down just after sunrise to Markos's compound and caught him going to the outhouse.

"You owe me money." He kept his voice low, walking along beside Markos to the shithouse. "You cheated me—"

Someone else was coming; he bit off his words, looking down the wall. Markos froze. Out the door came Irene, Ruskas's widow, plodding along down the path to the outhouse.

They waited, both utterly still, until she had gone inside and shut the door. Then Markos turned to him.

"I have no money. Raef, I never meant to cheat you, I promise. Look. Wait here." He pulled him back behind the wall of the compound, away from the street and the water. "Don't worry about Irene, she's deaf as a rock. Stay here. I'll be right back."

He was only gone a few moments, and brought him a loaf of bread, a jar of raki, and a piece of cheese. Raef seized them, drained the raki at a throw, and began to chunk down the bread and cheese. Markos was watching him mournfully. He said, tentatively, "You could stay here, if you want."

Raef said, "No, it's too dangerous."

The Greek shrugged, looking relieved. Raef gave him the empty cup back, and went up along the harbor street, eating the last of the cheese. He was washing his hands in a fountain near the fish market when he realized somebody was coming toward him from behind.

He wheeled around, and a big yellow-bearded man in a long dark coat ran at him with a dagger. He gave a screech as he came. Raef braced himself, saw someone else lunging at him from the side, and dodged between them. The two men ran into each other. Raef dashed away down the street and into the first narrow lane he came to, went over a wall, and along another, doubling back around toward the harbor again.

In the shade of an arch, sitting near a bunch of beggars, he pulled his shirt up over his head to hide his hair and tried to figure out what to do. Blud was behind this, somehow; it had all started when he asked questions at the bath about Bjorn. Blud was trying to get rid of him. Certainly he had killed Bjorn.

He went to the bath, and waited, lurking in one corner, and then moving to an arbor on the slope nearby where he could see through the branches. The stocks of the vines twined thick as his wrist up the arbor walls. Buds were appearing on the canes and the space felt close and cool.

Blud had killed Bjorn for some reason, to keep Bjorn from talking, or from finding out too much. Raef remembered the Kievite prince's offer to him, and thought, He's betraying Constantinople to Phokas.

Near sundown he saw Blud leave the bath, trailed by half a dozen of his men. Raef followed him, staying well away. He saw the watch ahead of him and had to wind his way up a staircase and past a fountain thronged with water-sellers and their

donkeys, but he cut down across Blud's track and found him
again.

Blud went here and there, leaving men and sending others
off with messages. Following him was hard, tiring, boring.
Then at the end, all he did was go back to St. Mamas.

Raef waited on the far side of the bridge, in the cover of the
gate in the wall. This was also a favorite place of beggars and
by pulling his shirt up over his hair and hunching over he could
hide among them and still watch the bridge. When someone
came down through the gate, the beggars all called plaintively,
and their hands swung out, cupped, and he did that also, not
speaking, but putting his hand out. No one ever gave them
anything.

In the evening, Leif came out of the taverna, walked across
the bridge, through the gate, and slowly up the harbor street. A
few minutes later he came slowly walking back. He did not go
over the bridge, but followed the street on past the curve where
it met the great city wall, and then came back again, walking
slowly along, his head down. He went along the street and turned
back again, and as he came on the way back, finally, Raef understood, and he got up and went in through the gate and whistled to
him.

Leif ambled toward him, not looking in his direction, and
they walked together along the wall in the dark. Leif said, "I
knew you'd be somewhere around. You'd better get far away,
fast. They're looking all over for you."

"They. Who?"

"The watch. The Imperial people. Blud's boys. They're
hanging some plot against the Emperor on you, and blaming you
for killing Bjorn, too, for good measure." Leif slid one hand up

between them; in his palm he had a couple of coppers. "That's all I've got. You'd better get out of the City. Did you give Laissa a gold piece?"

"No."

"I didn't think so." Leif turned and walked away, back toward the gate to the St. Mamas bridge.

Raef leaned back into the dark shadow under the gate's archway. The beggars had all gone elsewhere, except for one who was drunk or maybe dead over by the wall. Someone was lighting the torches on the harbor street, the light coming nearer, but it would not penetrate here, beneath the cold stone.

He wasn't going to leave Constantinople. What Leif had said only hardened what he had already believed: Blud was making him the goat in some much bigger scheme.

He gathered up his hair and bound it in a club at the nape of his neck, and rubbed dirt on his face and his tunic, but he knew somebody would recognize him quickly enough. Eventually, curled up in the gateway where Blud had to pass, he slept.

All the next day he followed Blud around the City. Once someone saw him, and pointed, and he turned and went quickly away down an alley, twisting and turning, and then moving over to find Blud again. He felt prickly, as if a web of interest tightened around him. He thought somebody was sniffing out his trail, back behind him, but he fixed all his attention on Blud and ignored the tingle on the nape of his neck.

He bought bread, waiting until there was a great crowd at the baker's counter, and then just sticking out his hand with the copper, so she never looked up at his face.

In the harbor street near the St. Mamas bridge as he was waiting for Blud, Laissa saw him; she was walking by, part of a big crowd of girls, and her head turned, her eyes wide. She jerked forward and hurried off, passing the girls in front of her, going toward the taverna.

He waited then, on edge, for Blud's men to come rushing out of St. Mamas and grab him. But she went into the taverna, and stayed there. He drew back into the shadow of the gate, against the cold stone.

—⋄—

Leif sat eating lentils and sausage at his usual table; he was supposed to go on watch in a little while, a prospect that made him low. He told himself he was too old a man to stand around all day. Laissa came across the room toward him and sat down on the bench next to him.

"Leif," she said, "what if someone did something really wrong, that hurt somebody else—somebody the first somebody really kind of liked."

He scooped up the saucy little beans on a wedge of the flatbread and stuffed it in his mouth. He thought of Raef hiding out in the cold and was angry but he held his temper down. When he looked at her again, he saw how sad she was, and had to smile. "Well," he said, wiping his fingers on his sleeve, "you repay."

Her thin shoulders went up and down. "How?"

Leif pushed the plate away. "I don't know." He leaned his elbows on the table. "You like him, no?"

"This isn't about—"

She stopped in midword, her eyes going to the door. Leif

looked where she was looking, and saw Blud there, in the doorway.

He beckoned toward them, to her, surely, Leif knew, and he glanced at her. She was shrinking back into the bench, her knees drawn up. She shook her head at the big bluff figure in the light of the doorway.

"Send her over here," Blud called. He fingered up a coin and held it into the light, a gleam of silver. "Come, pussy."

Leif got up from the bench, moved around, and stood in front of her. The other half-dozen men in the room were silent, watching. Leif said, "Leave her alone."

Blud set himself, his feet wide apart in their high boots, his hand on his belt. "You tub of guts, keep out of this."

Leif strode up and thrust his fat belly at the Kievite prince. "I'll roll this tub of guts right over you, mighty mouth, if you bother her again."

Blud reared back, his fist rising, and then between them was a staff of wood, and Gregorios pushing his way after, thrusting them apart.

"Not in my place!" He waved his stick under Leif's nose.

Leif took a step back, his eyes fixed on Blud's; in the middle of the room Maria had her arms around Laissa. Blud sneered at Gregorios, but when the big Greek cocked his arm with the stick Blud backed hastily away. He gave Laissa a sideways glance.

"I'll get you, girl." He turned to go. The light shone on his sleek red beard, his curly fine-combed hair. "Alone." He went off.

Tryggve came in, his head turning after Blud, his brow furrowed. Leif gave up a sigh. Under his breath, he said, "And stay out, you shit-merchant."

Tryggve jabbed at him. "You're on duty. You're late. Get going." Leif glanced around at Laissa, still snug in Maria's arms, and went out.

—⚬—

Darkness fell. Raef thought he'd have to stay the night again there, in the cold stone arch. But then Blud came out of St. Mamas with a man ahead of him carrying a lantern on a pole, and crossed the bridge and came up through the gate. He went almost within reach of Raef, standing there by the wall in the deep shadow.

He let them get ahead of him, the little spot of light from the lantern glowing on the street, on the walls around, like a bait on the end of a string. Leaning on the wall, waiting, he became aware again that somebody was following him, and getting closer.

He moved off fast in the other direction, as he had done before, going any way that took him up the hill, in narrow lanes and over walls. High on the hill, he circled around toward where he had last seen Blud, and picked out the glow of the lantern, from a distance, in the harbor street. He started that way. Then, abruptly, he sensed Blud, one street over to his left, alone. He had sent the lantern off on a false trail.

Raef forgot about the men following him; he fastened all his attention on Blud, to keep from losing him. Going down an alley, he stood still a moment, so intent that the Rus prince seemed like a fire in the gloom, a warmth in the cold winter air. Raef went along the street well behind him, followed him even around corners, through a building.

Blud went into the building alone and came out the other side, where he met another man, wrapped in a dark cloak.

Who talked to Blud in Greek. "Glory to the Empire?"

"Good, you finally came."

"No, answer me! Glory to the Empire."

Blud said, "Oh, yes—glory to the Emperor Bardas Phokas."

"That's better."

They went off down the narrow street. They were close to the great double wall. But they did not go out; the gates were well guarded, as Raef already knew. Instead they went uphill into the fringe of the City, farmland, trees, old fields, barns, empty ground. Blud and the man with him went along the street until it turned to a dirt path, an unlit winding rut through stands of trees and scattered houses. Raef hung back, because there was no cover, but Blud and the man with him walked out along the dirt path a good way through the dark. Then they turned abruptly left and went off the path into the space between two houses.

Raef trotted down the lane, afraid now of losing the track; he kept his eyes on the place where they had turned. There was nothing to hide him except the tall grass along the side of the path and he hunched over and moved quickly.

They had gone through a gate, now closed, into a lane that led off between two dark peaked roofs. There were other gates on either side, and behind him, across the path, there were more houses and a garden. Raef, hoping now that whoever was following him was the watch and not just more of Blud's men, took his knife and scored the gatepost, a bright, deep mark, and went in.

He knew Blud was ahead of him somewhere. The lane ran between high walls of the two houses but there seemed no way into either. Blud he thought was on the right. He tried to narrow his mind now simply to the Rus prince, to find him, and grew sure he was somewhere in the house to the right.

He slid around the corner of the wall. The stone abruptly

gave way to a hedge of trees, and he slipped between two trunks, into a garden.

In the house ahead of him, a light showed in a doorway. Then right behind him, someone spoke.

"Put your hands out. Don't move. My spear is right at your back."

Raef's breath clogged in his throat. He did not know the voice behind him, which spoke Greek. He stood still while the man back there took his knife and groped him over for other weapons, and then pushed him forward.

"March. To the door. Try to run, and I'll skewer you."

Raef hoped this was not the man he had known for a while that was following him. Something sharp poked him in the back, hard enough to slice him. With the hand heavy on his shoulder he walked forward to the door, waiting for a chance to dodge, or jump, but quickly two other men appeared, one on either side of him, with more spears. He felt a rivulet of blood run down his side.

"Who's this?"

"Caught him in the garden. Take him in to Theodore." The man behind him suddenly jerked Raef's hands behind him and wrapped a rope around his wrists and knotted it.

One on either side, the spearmen gripped his arms and hauled him along into the house and down a short dark corridor. Raef kept his feet under him, but he hung back, made them carry him. They kept good hold of him, and pushing open a door, they dragged him into a lamplit room where Blud stood.

They threw him down on the floor. Raef blinked his eyes against the dust. Besides Blud, there was the other man, a chinless round head on a short body, who looked Greek.

Blud nudged Raef with his boot and grunted in surprise

when he saw who he was. He kicked him hard in the hip. The other man, who looked Greek, said, "Go back out and stand watch." The spearmen left. Raef got up onto his knees and then stood. His hip ached.

"Who is this?" the Greek asked.

"A purebred nuisance," Blud said. "He's a Varanger. Goose. You stuck your damned neck in the wrong place this time."

"Kill him," the Greek said. He took a stick from his boot; there was a cord looped to one end.

Raef backed toward the wall. Behind him, he was trying to pick apart the rope around his wrists. The guard had used a slipknot, which got tighter if he pulled; behind his back he began to push the knot together. He watched the Greek's stick, tensed to jump. If he could knock one down—

"No," Blud said, "not yet." He walked up to Raef and pushed him around so he could tug on the rope around his wrists, which was still secure in spite of Raef's work. Satisfied, Blud shoved him over to the wall opposite the door. "There's a way to make some use of him. A lot of the old Varanger like him. If we make it look like Basil killed him, so much the better." He walked back into the middle of the room. "Where's the money?"

"It's coming," said Theodore. Raef began to wriggle his hands in the bonds again; the blood was leaking through his tunic and he managed to smear some on the rope. He glanced at the door, thinking someone was out there.

"You said you had it here already, didn't you. Five thousand nomismata! Otherwise, I can't—"

There was a knock on the door. Raef had gotten one hand almost free of the slick loop of the rope. Blud said, "What's that?"

"The money," Theodore said, and went to the door.

"Make sure to get the password." Blud laughed. He turned

heavily toward Raef, and said, "I said the Emperor would kill you. One way or another. Volodymyr will even give me gold for killing you. I'll take him your head in a jug of raki."

"Make it Gregorios's," Raef said. "The best raki in Rome."

"Ah, you fool."

At the door, Theodore called, "Glory to the Empire!"

The door slammed open, cracking at the hinges. "Glory to the Emperor Basil!"

Michael Lecapenus walked through the gaping space. Tryggve came on his heels. Blud wheeled around, snatching at the sword on his belt, and Raef lunged forward off his feet and tripped the big Rus down hard, landing on the floor beside him. Leif and Ulf and two others of Tryggve's men burst into the room, and when Blud leapt up Ulf slammed him down again.

Raef got his feet under him and stood up, peeling the rope off his hands. Tryggve had the Greek Theodore by an arm around the neck; he said to Michael, "What about him? You need to talk to him?"

Michael looked as unruffled as ever. He said, "No, we have the others. We'll get what we need from them."

Tryggve snatched the stick out of the Greek's boot. The Greek knew what was coming; he screamed, "The Empire Forever! Many years to the Emperor Bardas Phokas!" and flung his hands up, but Trygge had the rope around his neck and the stick tight against the base of his skull. The Greek's face swelled, dark. His eyes rolled up and he slumped to his knees on the floor.

Blud began to babble. "You need me. You need me. My men will follow only me."

Michael said, "Then you will be the first, in every charge, in every march, in front of us all. Do you understand? Until we fight, you are living in the palace. Tryggve, good work."

Tryggve bowed. Leif said, "Come along, now, Lord Blud. Move sharp. Like a real warrior."

Most of the Varangians left, pushing Blud ahead of them; somebody dragged Theodore's body out. Michael remained, his gaze on Raef. "What are you doing out here?"

"What do you mean," Raef said. "I led you to the traitor."

Michael gave a harumph of laughter. "I suppose so. But it wasn't that simple. We intercepted more of that money."

"What money?"

"As I said, it wasn't that simple." Michael nodded at the door. "Let's get out of here. I have to tell His Imperial Majesty what's happened."

Raef went ahead of him down the corridor to the garden; on the threshold he almost tripped on a body. Michael was right behind him. More of Tryggve's men stood in a solid rank around the garden. A torch burnt at the garden gate, which was farther down the hedge than where Raef had come in. On the ground between it and the house lay two of the Greek spearmen. Leif came up and gave Raef a toothy grin.

To Michael, Leif said, "It's all done, Magister. We have everything."

"Good," Michael said. "Go get my horse, will you?"

Leif grinned again at Raef, clapped him on the arm, and went off into the dark.

"I should at least get some reward," Raef said to Michael.

"You did," Michael said. "They were going to kill you. They didn't."

"I admit I was glad to see you."

Tryggve's men dragged some more bodies around into the garden. Most of these men were dead. The rest were about to be dead. "What was that about money?" Raef remembered what

Leif had said, about Laissa giving him a gold piece, and how she had looked frightened when she saw him on the street.

"Nothing of your concern. We have two more of Phokas's agents. By tomorrow morning we'll know everything about what they were plotting." Michael stood with his hands folded before him. When he moved his splendid cloak glittered faintly in the light from the torch. His voice took on a light note. "Somebody told me your father was a wizard. Do you believe that?"

Raef thought of Corban, gone forever over the edge of the world. Who was not his real father, anyway, which seemed to matter more than before. "No," he said. "Corban had no power." He remembered Corban with a sudden, deep, uplifting love.

"Aha," Michael said, as if he had known this all along.

"But my mother could fly."

A gurgle sounded in Michael's throat. Somebody not Leif was leading up his horse; the thin white stripe down its nose was bright in the dark. Michael took the reins. He asked, "Where are you going now?"

"You keep Blud close and call the watch off me. If you aren't looking for me anymore, I'm going back to the Do-Dokos taverna. I can talk her into giving me something to eat."

Michael said, "Don't worry about Blud. Or the watch." He looked back at the house, where Tryggve's men were dragging bodies into rows. "I'll see about getting you some money." He turned to his horse and swung up into the saddle and rode off.

—⚬—

Michael said, "Unfortunately Blud may be right; if we kill him, or even just send him off, the rest of the Rus may go, too. Although I doubt any of them really knew what he was planning."

Basil leaned over the sand table; he had moved Constantine's army slightly down the long line of the road. "The main thing was getting those agents and the money. That was clever."

Michael lowered his eyes. He said, with what he hoped was appropriate modesty, "I knew those coins weren't coming from inside the City."

Basil braced himself with his hands on the side of the table, his arms straight, looking down at his battlefield. "I'm still waiting for the astrologers to give me a day," he said. "We can't find an honest birth hour for Phokas." He turned his head toward the wall, where John Barbos waited. "Has Helena left?"

"Yes. Sebastos, she made all her arrangements through Constantine's offices, but I oversaw everything."

Basil muttered in his throat. "If she'd used my offices I would have sent her in a pigboat." He turned back to Michael. "This is the second time that white Varangian has gotten himself into the middle of everything. What is it that they call him—Goose?"

"One of them told me his father was an Irish wizard."

"Really." Basil snickered. "With a magic wand?" He moved around the table, and Michael saw how he had Phokas bottled up there on the tip of the land, between Constantine, the hostile sea, and himself, looming across the Propontis.

If the Varangians obeyed him. Without the Varangians, Phokas would take Constantine and Nicephoros at leisure, and then come across the Bosporus on a defenseless city.

Basil was moving figures around on the table, his body blocking Michael's view. Michael knew what lay there; he was putting the Varangians into the battle. Michael crossed himself.

For an instant he thought, He's mad, we're doomed, they'll desert us, and we'll fail; the doubt swelled like an abscess. He forced his renegade mind still. He crossed himself again. God's will be done.

"I could use a wizard now," Basil said.

"I asked him if he believed that, about his father, and he said no."

"Good," Basil said.

"But he said his mother could fly."

"Hunh." Basil straightened, and stared at him. "He's joking with you."

Michael smiled, amused at the look on his face; he was glad Basil was as disturbed as he was. "Perhaps. He's got an odd humor. Certainly, he was useful. He knew I was trailing him, too, he left me signs."

Basil snorted again. "Keep him in the City. He still owes me submission. I haven't forgotten." He leaned far out over his sand table, planning his attack. At the door, the Varangian Ulf leaned, half-asleep. As he went by, Michael saw the glint of his eyes under the lowered lids; he was watching, anyway, bored as he looked. Tryggve's men had done well. It seemed like a false assurance, but it was at least something. Michael went off through the palace.

—⁖—

Raef went back to the taverna, where Maria saw him coming and stood in the doorway to shoo him off. "No. We don't want trouble." Gregorios came up behind her, scowling, his stick in his hand.

"I'm not in trouble anymore," Raef said.

"Besides, you owe us money."

"I'll pay you."

They hovered, caught between greed and suspicion. Maria's cheeks were soft as risen dough. Her eyes were hard as river rocks.

She said, "We'll send for Tryggve. He'll know."

"Good," Raef said, and sat down on the bench at the door. "Send for Tryggve." Laissa peeked around the corner, saw him, and fled. He put his head back against the wall and went to sleep.

CHAPTER FIFTEEN

When he woke up, still propped against the wall by the door, Tryggve had come and gone, headed back to St. Mamas to sleep, and left a purse on the table for him. Leif was there, loudly guarding it. When Raef went in and sat down Gregorios and Maria together came bowing and smiling up to him. Out of the purse he paid them what he owed, and sent them for something to eat.

Leif said, "Now everybody is happy. All we need now is a good fight and another victory and more gratitude from the Greeks."

Raef said, "I'm not waiting around on the chance."

"No, no, you can't go. You're too lucky for us. Besides, they want you to stay. It will be soon. Winter's over. Time to fight."

Maria herself brought Raef a mutton shank, and he picked it up and began to eat the meat off the bone. It was delicious; they soaked it in something before they cooked it. He thought, I saved this place. Phokas could have taken over, if I hadn't led Michael to his men. Maybe it's my place now. But he did not want to stay at St. Mamas. There had to be some better place to sleep besides the monastery and the streets.

Leif said, "Laissa's afraid to come in here." Some of the other Varangians came in and called to Raef, who waved his hand, his mouth full.

He swallowed; his chin was greasy. He wiped his beard with his hand. To Leif, he said, "I'm not after her. She's a stupid little slut, she was spying on me for Blud from the beginning. But she saw me yesterday and she didn't tell anybody. I don't care what she does." He put the gnawed bone down on the table, his stomach full.

"That's not very nice," Leif said.

"Little whore," Raef said, and got up and went to ask Gregorios if he had an extra room.

—⚬—

That night, in the little room at the back of the taverna, he dreamt of the hawk, but this time, as she really was.

He sat in a long hall, plunged in the gilded light of lamps, draped in fine hangings, the table before him heaped up with piles of gold coins. He himself wore a tunic woven of gold, with silver designs all over it, like the Greek runes. She sat across the table from him, more beautiful even than he remembered, much older than he remembered, her hair abundant still, but white, her face elegant with age, the fine wrinkles like creases in silk, her eyes as blue as stars.

He looked away, as he always had, shy before her, overwhelmed.

She said, "I'm glad you still have some humility. This City is corrupting you, as she does everybody who falls into her grasp, she is a witch of time. You are being seduced. You have lost sight of your purpose, of your journey."

"What purpose? If I'm free, how can I have a purpose? And why should I go on? Nothing is as fine as Constantinople."

"But she is not yours. And her destiny is not yours." Her arm lay on the table and she tapped impatiently with her fingertips on it. Her magnificent eyes regarded him candidly. "All my life I have seen men fail because they took the wrong path. As the White One said, they fell like seeds among stones and they withered. You have your place, your work, your life's purpose. And it is not here."

"What work?" he said.

"You must go where your father was King."

"My father," he said. "My father was Bloodaxe, a ravisher, a beast in the night. Or was Corban really my father? Where he was King was the island, which is lost now. Where are you? You are the only woman I ever loved. Where are you?"

Then suddenly he was awake, lying on his side on the floor of the little room in the back of the taverna, in his ears some distant rumbling.

The low general roar got louder. He heard someone scream, in another room. He got to his feet and the floor began to shake under him so hard he fell down again. Something crashed behind him. The whole building swayed back and forth. Then with a last, almost liquid quiver the trembling stopped.

On his hands and knees he waited, tense, for the quaking to start up again. The floor stayed still under him. He realized he had never understood before how important this was. He got up slowly onto his feet, hearing, outside, running feet, and yells, and another scream.

He went out the door through the public room of the taverna, where the barrels full of raki and wine had fallen off their racks and smashed on the floor. One of the rafters had broken in the middle and crashed into the middle of the room, and by the door a crack two inches wide ran up the front wall from floor to ceiling. He saw no dead people. Everybody had run outside. He waded through the puddles of spilled drink to the door and went out to the yard.

Laissa stood with her arms around Maria, who was patting the girl's back while herself all sobs. Gregorios walked up and down the yard swearing. Leif and Ulf and three or four of the other Varangians were running off toward St. Mamas. Raef said, "What was that?"

"The earth shook, stupid!" Gregorios roared, and swore at him in Greek and dansker. The big tavern-keeper's face was white, his eyes haggard. His voice babbled on. "I'm leaving. I'm going somewhere quiet to live."

Raef turned, looking around. The building looked good enough still, except for the crack and the broken rafter, where now the roof sagged into a three-sided pocket. The great old wall behind it was whole. Down at St. Mamas, another roof had fallen in.

"Not so bad," Maria said with a sigh. She hugged Laissa again, and looked around, at Gregorios pacing up and down shouting, and the scullions trying to creep in the door and lick up the spilled wine. "Laissa," she said, "stop crying and let's get out the big pots. You, Raef, make a fire."

"A fire," he said, startled. "Where?"

"Out here. In the yard," she said. "Do as I tell you, blockhead, you live here now."

Raef made her a fire in the center of the yard, using the kitchen wood and some rocks off the wall for a ring, and she and Laissa and eventually Gregorios built a big tripod over it and she started making a great pot of soup.

Almost at once people began to come in through the gap in the low wall. The Varangians from St. Mamas came up, but also people from the houses just across the bridge. Everybody was afraid to go back inside, in case this was just the beginning. They all told stories of other, more terrible earthquakes, in which people had been mangled and crushed and the earth had gaped and swallowed palaces whole. The story passed around of the place in the east where sometimes when the earth quaked, fire burst out of the cracks. Every now and then, the ground gave little quivers, like something settling back down to sleep.

One of Blud's men shouldered up to Raef and said, "What was going on between you and the prince?"

Raef recognized him. "Yaro, right?" He held out his hand, and the Rus shook it. Like most of them he was probably a younger son, who had answered Volodymyr's call without much thinking. And gotten himself into the middle of this civil war. Raef said, "It was just a difference of opinion."

"He had us all looking for you, up and down," Yaro said. "Didn't care if you were hurt, he said."

Raef shrugged. Gregorios had found an unbroken cask of raki and was ladling it out for a copper a cup. Yaro said, "Well, it doesn't matter, since he's been promoted. He's up in the palace now."

Raef said, straight-faced, "Well, he deserves it."

"Oh," Yaro said. "I don't know about that."

Later, as the sun went down, the Greeks danced in circles, the girls on the inside, the men on the outside. There was a flute, a drum, a stringed wheel of a harp. It seemed as if half the City was there, filling the space on both sides of the bridge. Markos came, with his family, bringing bread and fish to grill and jars of wine to drink. He smiled at Raef but came no closer. Raef thought, He thinks I've forgotten he cheated me.

All anybody talked about was the earthquake. Nobody wanted to go inside again. The children slept in drifts by the walls; everybody else stood around and drank or danced. Gregorios talked grumbling about where else he could live, somewhere the earth kept still.

Maria came and got Raef by the hands. When she moved her fat jiggled around her, and watching this lured him into the dance. He spun her, to see her big breasts shake and her backside ripple. The turning of the two circles carried her away but he saw that Laissa was coming around toward him. She gave him a frightened look, and held back, but the circle bore her along. They had to dance together, back to back, and then turn around each other, arms linked. He was not good at this and she laughed, suddenly, not afraid, and looked up at him. He smiled at her. She gave a whoop, and danced away.

⸺⬥⸺

The earth lay quiet through the night. Everybody slept outside, bundled in blankets, crowded together near the dying fire. In the morning Maria had Raef build the fire up again, and was cooking another soup; the yard filled with the local people, carrying bowls and jugs, and Gregorios had uncovered another cask of raki. Raef tasted it and decided it was more like water in a cask that had once held raki. He was going toward the building when he looked up and saw the horsemen riding over the bridge.

The people in the yard saw this only a moment later. A call went out, tense. They began to kneel down, their eyes sharp, and then abruptly they were all facedown on the ground, and Raef turned and looked for the Emperor.

He rode in the midst of his retinue, undecorated, uncrowned.

Raef drew back into the dark shade beneath the eave. Most of the men surrounding Basil were Tryggve's men, with their axes, but Michael Lecapenus rode closest to him, and his other officers trailed him, John Barbo-something, and Leo Agyros. Ulf was one of the men guarding the Emperor. Michael dismounted, and walked in the gate and through the obeisant crowd into the building.

He was inside a long moment, and Raef, in the shelter of the eave, looked through the doorway and saw him poking at the roof. Then he came out.

This time he noticed Raef, and his head went up, like a startled horse, but he walked on and out the gate again.

He did not get on his horse. Instead, in clear Greek, he called, "One of you is—" and turned to somebody else, behind him, for the name. "Gregorios Philippiposes."

Gregorios stood up. He was just the other side of the low wall, and he wrung his hands, bowing. "Your Majesty. Your Majesty."

Michael said, "Was anyone hurt here? Killed? Are you going to be able to fix this?"

Gregorios was still scrubbing his hands together, bouncing up and down, babbling, "Your Majesty, Your Majesty."

Maria stepped out the gate. She knelt down and spoke to Michael. "No one was hurt, Magister, Patrician. We can fix it, we always have."

Michael held out a handful of coins to her. "See everybody is fed."

Maria's face shone; she held up her hands, and he poured money into them. Her voice rose, triumphant.

"Glory to Rome!"

Then all the yard people were shouting, "Glory to Rome! Glory to the Emperor Basil!" They surged up straight on their knees, their arms waving in the air. Michael turned to his horse and mounted. In the midst of the others, Basil lifted one hand in response and galloped off toward St. Mamas.

The crowd around the taverna whooped and sang and cheered for a long while. The Emperor and his followers came back from St. Mamas, galloping by without stopping, and thundering back over the bridge into the City. Raef stayed to one side. These people weren't just afraid of the Emperor. They loved him also. He remembered what the hawk had said: that he did not belong here.

The people were chattering away again, not about the earthquake, but about what had just happened. "He came here! He bothered with us!" Laissa came up to Raef, her face glowing. "See? What I told you. He's one of us." Gregorios had gone back into the taverna. Maria was stirring her soup; she tipped a handful of herbs into it. Raef went around to his room, to make it ready to sleep in again.

⟶⟵

Basil rode everywhere in the City. Although everybody was outside, and some of the buildings had lost walls, the streets were sound, the city walls, the Mese, the Hippodrome, and the bridge and the aqueduct. He arranged for supplies where they were necessary and gave orders to the Eparch to make sure things were fixed.

Back at the palace, they sent off the Varangian guards, and Basil and his friends went into the Hippodrome, where the stables were. While the grooms were leading the horses away, the Varangian Tryggve suddenly reappeared.

"My lord—" He hung back, knowing he should not approach directly; another lowborn man followed him, his face stiff. Tryggve nodded emphatically at John Barbos, who went over to him.

Basil stood where he was. The night was stealing over Constantinople, and the vast space above the Hippodrome was alive with shrieking seagulls. He could tell by the sudden alarm on John's face that something had gone wrong.

His gut twisted. John turned on his heel and walked straight toward him, and bowed deep.

"Sebastos, I—I have bad—"

"Say it."

John forced himself visibly into speech. "This man's father is in Lampsacus." He waved toward the man with Tryggve, who went down on his knees at the mention. John went on, "He sailed up the seacoast and they used the lights there to send us this. The Empress—the Empress seems to be there."

Basil blurted out, "In Lampsacus."

This was the old harbor at the mouth of the narrow water down to Abydos. If she were in Lampsacus she was practically in Phokas's camp. His mind churned. Understanding blazed in him like a cold blue flame. She had tricked him, she had fooled him. She had meant to do this from the beginning, before the banquet, before the uproar at the banquet when she announced she was leaving. He had played into her hands.

He felt like ice, still and hard as rock, the rage packing him solid as a rock, crystalline with fury.

John was bowing and bowing in front of him. "Sebastos, I

checked everything, I made sure of everything. She's supposed to be going to Thrace."

Basil said, "Did anyone meet her?" His lips felt too rigid to form words. Through him the desire rose to strike John down, kick him, poke his eyes out with his own hands.

"They think—they think—it was soldiers."

"Phokas, then." If she were with Phokas, no telling what she could get Constantine to do.

John was still bobbing up and down. Kick him. Kill him. "Sebastos, I accept all blame—"

"Shut up." He made himself pace around, up and down on the Hippodrome sand, to get his mind moving past the icy rage. It would do no good to kick John. Night had fallen but the lamplighters were around and slowly the great arc of the track was appearing in the darkness. The sand crunched under his feet. The other men stood there watching him. They needed to be told what to do. He set his mind on understanding this, on composing some response.

"She must have bought off the captain. There's a sailing record?"

"Yes, Sebastos—"

"And you made sure of the names on the licenses?"

"Yes, Sebas—"

"Catch him. That damned woman foxes all my calculations. I'll throw him overboard with his anchors around his neck. This makes a mess out of everything. Oh, that she were a man, and could be blinded."

All three of them, together, said, "Sebastos."

He strode past them, his hands fists, his eyes lowered. "It could be all in my grasp and a woman's whim knocks it away from me. Has a woman ever been blinded?" He wheeled, facing Michael. "You would know."

Michael stood with his back to the great brass column, spangled with torchlight. He said, "I don't remember that there has been, Sebastos." His face was rigid. He made a gesture, tried to brush this aside, as a joke. "Rolled on hot coals, and Saint Cecilia was steamed."

"Shut up."

Silence. Basil walked up and down, until the coldness left him. He remembered he was tired, and there was still much to do. He crossed himself. "God will defend me from her." He turned back to John.

"I hope you're keeping better watch on Blud?"

"Sebastos. Many years, many years. I swear—"

"Shut up."

John's lips snapped together. Basil, looking from one to the other, saw each of them tired and worn and gaunt of face. They were using themselves up waiting. At last he found some calm, some broad way to see this all.

He said, "We have to strike. And soon. This is sapping us all."

Michael said hoarsely, "What about Helena?"

"Well, I think we should try to recover her, somehow. Before she distracts Constantine." He saw another purpose before him. He turned, considering it, and nodded.

"Send the white Varangian."

"What?" Michael said blankly. "She hates him. She won't go anywhere with him."

"Good," Basil said. "Maybe he'll have to hurt her to get her away."

"He knows nothing of Abydos," Michael said. "He'll just get himself killed."

"Then he'll have died in the service of Rome," Basil said. "Redeeming himself." He smiled at Michael. "Do as I say."

—⋄—

They had sent Leif for him, who led Raef into the Great Palace, not through the Chalke, the main gate with its double bronze doors, but by way of the Hippodrome, through its big main gate with the chariot on top. Raef looked along the spine of the track, where Delphinas had been impaled, but even the spiked pole was gone.

Leif went ahead of him between two of the standing stones on the spine to the palace side of the racetrack. As they came out onto the other side a boy galloped by, riding bareback on one horse and leading a string of half a dozen more, their hoofs scattering sand like a wake behind them. A crew of servants was sweeping the sand down out of the first tiers of the seats back onto the racecourse. Raef remembered the little hippodrome at St. Mamas, so overgrown. Twice, maybe three times that size, this place was kept like a housewife's kitchen; they were already raking away the tracks of the horses on the golden sand.

They went past the high square tower on the side where the Emperor watched the games, and the platform beneath it where Raef himself had stood once. They were coming to the lower curve, and just at the beginning of it, in the high, sheer wall, there was a gate.

Three human heads had been nailed up to the crossbeam. They were new; shreds of flesh hung from the skulls, and their jaws were attached, hanging open as if they were still surprised at finding themselves dead. The eyes of the two on either side were charred black hollows but in the middle was the frog-faced man Theodore, whom Tryggve had killed. His eyeballs and lids were gone but the sockets were unburnt. A raucous flapping flock of crows hung around the gate waiting to descend again to the work of picking the heads clean.

Leif said, "Friends of the Emperor." He gave a jeer of laughter. "Like that eye makeup?" They went in through the gate, into a broad ramp going down, turned left to a doorway and out, and climbed a little flight of steps.

"Which Emperor?"

Leif said, "The wrong one." He laughed again. The steps took them up into the middle of the palace grounds, with buildings on three sides and the great Hippodrome wall behind. "I think he had them stuck up there to remind him. He goes in and out there all the time, he keeps his horses down in the Hippodrome stables."

Raef said, "Blud's lucky it isn't his head."

Leif chortled with mirth. "Maybe soon." He led Raef around the corner of a long hall. Through the window Raef could see a servant swabbing the floor, another on hands and knees scrubbing. They went past a church. He supposed they were going to Basil's sand table room, which was somewhere in the next building, with its colonnaded porch, but instead Leif went off across the broad stretch of grass, toward the seawall.

Out on the open terrace three women were spreading linen on the bushes to air. One of them was singing, and the other two joined in on the refrain. Leif led the way down a few steps, past strips of gardens, turned under for the winter. Beneath a line of the plumelike trees, two men gathered up the huge cast-off brown fronds. The broad blue glinting sea spread out beyond the abrupt end of the land. They went left through the trees onto a circular pavement before a building faced with white and purple stone, which curved around the far edge of the promontory. This building was so close to the sea that Raef guessed it was built partly on the seawall. Somewhere someone was practicing badly on a flute, all squeaks and whistles. The wind was fresh and clean. On the side of the building, the lawns were full of roosting seagulls.

"This is the Palace of the Bucoleon," Leif said. He sounded proud, as if it belonged to him. "See?" He pointed at a broken statue in the center of the pavement. The marble figure was worn and pitted with age but Raef could make out long sweeping horns, and a lion's paw. "The Lion and the Bull. This is where they live."

Raef said, "What is this about, anyway?"

"I don't know. They said they wanted to see you." Leif led him around the side of the building and in through a little side door, standing ajar. The battered shoes of servants lined the wall just inside. They went up through a corridor and out to a wide hall, the floor inlaid in stone circles and zig-zags, great golden lamps like bunches of apples dangling from the ceiling.

Ulf was standing against one of the far doors, his axe against the wall; he lifted his hand, and Leif answered with a wave. Leif turned and walked across the hall to a doorway trimmed in marble and gold, and out onto a balcony.

Raef followed him into the caress of the wind. The balcony stood far out over the sea. The air was full of the mist of the sea. He went straight to the railing and stood there, his head lifted into the salt breeze. This was not the narrow Bosporus but the wider inland sea, the Propontis, blue under the broad sky, dappled with leaping white foam, and he felt a sudden, strong tug to be going west, to be sailing again. He drew in a deep breath of the free air.

"You came at once. I appreciate that," Michael Lecapenus said.

Raef turned. Drawn by the sea he had not noticed the Greek where he was sitting in the corner of the balcony rail. He looked quickly around, but Basil was nowhere. Nearby, one of the doorways onto the balcony stood open, a fine white drapery blowing across it. Raef turned his gaze back to Michael.

"Not much else to do."

"Well, I hope to remedy that." Michael lifted a finger and pointed, and a servant slipped off into the interior of the palace. "We would like you, first, to enroll in the Guards."

"No," Raef said.

"There would be a handsome amount of gold, and a nice title."

"No."

"You talk of honor. For honor's sake, you should want to serve Rome. The plot Blud was in? Phokas's men confessed. They were to buy the Varangians to murder us all, and then open the gates to Phokas, and sack the City. Destroy the heart of the world, like cutting it out with a knife."

Raef thought of the heads above the gate. He thought of the great City pulsing around him like a heart. "Likely they would have confessed to killing their own mothers, by the time you were done."

Michael shrugged one shoulder, unperturbed. As always he was perfectly dressed, his neat, close-trimmed beard and tight gray curls like a helmet. Like his master he wore no jewels but his dark red dalmatic with its deep bands of gold trim was worth a small city. He said, "You heard the one we caught that night. He died screaming Bardas Phokas's praises." The servant came back with a table, an ewer, cups.

Raef waited until the servant had gone, and they had both drunk of the wine. They were not bringing him a stool and he leaned back against the balcony rail. He said, "Yes. They thought they were right. You think you're right. What's the difference?"

Michael's head rose sharply, his eyes hard. "We are right. We are the Empire of Rome."

"You kill anybody who gets in your way. So does this other one—Phokas. So do I, I admit, but my way is a lot narrower than yours. You want the whole world. Everybody is your enemy."

"The world is better off without those who are the enemies of Rome. It is our sacred duty to order the world. That means one Emperor. One Empire, one God in His Church." Michael's voice rang with certainty.

"I wish I were as sure of anything as you are of this one thing."

But he looked around, at the magnificent marble face of the building, and he thought, They can do whatever they want.

Michael said, "You are impossible to argue with. You challenge the most obvious truth. Nonetheless, I admire you. You have a rare kind of honesty. Honor. That, of course, leads to this. I believe, according to your own sort of reckoning, what happened the other night put you in my debt."

Raef shifted, uneasy. He could tell now they were coming to the reason for all this. He glanced at the open door again. "In a way. What's your point?"

"I saved your life. He would have killed you."

"All right." Raef said, "I've been nearly dead before. I wouldn't say there's a high wergeld for it."

"Yet you owe me something."

"What do you want me to do?"

"There is a certain delicate matter we need you to take care of."

Raef kept his gaze off the open door, just across the way, the white silk curtain blowing through at the corner of his vision. He knew Basil was listening. He said, "Which is—"

"The Empress Helena has disappeared. We believe she's with Phokas, down by Abydos. We want you to get her back."

CHAPTER SIXTEEN

"Helena was going, she said, and the records show she was, to St. Anthony's, in Thrace. Maybe her ship was blown off course, or attacked, although the weather has been decent and we control the Propontis. However it happened she seems to have gone ashore near Lampsacus and met Phokas there."

Michael rubbed his hand over his face. He thought to himself that if Constantine had only some of Helena's will and ambition, he might actually have made an Emperor. He brought his attention back to the sand table in front of them, and pointed to Lampsacus, on the lower edge of the mouth of the Strait of the Dardanelles.

"Helena is potentially extremely dangerous to us. At the very least, she's a hostage, whom Phokas can use to buy himself out of anything. Or, she could actively talk Constantine into joining with Phokas against Basil."

"I thought your friend Nicephoros was with him." Raef Corbansson folded his arms over his chest.

"Nicephoros has only eighty men. And the other twelve centuries have no real loyalty to him, Basil or Constantine, they're themata from Caesarea—they were Phokas's men, remember." Michael studied him. He had seen how Raef looked when he realized it was Helena they wanted him to find—how his eyes had glinted. Like putting a hound on a deer, he thought. He remembered the brief previous collision between the Empress and the Varangian, which had not seemed to him evidence of a passionate attraction. There were times he thought his innocence of women was a liability. He had never considered that one could be so devious. He said, "Find her. And get her away from Phokas. Whatever it takes, and quickly."

"All right," Raef said. "But I need a few things."

"Name them," Michael said.

⸻∘⸻

Helena knew she had made a mistake. She knew when her greeting at Lampsacus, early that morning, was a centurion and some cataphracts, not a carpet of roses and an adoring Phokas. It had been a raw, blustery day, and she nearly fell getting down off the boat.

Then with no explanation and no courtesy the centurion and his men carried her away bodily to this country house in the hills and pushed her into this bare little room. She had not even seen Bardas Phokas yet. She was hungry. They had brought her chest, fortunately, but she could hardly change her clothes by herself.

She paced across the room, unable to be still. She had practiced in her mind what to say, how to say it, so many times that it ran through her head like a memorized rhyme. Yet even now she saw how flimsy it was. How much it needed Phokas to believe it already.

She had seen little of this place, coming in, enough to know it was no fortress or castle—a country house, she thought, a spread of rooms and courtyards inside a single wall. Anticipating a long siege of Abydos, Phokas had chosen something comfortable for his headquarters. She remembered the vines growing in rows on the hills. There would be mere peasants for servants. She wasn't even in one of the good rooms. She walked its length in seven paces. There was a long window, above her head on the wall, through which she saw a patch of sky, the top of the outer wall, but otherwise this was suspiciously like a storeroom.

Worst of all, there were no other women, no servants, no eunuchs, nobody to attend her. She had eaten nothing all day. Drunk from a simple pitcher on the table, which was probably wash water. The walls were bare mud-brick. Save the narrow straw bed, overlaid with a gray soldier's blanket, a chamber pot, and the table with a small lamp, and the two braziers by the wall, the only other furnishing in the room was the chest she had brought with her.

She should never have come here. She had gotten no answer to her last message; in fact, she hadn't heard from his messenger for a while. But she had been sure, from Phokas's letters, that he was devoted to her. If, for some reason, her message hadn't reached him—he would be happily surprised when she appeared. Now she suspected he had been playing with her, all along. And if he was glad at all she was here, it was not to her advantage.

Then she heard the heavy tramp of feet at the door, and whirled around, her heart hammering.

The door sprang open, and a file of officers in plumed helmets and breastplates marched in, turned to either side, and made a corridor between them. Two other men came quickly down it scattering flower petals on the floor. At a sharp order, all these men knelt down and put their foreheads to the ground. Between them, Bardas Phokas marched through the door.

He was a head taller than Constantine, who was tall, and his crown made him tower up like a great tree. He wore a magnificent dalmatic fastened with a brooch studded with diamonds and garnets, and under the hem she saw the purple leather of Imperial boots. She bowed down, her arms spread.

She was glad to turn her face down. It hid her shock. She had not seen him in a long while—three years. He seemed so old, much grayer than she remembered, his face creased and wrinkled. He wasn't even handsome anymore.

"You may rise," he said, in a thunderous voice.

She straightened. He was as broad as before, as strong. His eyes were bright, and his color was high. She lifted her gaze to his and performed another bow.

"I salute the proper Emperor of Rome."

He said, "Augusta, what are you doing here? I sent to you not to come."

She straightened to her full height, throttling down her alarm. She was Empress of Rome and not to be slighted. He had not bowed to her. She needed to make him see how important she was to him.

"I got no message. I have not heard from you in weeks. There is much I have to tell you. Better we speak in person. We need to plan."

"Something has happened to our messenger." He scowled at her, his mouth kinked. "But I sent to you not to come. Such a perilous journey." The other men had stood up at his command, and were gathered behind him: young officers, waiting for orders.

"Oh," she said. "Yet you must still be glad to see me, now that I'm here." She smiled at him, her eyes on his, remembering how they had last met, and nodded at the other men. "Order them away."

His eyes narrowed slightly. His mouth softened out of its twisted frown. He remembered, too. He was old, but perhaps the fire still burned. He spoke briefly to the men behind him, and they went out of the room. The door shut. Helena walked away a step, her back to him, moving toward the bed.

"My lord, I congratulate you. You are on the verge of winning all you desire."

Phokas said, "All that is rightfully mine." His voice was harsh. He had not followed her across the room.

She went back toward him, reaching out to him. "Let me help you—I can help you."

He caught her hands, and held them stiffly away from him. "Tell me one thing. Are they afraid? Does he shake when he thinks of what is to come—that serpent Basil?"

She leaned toward him, knowing what to say. "They are terrified, my lord. Constantine pleaded not to march—begged Basil to make peace with you. And, yes, even Basil shivers. All the world fears you."

"Ah." He smiled a little, but not at her, his gaze passed her. "I shall see that nasty-tongued little cur whimper for mercy at my feet."

"I know them. I know much. I can help you."

"That's why you're here, isn't it," he said. His voice was cutting. "Because I'm going to win. You want to be on the side that stays in the purple."

"Bardas." She clutched his hands, but he was holding her away from him. She could not reach him. She flung words at him, desperate. "I adore you. You know that—I always have. I want Rome to have a true Roman Emperor."

He was breathing hard, like a horse at the bit. He laughed at her. His face was hard, his cheeks bright red. He gave her a shove, and knocked her several steps back across the room.

"You want to stay Augusta. That's why you've been spying for me all these months, isn't it? So you can keep the palace and the servants and the adoring crowds, once I take the throne." Phokas's lip curled. He paced toward her, loomed over her, so she had to look up; her face began to heat. He said, "But I don't need you, Helena. I'll do this by my sword. Mine alone." He leaned over her, his head jutting toward her, as if he would take a bite out of her. "Your Constantine—that snake Basil—those two greenlings who think they're Emperors now are going to suffer the way they made poor Delphinas suffer. And see then what becomes of you and those little girls."

He smirked, his eyes studying her; she knew how she looked, she could not keep the fear off her face. She said, "Bardas, I love you."

"No, you don't," he said. "You love power, Helena. Now stay here and remember what it was like, because you aren't going to have it anymore." He turned, looking around the room, where the light was fading; night was coming. "I'll have them bring you a loom," he said, and went out.

She sat down heavily on the bed. The light was fading from the room; the sun was going down. She fought against the urge to cry. Instead, she got up and lit the lamp on the table from one of the braziers.

The flame caught on the wick, floating in its bath of oil; the light flickered a moment, steadied, and swelled. She took it back to the table and set it there and sat in the little swell of light. She refused to lose heart. She did not think about the threats he had made—to her, to her children. There was always a chance. If not, she thought, there was always revenge. The room was cooling off, as the day ended, and she drew the rough blanket around her shoulders, and sat there, wondering what to do next.

⎯⎯⎯⎯

Bardas Phokas put guards on the Empress's door, and sent a servant across to the kitchens to find something for her to eat.

To his aide, he said, "It would not do to let her starve," and laughed.

The aide said, "Megalos Sebastos, you are always wiser than anybody."

Phokas grunted. He knew flattery but he liked it. He thought it was true, too. Everything was working in his favor. At first the whole notion of her coming down to join him had struck him as madness—what could she spy on, if she were here with him?—but now he saw great advantage in having her in his control. This could be the final blow.

"Send a message to the milksop Constantine—where is he—barely out of Chrysapolis? Tell him I have his wife."

The aide bowed. "Megalos Sebastos." He turned, gave orders, and there was a flurry of action among the waiting officers. Phokas thought, I have only to speak, and all obey.

To the aide, he said, "At the very least, he will not join battle with me."

The aide murmured, "Nicephoros Ouranos is with him."

Phokas wheeled toward him, angry. "Do you think I do not know that? That's my whole point, you fool. Basil has only one good strategic head, and Nicephoros is it. Keep him out of the way, and Basil will fall at my feet like something rotten."

The aide was bowing down. "Once again, Megalos Sebastos, your understanding far outstrips everyone else's."

Phokas was no longer angry; he was in a bouyant mood at the prospect of bringing this finally to a close, of seizing what should have been his following the reign of his uncle the Emperor Nicephoros Phokas. He thought briefly of Helena. Even after the rough journey she was beautiful. She certainly hoped to seduce him. He straightened, his hands folded before him, proud to know himself cold to her. She could not sway him. But he could use her. He smiled again, anticipating that.

—❦—

The dark water slapped at the wharf, glinting in the light of the torches along the shore, and above, on the balcony of the Bucoleon Palace. The tide was almost to the top of the little wharf. Raef went quickly through the boat, three thwarts, a boxy stern, and a high prow; the mast lay in its crutch down the midline. It had about the same freeboard as a dragon ship. There were two sets of oars, two sets of sails and booms.

They had supplied him with a big boat cloak, a sack full of food, water in a jug. Now Michael said, "You wanted something that would show you acted for us." He held out a grape-sized yellow crystal, set in a gold ring. "Everybody would recognize this. It was John Tzimisces's. Basil doesn't like jewels but John wore this one everywhere."

Raef's heart jumped. He made himself take it, although he shuddered at the touch of it. He wrapped it into his cloak until the layers had muffled its uncomfortable tingling and put it under the forward thwart. He was in a hurry to be sailing again. The sea air was crisp and clean in his face. The year had turned, days were getting longer, the spring coming, the wind rising, sweet and clear as opening flowers. Even through the layers of the cloth the crystal poked at him.

He stowed away the supplies. Besides the water there was a smaller jug of raki. Michael said, "You know the currents out here are legendarily treacherous."

Raef said, "I'm not surprised." He climbed in, sat down on the middle thwart, and ran out the oars. "Cast off." When the line hit the bow thwart he began to row.

At once he felt the sea around him as if the land had faded instantly to nothing and in all the world there was only water. The oarlocks were well set, and the boat was nimble. He stroked out the gate of the little harbor, zigzagged over the riptide there, and let the current carry him off out to the north, where he could pick up a fair wind and sail southwest.

Under him the currents fought and tumbled but once they were clear of the riotous mouth of the Bosporus the water quieted, eddying, wind-ruffled, picked out with a white froth luminous in the blue night. Behind him, the lighthouse by the harbor, and the little pinpricks of torches on the hill above, grew dimmer and farther away.

When he was all out of sight of land he shipped the oars and lay down on his back across the thwarts and looked up at the stars. In cities people didn't look at stars. Yet now, free of the City's spell, he knew that the night sky was more beautiful than anything in Constantinople. Through the scattered brilliant points of the stars the great white river blazed across the blackness, swirled like a current. Near the horizon he found the big blue wanderer, one of Corban's stars whose name here he knew was Jupiter, that drifted all over the belt of the sky.

Corban had always known what to do, he thought. That was Corban's magic.

He was free, now. He was alone, and masterless; he felt as if he were the only man alive, floating on the endless world-blood of the sea. Now when he thought of the Magnaura, and the roaring brazen lions, he knew that was not magic, not like

Gunnhild's shape-shifting, or the way Benna could draw up something from nothing. The Greeks had only a cleverness about the world, not knowledge of it.

He remembered the City as if he flew above it like a hawk, seeing it sprawled out beneath him over the land, everything divided by streets and roads, all dominated by the things of men, and he thought, They have built a way to be out of the real world. To make their own world, where what they want happens.

But the real world went on, shifting and whirling, shaking with its own fierce force, and in the end theirs would crumble away.

He watched the stars wheel over him. He was free; he could do as he pleased. He could just sail on, go on past Abydos, keep on going home. But he remembered her dark eyes, and her wide, ripe mouth. He remembered, more, the fierce longing in her, that deep untouched desire. He wanted to touch her there, where she was still virgin. And now they were giving her to him, at least for a moment, if he could find her.

He had pledged this to Michael Lecapenus; he was discovering, now, that he wanted to keep his pledge to Michael Lecapenus as much as he wanted to lay the Empress down under him.

He put the mast up, and set the sail, caught a good wind all night, and sailed steadily southwest. He did not sleep much. By sunrise he was passing a big island to the south, and he could feel the next narrows just over the horizon to the west, another confusion of currents, the water piling together into a race toward the sea. As the day warmed up the wind died and he took the sail down and rowed. Nearer the island, he saw a big galley, high-prowed, still at anchor for the night. Another ship was moored even closer to the island. Here the sea roiled and churned, chopped and backed, and he steered a way through the tows and the crosscurrents, passing this island and several more, smaller, angling south and west most of the rest of the day, until he was heading into the swampy, lagooned southern coast of the narrows. With the sun going down, he picked his way through the shallows deep into the coast, staying far wide of a fishing village on the edge of the marsh. That, he thought, was Lampsacus. Finally, in the half dark, he found a place to tie the boat up, and got onto dry land.

He ate most of the rest of his food, drank some of the raki, and sat down and took the crystal out of his cloak.

Even in the dark it seemed to him bright as a lamp. It burned like a cold fire on his palm. John Tzimisces, he remembered, had murdered his way to the throne. The ring felt hungry. Felt bloody. He looked down into it, fighting against the warning flashes of the lights, the daggers of its beams. He had never tried to use a crystal before; he thought of Helena, trying to see Helena in it, her almond-shaped dark eyes, her wide, unhappy mouth.

In the yellow ice-heart of the stone he saw purple berries, clustered in dark green leaves. He saw a crown rolling around and around on the ground. He saw a horse rearing, and the crown falling, and rolling on the ground.

None of this meant anything to him. His eyes hurt unbearably and he folded the crystal away again in layers and layers of cloth. Night was coming; he moved on inland, across the swampy lowlands, to a road, and there slept, the crystal under a stone.

He dreamt, trying to find the hawk, but he could not.

—⚬—

Sitting at a little table in the corner, Basil ate bread and cheese and olives, while John Barbos read him a dispatch from the city of Dyrrakhion, off on the western sea. The tone of the dispatch led Basil to believe that by now Dyrrakhion had fallen to the Bulgars. He pushed the dish away, his mouth sour. He cursed Phokas for keeping him tied up here when he should be defending the Empire.

Since the Bulgars had humiliated him, three years before, in his first attempt at a campaign, he had itched to attack them again. Now they were taking his cities and because of the rebellion of Bardas Phokas he could not even send an army. He gripped his hands into fists, burning to hit someone.

Dyrrakhion was on the west coast of Greece, at the end of the old Roman Road that stretched from there to Thessaloniki on the east coast. Losing it meant losing the straight road to Italy. He had to control that road. As soon as he was done with Phokas, he would start on the Bulgars. After he had conquered them he would move east.

As soon as he was done with Phokas. His mind leapt toward that, when they came at last face-to-face in front of armies. He struggled to imagine what it would be like. Phokas loved to fight hand to hand. He might challenge him. Basil's belly knotted. He could not practice that on a sand table. He wondered if he was afraid—if he would run. Suddenly his body felt like someone else, who might betray him.

"Sebastos," John said. "Leo is here."

"Send him."

Leo came quietly in, did the obeisance, and rose. "Sebastos." His voice was taut. He looked tired, his down-tilted eyes sad. "I am convinced now this is the right chart for Phokas. And I did yours again. As I told you before, there are some good days ahead for you, in such a matter. After Easter especially."

He drew a step nearer. He wore a long yellow dalmatic with

a green trim; it made him seem even more sallow, like a mummy. His voice was thin with excitement. "But for Phokas, there is one day in particular which is very bad. Not good for you especially but for him, very bad. He loses something." Leo glanced at John and turned back to Basil, his eyes gleaming. "Maybe he dies."

Basil started. "When?"

"In four days. April 13."

"Four days." It was too soon. He got up, walked around the table; the stool was in his way and he kicked it aside. He had no idea if the Varangian had gotten Helena out of the way. Constantine would still be several days' march to the north. He had to find boats, get all his men armed, supplied, and on board and across the Propontis, and force Phokas to engage him, in four days.

He wheeled toward Leo. "Yes. We will sail. I'm sick of waiting anyway. Find Michael. Tryggve the Varangian captain. John, go bring me that Rus, wherever you're holding him. We'll sail tomorrow. Quick!"

⸻

After the terror of the earthquake faded, Gregorios had pushed the bricks back into the wall, thrown a layer of plaster into and over the crack, and braced up the rafters with timbers. People began to live inside again, instead of in the yard, or in the street. One day Leif was sitting in his corner, drinking some raki and picking at the last of one of Maria's delicious fish stews, and Laissa came up.

"Where is everybody?" she said.

"Ulf's on duty," Leif said. "Tryggve is at the palace. Raef, I don't know, he went somewhere. I hope he didn't leave. He keeps saying he's going on."

He looked at her, frowning; she wore a dress so shabby there were holes along the seams. She was thin; she already looked worn, and she was only a child. He thought how she was living, in the cracks of other people's lives, and his heart was heavy for her. She leaned on his shoulder, as she often did.

"Nobody leaves Constantinople. Where is he going?"

"I don't think he really knows."

"Where is he from?"

"That's kind of a riddle, too. Like you." He slapped the bench beside him. "Come sit next to me. No, not on my lap. Next to me."

The girl perched on the bench. She gave him a long slow look. "What's the matter with you?"

"I'm getting old," Leif said. "I think too much. Where are you from?"

Laissa said, "I'm from here." She frowned at him, and he smiled. Finally she looked away. "I wish I were from here."

"What do you remember?" Leif asked.

"Look, I don't want to talk about this." She whirled toward him. "You want to do the Greek thing, or I go. That's all." Her voice was shrill, and she cleared her throat afterward.

Leif said, "Talking costs you nothing."

"You don't even have any money!" She jeered at him, but she stayed perched like a bird on the bench, her bare feet raised. Her hair was dirty. She bent to investigate her toes.

"I'm getting paid now," Leif said. "Standing guard isn't that much better than whoring."

She struck at him with the back of her hand. "It's all right.

Being a whore. It's good. Sometimes." Then she looked away again. "You don't like me anymore? You haven't asked in a long while."

Leif said patiently, "I like you too much."

That made her smile. She gave him a sideways look. "Oh."

"What's the earliest you remember? Not here."

Her face slipped out of its happiness. "I only remember here," she said, looking off. But her voice was trembling.

"Something else," Leif said. He was leaning in close to her, sheltering her. He could see she was getting ready to cry.

"A man." Her voice was low. "With yellow hair, like mine. He carried me on his shoulder. He fed me bread. I think he was my father." Her face twisted, falling apart. "Ma p'teetcher." She sobbed. Leif reached out and pulled her into his lap and stroked her hair.

"Do you remember any more?"

She stared away, her head against his chest. A few more sounds stumbled out of her. "Mo—Monam. Sacure. Sacercur. Rawn." Tears brimmed out of her eyes. She leaned on his chest and sobbed.

Leif held her awhile, until she was done crying. He said, "Now, listen. A lot of people never go back home. Sometimes, it's better to leave. I'm never going back home. Iceland is the most piss-poor country I've ever been in. But if you want to, likely you could go back." A shadow passed across the edge of his vision, and he looked up.

He frowned, looking toward the door, where someone was standing in the sunlight. Laissa sat up.

"It's Markos," she said. "Raef's friend. Markos!" She waved her hand. "Have you seen Raef anywhere?"

The Greek came into the taverna, blinking against the dim light. He said, "No—in fact, I'm looking for him. He's not here?"

Leif said, "No, he isn't. What's wrong?"

"I need his help." Markos leaned over the table. "I just bought a new boat, and the Eparch came and took it." His hands twisted together. "I don't know why—Raef knows the Emperor, everybody says so. I need him to help me get my boat back."

"Your boat," Leif said blankly. "Who's taken your boat?"

"The Eparch. They brought me a paper—"

A suspicion sprouted in Leif's mind. "Just yours? Or everybody's?"

"They've taken all the big boats in the upper harbor. Just this morning. But I need—"

The suspicion came to full bloom. Leif stood up. "Maria," he roared. "If anybody from St. Mamas comes in, tell them to go down to the refectory! We're marching! Or sailing. Or something." He turned to Laissa, wishing he had some money. "Go buy a new dress. Get Maria to loan you the cost. When I come back, we'll celebrate."

Her face gawked at him. She said, "You're fighting? Again? But—"

"What about my boat?" Markos asked.

"I can't help you with that, boy," Leif said, and went on out of the taverna and down to St. Mamas, to tell them to get ready to leave.

CHAPTER SEVENTEEN

Raef followed an old and well-worn road along the coast toward Abydos. Paved with large flat stones, the road was obviously much used, but no one was using it now. He saw no one all morning. For the first several miles the way followed the narrow brown beach, but then it swerved inland to skirt a swamp. Before he saw the ducks he could hear them on the marsh; they were sprinkled in great flocks on the shallow shining water. The low inland hills were just turning green with spring grass. Along the road new leaves were starting to unfurl in the baskets of the tree branches.

Every so often, as he loped along, he passed an upright stone, with runes cut into it. He saw the smoke of a village, off inland, and trails leading toward it. The road took him over an arched bridge across a stream, like a little section of the St. Mamas bridge, and out onto the wide meadows that lay beyond it, deep in grass. Ahead the hillside pinched down sheer to the water and the road led up the back of the rise.

From the hilltop he looked out over the strait, pale blue along this coast, darker in the middle, the far side steep and rocky. He saw ahead of him, beyond a stretch of marsh, the water sweeping away toward a distant cape.

At the edge of the cape he could make out walls and towers: Abydos.

The crystal was burning him, stronger and more piercing with each mile. He went on, pressing himself into the pain like a needle of fire, the sack with his food and water and raki slung over his shoulder, and the cloak bundled around the crystal under his arm.

A column of horsemen jogged down the road toward him; he got out of the way and let them pass. They wore the breast-plates and crested helmets of Roman cavalry; they carried spears. He watched them trot in their neat rows on down ahead of him, on their way to Abydos. Phokas's men, he thought. He thought of them fighting Varangians and his blood quickened.

Then in the midafternoon as he was striding along, the burn against his left arm slackened, cooled. He turned around and went slowly back up the road and with each step it grew hotter. Where it burnt hottest he turned south, off the road, forc-ing himself up along the thread of heat. Quickly he came on a path into the inland hills. In the dusk he went on south and west, crossing the little brushy slopes, the crystal hurting his whole side now.

At moonrise, walking up over the top of a hill, he saw a sort of farm ahead of him.

He sat down under a tree, to look it over. Torches burnt at the four corners of the square outer wall, and more torches at the tall gate, so he could see it well. It crowned the next hill, with the leafless stocks of vines around it in rows, like a skirt. In the middle of the vines the great square of wall gleamed white in the light of the rising moon.

A man with a spear paced along the top of the wall; Raef saw other men on the walls leading away from him. There were guards on the tall front gate, and other men, porters maybe, slaves. Two horsemen rode up to the gate. The guards stopped them and one of the horsemen held something down, bending from his saddle. The guards waved them inside. A few moments later another guard, this one mounted, rode slowly around the outside of the place. At the corner, he met a second rider coming the other way.

Raef moved deep into the shelter of the tree and unwrapped the ring with the crystal again. When he touched it the pain shot up his arm as if somebody plunged a dagger up through the bone into his shoulder, but he held the crystal in his palm and looked into it, and thought of Helena.

The blaze dazzled his eyes; the front of his skull felt boiling. In the crystal he saw Helena.

But not as she was now. In the yellow glow she was much older, and she wore the black hooded gown and white veil of a nun. Her eyes, without paint, were dull and sad.

Then out of the crystal, floating up toward him, came her face, fluid with grief, and her lips moving, saying, "I'm sorry." Through layers of time their eyes met and her lips moved in his name and, again, "I'm sorry."

He dropped the crystal into the dirt. Instantly the pain faded to a steady burning throb. He lifted his eyes to the walls crowning the hill, thinking that at least he knew she was in there. He didn't know what the rest of it meant, but it made his skin crawl. He dropped his cloak over the crystal, and pushed it away.

⸺⸱⸺

Ship by ship the Emperor's army crept out onto the crinkled waters of the Propontis. The Harbor of Justinian on the south side of the City was still packed with the Varangians waiting to board but they had found enough ships, and the Varangians had gathered without problem, each century with its centurion, armed and ready. Leif the Icelander walked up and down the wharf, directing a steady stream of men onto ships. As soon as each ship was loaded, half of the Varangians sat to the oars, and the ship started off across the inland sea.

"This is better than the last time," Basil said.

Michael said nothing, his gaze moving constantly over the crowd of the Varangians, the steady outward motion of the ships, stroking on their oars like walking ladders. Blud had gone in the first ship, with John Barbos right beside him.

John had said, "I should take a garrote. Keep him focused."

Michael had said, "If he has betrayed us it's already happened." He had already considered several ways Blud could destroy them.

Basil said, now, "Let's go." They had been watching from the hillside, and the Emperor turned and went along the top of the seawall, around the southwestern edge of the promontory, toward the Bucoleon. Just before the palace were the steps down to the Imperial harbor. Basil broke into a trot going down the stairs. He was impatient as a horse before the race, Michael thought, fighting off his own doubts. He had not come this far to falter. He had loved Basil most of his life and he would not fail him now. At the foot of the steps, the Imperial barge was already at the wharf, an eighty-man dromon, with gold trim and a silk-covered sterncastle. He followed Basil onboard, and they set off for Abydos.

Raef slept under the tree the rest of the night. In the morning two columns of horsemen, with a great blue pennant and trumpets blowing, rode away out of the big farm. Watching from the hillside, Raef thought the second column was the same that had passed him on the road the day before. It came to him they were coming down from the north ahead of Constantine's army. Basil had been right: Phokas would not challenge his brother.

He hid his cloak under some leaves, took his shirt off, and tore a strip from it to tie his hair down. He took his shoes off. The crystal was lying on the ground. He had to take it with him, but now he had nothing to muffle it. Finally he put the little finger of his left hand into the ring and tucked the crystal itself into his palm.

He gasped at the agony, but he had already seen the pain caused no injury. It was phantom, like the crystal's images. His palm burned as if the flesh were melting but the skin was whole and smooth. He could endure that, he thought, as long as he knew it would not last.

He circled around behind the farm, outside the ring of guards, and crossed a road, and a steep pathway that went up through rocks and stands of trees to a back gate. Along this pathway the servants and slaves went in and out, delivering goods and taking off refuse. Here, too, a man with a spear walked on the high white wall, and the gate had guards on either side.

A wagon full of firewood rolled up to the foot of the pathway. Raef got in line with some other men, shouldered a great basket full of firewood, and stooped under its weight walked up the pathway. At the gate the guards were leaning on the wall talking. Nobody looked at him. He walked in through the gate, into a great dusty courtyard.

This was full of horses and soldiers. Backed up to each of the four walls of the court was a building. The biggest was a great colonnaded hall on his right. As he came in the gate, bent under the weight of the basket on his back, there was a sudden trumpet blast, and everybody around him went down on his knees.

Raef set the basket down and squatted behind it. He looked up behind him, at the guard on the wall, also kneeling. A shout went up from all the people in the courtyard.

"Glory to the Emperor Bardas Phokas!"

Six or seven men came out onto the porch of the colonnaded hall. One was tallest by a head, a giant, with broad shoulders, a barrel of a chest, a belly under it that pushed his breastplate out. He wore a helmet with a golden crown set on it. He held his head high and his shoulders back, his mouth turned into a scowl. He stood a moment looking majestically all around at the people bowing to him. His officers clustered behind him.

"All glory to the Emperor! All hail Bardas Phokas!"

Then the giant came down the steps, to a horse led up to him, and his officers followed him. The crowd hustled out of their way, bowing and stooping and crawling, and the would-be Emperor and his men rode two by two out the front gate.

At once everybody in the courtyard stood and went back to their work, the guards chatting at the gates, women carrying bundles of linen out of the big house. Raef picked up the firewood and hauled it off to the kitchen.

This was a slope-ceilinged building opposite the colonnaded hall, with the farm wall for its rear, and two big rooms, one full of baskets like Raef's, and the other of people cooking. The firewood was stacked outside the kitchen, against the inside of the farm wall there near the ovens, and he put his basket down and unloaded it piece by piece, all the while looking around him. Another column of soldiers marched on foot out the front gate. A boy led a donkey out of the stable next door. Chickens pecked on the ground in front of the gate. A few girls from the kitchen sauntered by the back gate, where Raef had come in, and made quick talk with the guards there.

The crystal was pulling him steadily toward the big columned hall. When he had the firewood unloaded he found a broom and swept his way across the courtyard toward it. Industriously he cleaned the front steps, starting at one end. By the time he reached the other end, the crystal was burning a hole through his hand.

He went around the side of the building, sweeping, but there was no door. This building did not butt against the farm wall; six feet of open ground separated them. Here, at last, he found, if not a door, at least a window into that room, high on the building wall.

The window was a good size; he thought he could fit easily through it. But it was far above his head, just below the steep overhang of the roof, and the wall was plastered slick as a wet rock.

A trumpet sounded. Out there in the courtyard someone with a bull voice was shouting encouragement to a crowd. Sweeping back and forth, the broom whisking on the packed earth, Raef narrowed his interest to the window.

He thought at first of getting up onto the roof. He turned toward the outer wall, to see how much of the roof the sentry could see.

The farm wall was made of stone. Along it, about four feet from the top, a wooden rampart ran, which was where the sentry walked. That rampart passed within three feet of the window. At each corner of the outer wall was a little guardhouse, a three-sided box of wooden walls, where a ladder ran down to the ground.

They had just built the rampart, he saw, when they made this country farm into a military post. It was all braced up with a scaffold of wooden struts, lashed together and connected with beams butted to the ground. With his eyes he traced a path up through those struts. He wouldn't even have to go up on the rampart itself, just climb to the level of the window, just beneath the walkway.

The sentry paced back and forth on the rampart, looking outward, dragging his spear along. Raef went around to the kitchen again and in the storeroom found something to eat.

At sundown Phokas came back, with another great show of submission and power. Raef came out to the doorway of the kitchen storeroom to watch; he half expected Helena to appear, to greet Phokas, but this did not happen. Then there was a great coming and going of men in crested helmets and stamping horses.

With the night the place settled down, save for part of the big house, where lights showed, and faintly he heard people laughing, and once singing. The kitchen emptied. Raef went out of the storeroom and padded quietly around to the dark end of the big building. The yellow crystal lanced him; Helena was in here. She was having nothing of the lights and laughing. He hunkered down by the outer wall, in between two sets of struts, listening to the sentry pace along above him, his spear dragging behind him, bump and bounce on the wooden rampart.

Directly above him was Helena's window, and only a faint light showed.

She was not part of the celebration. That was interesting. Or, maybe, Phokas was there, and they were celebrating together. He pressed his lips together, considering that. This could get messy. The sentry went by him again, going to the guardhouse at the corner, where he sometimes lingered for a few moments—he probably kept a jug hidden there.

The moon rose. All around him he felt the people sleeping. Helena was sleeping, just beyond the thick stone wall between them, and she seemed to be alone. In the kitchen the scullions were asleep on their straw beds, and in the stables the horses were asleep. Above him the sentry paced with his weary stride, back and forth. Went into the guardhouse at the corner, loitered sometimes a long while, then turned back.

At last, in the depths of the night, Raef waited until the sentry had reached the corner, and he climbed up through the struts. They were raw new wood, pine, with long splintered edges, crossed and braced, and he climbed easily up toward the walkway. Halfway, he stopped and listened.

He heard the night sounds, crickets, and the wind. He saw bats, out in the moonlight. The sentry's pace came slowly nearer, an even beat on the boards over his head. When he had passed, Raef climbed up into the last X of the scaffold. From there he could see, across the way, the whole of Helena's window.

It was long enough, and wide enough, and the ledge was three feet deep, and there was a grille across the inside opening.

His heart turned over. He had not thought of that. The crystal ate at his hand; the sentry paced by again over his head. The grille looked like metal. He hadn't even brought his knife.

He had come this far, he had to keep going. He waited until the sentry had reached the corner where he sometimes lingered. The fading footsteps sounded like his heartbeat. He stared at the window, the squares of the grille across the faint light from inside.

Whatever happened, he would not stop now. He put his head cautiously out, and looked up the rampart. The sentry had gone out of sight. He braced his feet on the strut beneath him and jumped onto the window ledge.

He hit the back half of the opening, started to slide off, and reached out and gripped the grille and pulled himself sideways into the window space. Pushing against the iron grille, his legs doubled up, and his shoulders hunched, he fit entirely into the deep space. Through the grille he could see down into the room.

It was small, almost empty, save for a table, braziers, the bed. The light came from a little lamp on the table. On the bed lay a woman, under a gray blanket, asleep, alone.

He thought, Then she isn't Phokas's ally, she's his prisoner.

The sentry was walking by, looking out over the wall, watching for an enemy coming over the hills, dragging his spear. Raef caught a whiff of raki in the air after he had gone.

He put his hands flat against the grille. It was solid, of iron bars, set into an iron frame that ran two inches high all the way around the window. He felt along the frame on the outside, felt bolt heads, knew he could not dig it out, even with a knife.

He laid his head against the grille, tired. The grille moved slightly.

He drew his head back, put his hand on the iron, and pushed a little. It gave, not much, but some. With his foot, he pushed on the iron down at the other end, and it gave a lot more.

He stuck his fingers out the spaces at the very end, near his face, and felt along the side of the grille. His fingers ran over the flats of hinges on the stone. The grille was made to swing open and closed. It was latched. Carefully he turned himself around in the window space. He lay still, hardly breathing.

He could hear the sentry on his way up the rampart again. The even pace of his steps. The bump-bump-bounce of his spear. Grew louder and louder and then faded. Down below him, she slept, her back toward him, her hair spread out on the bed; he could see the nape of her neck in the parting of her glossy hair. Across the way was a door. He knew there was a guard at the door, maybe two, but everybody down there was asleep.

He put his fingers in through the grille and felt carefully over the latch and lifted it. He slid the grille open and let himself down into the room.

He went to the door, opposite the window, and listened. There was no sound. He felt everybody around him sleeping as if they breathed something into the air. He turned and went over to the bed, where Helena lay on her side, her head curled on her arm. He knelt down beside her, turned the ring around, and put his left hand over her mouth.

She startled awake, and he gripped her shoulder hard with his right hand, to keep her still. He let her turn toward him. Her eyes flew wide. Against his palm, her lips moved.

"You!"

He took his left hand away, and showed her the ring. He saw her recognize it. Her face settled. He put his head down close to her ear. "Either you go with me willingly, or I have to take you off by force."

Her eyes looked from the ring to him, and he saw something change in her look, as if a veil rose. "I'll go." She seemed suddenly livelier.

"Sssh." He put his finger to his lips. "Get up. Be quiet."

He stood up; he pulled the ring off, and threw it on the bed, glad to be rid of it. His hand instantly stopped hurting.

She wore a long nightdress. When she threw the blanket back and sat up, the silk flowed over her breasts, her arms, her thighs. By the foot of the bed was a carved chest full of clothes and woman's gear and she went to it.

He went around the room, silent, restless, and listened at the door a moment. When he turned, she had flung on a heavier gown, and was sitting on the bed putting the crystal ring onto one finger after another. It fit none of them. He wondered how she could bear to touch it, and yet she acted as if it were a common stone. He turned back to the door, found the inside latches, and pushed them noiselessly shut, top and bottom.

When he faced her again, she was still sitting there, turning the ring around in her hand; she lifted her head and whispered, "How will we get out of here?"

He pointed to the window.

"I can't—"

"Ssssh." He nudged her toward the window.

"Wait." She went back to the bed, to the chest. When she came back she did not have the ring but she had wrapped a dark blue cloak around herself. "Show me," she said quietly.

He put his lips to her ear. "When you get up there, squeeze to the side. Give me all the room you can."

She nodded. Her eyes were bright. He saw she was eager for this. He knelt down on one knee, the other raised, and she stood on his knee. He patted his shoulder with one hand, and she stepped quickly up, one foot on each of his shoulders, her hands on the wall.

"I still—"

"Sssh." He stood, his hands on her ankles, lifting her to the window. She threw her arms into the space, trying to drag herself up, she who had spent her life in palaces with other people doing all the work, and could not. He put out his hand, palm up and flat, and she stepped on it, keeping her balance against the wall, and he boosted her up until she had only to crawl into the deep ledge.

She huddled immediately over to one side. Raef backed away from the wall. Stooping, he could make out the top of the rampart in the darkness outside. He waited. In the window, she frowned at him, and he waved his hand at her. Finally the legs of the sentry scissored by, and the trailing haft of the spear. He counted, in his mind, the steps down to the corner, and the jug of raki. When he thought the sentry had gone, he ran at the wall and jumped.

His fingers gripped on the iron frame of the grille, and he kicked the wall, caught a toehold, and thrust himself up into the space, his left shoulder brushing hard across her breasts, and then doubled one leg up into the window, braced his foot against the frame of the grille, and launched himself outward, across the open air, to the scaffolding of the rampart.

Sliding, he clung with both arms to the wood. His knee hurt. He had splinters all in his hands, his arms, his chest. He lowered himself down to the ground, listening for the sentry, and when he did not come right back, went out below the window, and waved to her to jump.

She looked down at him, her eyes wide, afraid. Quickly she looked down the rampart. Her lips parted. She swung her legs over the edge and dropped feetfirst into his arms, the cloak fluttering around her.

He swept her up, one arm under her legs, one around her shoulders. She gasped at the impact, and clapped her own hand over her mouth. He gathered the cloak around her, and took her off to the storeroom of the kitchen, to hide until daybreak.

CHAPTER EIGHTEEN

Basil did not sleep all night, but prayed, and watched the sea ahead of them, his eyes straining for some sight of land. Beside him the other men dozed and dreamt. It was all to happen now, everything he had been planning since he was a child, everything he had gathered these men around him to do. The excitement coursed in him like an electric surge. He had begun to long to fight Phokas, hand to hand.

At dawn they reached the coast and traveled along it through the wakening day toward Lampsacus, the ancient city, where now the hovels of fishermen stood beside the white columns of temples and the long solid Roman road. What mattered to Basil was the harbor there, a wide beach inside a natural breakwater of sand.

His fleet was scattered back across the sea. His barge was second to grate ashore on the shelving beach and they brought the horses off, but then the boats began coming in fast. With Michael, he galloped along the sand, directing the Varangians as they poured ashore. Tryggve's guard came in and he sent them at once up onto the road toward Abydos, first to keep watch, and then, when he had twenty boats ashore, to march.

John Barbos and Blud came together off a barge, and a groom brought their horses. Basil rode over beside them, so close to Blud his horse's hoofs cast sand on him.

"You will lead your men, first of all. Keep close to Tryggve. John will be there. Stay so close you can smell them."

Blud looked darkly up at him, and did not bow. He grunted something, put his foot into his stirrup, and swung up onto his horse. Basil reined away and galloped off toward Leif the Icelander, who was sending men ashore in waves from the incoming boats.

There was no sign of Constantine, who would probably be coming down this same road, no indication either that he was near or that he had already passed. In the low hills that began just south of Lampsacus he knew there were thousands of spies, hurrying now to tell Phokas that Basil was advancing. His hands tingled. He had to stay back on the beach, to see the last of the boats brought in—getting the empty boats out of the way, which was as hard as unloading the full ones—but the fat Varangian Leif was excellent at that, and when Basil saw him managing it well, he rode off to a meadow and got off his horse, sent his officers to do as they would, lay down on the ground, and slept, toward noon, for a few hours.

Michael stayed by him, as he had expected, sat there by him all the while.

Then with the whole army ashore, he and Michael with a few other officers galloped to catch up with Tryggve.

Tryggve's guard moved fast, and they sang as they marched, tossing their great axes up and catching them on the way down. The guard gave a cheer when they saw the Emperor, and many of them bobbed in a sort of bow, or a kneel, something obeisant, anyway. They were turning into Romans. He would make the whole world Roman. The sinking sun cast a rosy veil across the sky. Basil's horse was panting for breath, its sides slick with sweat, and he let it walk along, watching the Varangians with their axes. Twice he saw men nearly sliced, catching the whirling hafts.

He looked behind them. Blud's first band was keeping pace, and behind them, the rest of the Varangians, in no order, no ranks, no marching rhythm. But they streamed along, yelling and singing, high-spirited, as if to some festival, a vulture feast. Basil rode up beside Tryggve, walking like a proper centurion in the middle of his century, and Tryggve angled over to meet him. Michael was still just catching up with him, the other officers well behind him.

"Have you seen any sign of the enemy?" Basil asked Tryggve.

The Varangian bowed, but on the upswing his gleaming eyes met Basil's. He was forgetting his Constantinople manners. The wolf was coming out, Basil thought, and smiled. Tryggve said, "Nothing, so far. I say we keep on going."

"There's a place on the coast ahead," Basil said. "Where a river comes up from the south. Across the bridge, there's a meadow. Make camp there."

Trygge gave a little shake of his head. His face shone with sweat. He waved his arm around at the sky, the land.

"See? The air is full of blood. It's an omen. The War God calls us. We should go on."

Basil lifted his head. It was true; the deepening sunset streamed red over the world, thick as fireglow. The hair on the back of his neck tingled. He looked west toward Abydos, and the urge came on him powerfully to keep on the march.

The wolf, he thought. My wolf.

"Michael, what is the day?"

"Sebastos. April 12."

One day more then. He lowered his gaze to Tryggve. "Make camp ahead, as I told you." He took his foot from his stirrup and shoved Tryggve in the chest with it. "Remember who you are."

Tryggve staggered back a few steps; his eyes flashed, but he laughed, and he bowed again. "Sebastos!" He went back in among his men. Basil turned to Michael again.

"We're going to need a change of horses."

"I've arranged that," Michael said. "But we've outridden them."

"Let's go." With Michael he jogged his weary horse back along the line of the army. From here he could see east along the dusty stretch of flat ground between the blue of the strait and the first rises of the hills to the south. Blud's Varangians were coming up behind Tryggve's men now, and they straggled back halfway to Lampsacus. Impatient, he kicked on his exhausted horse.

—⚬—

Helena even slept a few moments, in the stinking kitchen storeroom, wrapped in her cloak; but she woke at once when he touched her arm. He put his finger to his lips. She could hear people nearby, in the next room maybe, singing. Wherever they were the space was dark and reeked of burnt garlic. He half lifted her and half helped her into a huge empty basket, covered with dirt and wood scraps, a dirty pair of shoes at the bottom.

She sneezed. He piled something on top of her—cloth, maybe a cloak; it was too dark to see, and she touched it and realized by the texture it was base wool. Then the basket heaved up into the air.

He was carrying her. She was afraid to move, for fear of

unbalancing him; she turned her head, slowly, and pressed her eye to the woven side of the basket, trying to see out. Carefully, she shifted until she had a good view of the courtyard going by, then the gate. Chickens. A yawning guard. She lurched forward; they were going downhill.

He carried her a long way, up and down; she saw the hills turning green, and vines curling sweetly on their stocks, and some trees. Her legs began to throb from being so long doubled up. He stopped once, and something else landed on top of her, heavy enough to push her head down a little. She said, "I'm thirsty."

"Wait."

Then off again she went, curled up, like a baby in a wicker womb, rocked along as he walked. She dozed. She woke up to the scratch of her thirsty throat. Then the basket was still, and on solid ground.

The piled cloth above her lifted, and she looked up, poking her head over the edge of the basket, and he kissed her.

The tenderness held her a moment, a warm and sweet touch, so rare. Then she reared back and slapped him.

"How dare you slobber on me."

He said, "Here," and gave her a jug. "There's food. Come up." He put his hands on her as unceremoniously as a nurse and lifted her out of the basket.

They were in a cave, a vineyard cave, with a broken barrel at the entrance. He had laid the cloaks down on the dirt floor. She sat down gratefully and stretched her legs and drank deeply of the jug, which was half full of a wine gone bad from jiggling.

He sat on his heels before her. He wore only a sort of loin-cloth. A bright strip of silk held his hair back and he reached up and pulled it loose, and his hair swung down over his shoulders, white as dirty linen. His blue eyes were direct. She thought he looked like a faun, his ears poking through his long hair, his long arms ropy with muscle. She remembered him leaping into the window, that whole lean body flexing like a cat in the air. She wanted him to kiss her again. She lowered her eyes, her heart pounding.

—◦—

Bardas Phokas pounded his fist once on the door and wheeled toward the guard. "Break it down." He would beat her for delaying him like this. She had no right to bar her door against him. The guard hammered on the door with the hilt of his sword, until the panel cracked and broke.

Phokas laughed to himself; in there, she would be cowering. Knowing he was getting to her anyway.

The guard reached into the hole and opened the bottom latch of the door, and the two guards together slammed against the door, forcing the top one. Phokas strode in, looking at her bed, expecting to see her frightened, beautiful, and soft.

There was no one in the room. He wheeled around, looking, refusing to believe this. The guards fell on their faces, babbling their innocence, their ignorance, and he kicked one of them, glared at the strategos in the doorway.

"Where is she?"

"Sebastos. Megalos autokrator." The strategos went down on one knee. Phokas whirled around again, determined to see her in the room.

Instead, he noticed a yellow jewel on her bed.

"I remember that ring. John Tzimisces wore that ring." He took it. It was dirty, as if it had been lost. He put it on. "It fits me."

"Sebastos!" Someone burst in, past the strategos, and fell onto the floor, arms out. "They're coming—they're on the road already from Lampsacus—"

"Them."

"The Emp—Basil, Megalos Sebastos—Basil the Macedonian boy."

Phokas turned. His heart quickened. "Basil. It is begun." He fisted the hand with the Imperial ring, shut his eyes, and drew a deep breath. His apotheosis was at hand. Helena could wait. He strode out of the room, the men trailing him.

———

Raef let her eat her fill, and drink the rest of the wine. She gave him a long sideways glance. She was not frightened, he saw, glad. "Where are we?"

"Safe. Out of Phokas's reach. I only kissed you. I've wanted to kiss you since I saw you on the Mese almost the first day I was here." He made no move toward her yet. He was between her and the opening, and she did not intend to escape him anyway; he felt that in her, a warming, a quickening. He folded his interest around her like wings. Remembering that momentary answer in her kiss.

He said, "Let me kiss you again. You liked it."

She said, "I don't—" and he leaned toward her and brushed his mouth over hers.

She trembled under his touch. He drew nearer now, and pressed the kiss, slow, tender, all his mind on her, feeling every awakening of her flesh as if she were part of him. Teasing every fiber soft and quick. It had been a while since he had done this and he wanted it to last. After a moment her lips parted under his and he slid the tip of his tongue over the soft inside of her lower lip. One of her arms went around his neck. Her eyes closed. Carefully he moved in beside her, and laid her down on the pile of cloth.

She stiffened in his arms, resisting. He lay down beside her, his tongue inside her mouth, aware of her in his whole body, her wariness, and her hunger. He let her feel safe again, and then she was pushing into his mouth, and he sucked on her tongue, and slid his hand down inside her gown, his fingers stroking her belly through the silk.

He felt her whole body rouse at the touch. He curled one leg over her legs, opened the front of her gown, and stroked his fingertips over her breast, the nipple standing upright like a bud.

She moaned, her hand on his hair. He moved his head down, kissed her throat, and then her breasts, big and full like moons, heavy in his hands. He leaned more of his weight on her. Like the sea, she stirred under him, rushing on the currents of her body. Like the sea she rose under him, lifting herself toward him. He slipped his hand down between her legs. He knew where she longed to be touched and he stroked all around that little whirl of heat, and she lifted her knees up, wide apart, and lay back and said, "Please."

He pulled his drawers off and lay down between her knees. "Please what." He rubbed his belly on hers, cradled her shoulders in his arms and her head in his hands and kissed her, his tongue stroking deep in her mouth.

"Please—"

"Please what?" He was stiff as a horn, and he felt her part

ripe and soft and swollen, aching to be pierced, but he wanted to hear her say it.

"Please—" she said, and gulped, and said a Greek word he had never heard before, not even from the whores. He knew what it meant and he did it, until she lay sobbing in his arms.

—⁂—

After, he kissed her face, tender and protective, and she turned herself into the crook of his arm, smiling. She felt warm all over. She touched his chest, the muscle arched under the skin. He was lean and hard as a blade. She had thought Nicephoros Ouranos was beautiful, with his horseman's legs, his barrel chest, but now she saw his manliness was sleeked over with a layer of good living. The Varangian was like a forest animal.

She said, "I hope I'm pregnant."

He muttered something. He sat up, reaching for the jug, found it empty, and picked up the last of the bread.

"What," she said, sitting beside him. "You think I am light? A son of yours could rule the world."

He gave her half the bread. "There is a little creek down there, I'll get some water." He left with the jug. She thought of convincing him to take her straight away to Constantine. Maybe she could talk Constantine into turning on Basil and Phokas both.

Then he was running back up the hillside to the cave. He had the jug in one hand, but he got her by the arm and towed her out, running before she had her feet under her.

"They're marching. Come on."

"What," she cried, dismayed. She could not run very far,

and he slowed down, but by then, they were between the hills, and she could see what he had seen.

In the distance, on the road, was a dark mass that surged along like a tide, bristling. With a sinking heart, she saw it was an army.

"Basil," the Varangian said. His voice was admiring. "He moves fast."

She sighed. He held the jug out, and she sipped cold, winey water. He was getting up, his hand out to her. "Come. Up there." He pointed up the hill. "We can see. Come."

She followed him, breathless, up the grassy slope, under some trees, and then out onto a bald hilltop.

Before them the broad stretch of flat ground opened up like a bowl between the hills and the sea. Abydos was at the head of it, its towers and walls buttressed by the shore on one hand and the high ground on the other; the road led toward it like a bolt. The army she had just seen was rushing out along the road, and its faint roaring voice came to her. The hackles of her neck stood on end. She sat with her legs drawn up, watching. Beside her, the white Varangian hunkered, silent.

—⋟—

Tryggve said, "There they are."

Basil stood in his stirrups. Here the hills curved around in a broad rim, with Abydos where the curve ended at the strait; he could see the red roofs of the town above the wall at the corner of the plain.

Down through the hills behind Abydos, he saw trains of men coming, ranks and ranks of horsemen.

He turned, and saw behind him, his own army, gathering around him. The night before, they had all come into camp early, and slept and eaten, and now they were moving in on Tryggve's left, bristling with axes and stretching out far into the plain. They yelled, and whooped, and waved their arms in the air, and they strained forward, ready to leap. Blud was riding toward him, John Barbos at his stirrup.

Not even Blud could call them off now; they had seen the enemy, and their voices howled for the fight.

Basil sat back. "All right." He turned to Tryggve, beside him, and found the Varangian already looking up, expecting orders. "He will strike toward the beach. Take your men and get between him and the water. Hold that beach, and keep him back on the plain. Michael—" He wheeled his horse, which had caught his excitement and half reared. "Go with him."

Michael shouted, his face shining. "Rome! For Rome and the Roman people!" Everybody suddenly was shouting. Basil's page was beside him, holding out his helmet, his shield in its cover of purple silk, his spear. Basil pulled the helmet on, snatched the shield and spear, his reins in one hand.

"The rest of you come with me!" He charged off, galloping across the front of his army.

"Attack!" he shouted, with every stride. "Attack! Attack!"

He was still shouting when he reached the end of the line but he no longer heard himself. The roar from the Varangians drowned everything. They were rushing forward, screaming as they went, their axes over their shoulders, their gazes fixed on the army filing out of the hills in front of them. First of them all was Blud, red-faced with rage; even Blud would fight for Basil now.

The Emperor's horse danced, its hoofs beating the ground, its head tossing. It snorted, fierce as a lion. He peeled the purple silk from his shield. Under it was the blessed icon of the Virgin, her clear blue eyes mild as milk. He kissed the shield and fit his arm quickly through the straps on the back. His officers were catching up to him, galloping up around him, shouting. In their midst, he wheeled his horse and raised his spear up over his head.

"Attack!"

They charged.

Basil had fought this battle fifty times on the sand table. He knew that the way the ground lay forced everything toward the strait, toward the beach, where an army could fix both ends of its line. Phokas's army, coming out of the hills, would swing toward the beach, away from the broken higher ground. But Tryggve would hold them back, would stop their charge into the defensible position, and at the same time Basil would strike straight at him from the flank. Phokas would have to fight on two sides at once. Basil spurred his horse.

Ahead, Phokas's cataphracts were pouring onto the plain. They kept good order. Their helmets gleamed. Their horses trotted in close files. On foot, the Varangians hurtled across the plain toward them like a pack of wolves.

The first mass of the cataphracts swung around, forming ranks, their spears lowered, and charged. Basil swept toward the oncoming line; he leveled his spear, but he held the shield close against his body, to protect the Virgin from harm. The wall of helmets, eyes, manes, spears, and shields rushed on him. He set himself. His spear struck something and tore through, and his horse bounded and crashed into another horse. His leg was jammed against somebody else's saddle. He struck again with his spear into the massed bodies ahead of him.

He swung around to his left, pulling out, trying to get where he could see what was going on. Looking back over his shoulder he saw the Varangians crush the first rank of the cataphracts. The axes slashed down horses in gushes of blood, flying hoofs in the roiling rising dust cloud, screams and neighs of pain. The second rank of cataphracts hurled a wavering line of spears, and some Varangians fell, but the rest surged past the first mass of dead, their axes high. Basil galloped back into the middle of the fighting, shouting to his men.

"On! On!"

He could not get to the front of the line; the Varangians were pushing Phokas's men backward in a screaming rush, and now, he saw Varangians also over on his right: Tryggve had broken in from the beach.

Phokas's army was coming apart. Basil shrieked in triumph. Their backs were turning. They were flying, battling their way back up into the hills.

Then, even in all the uproar he heard someone bellow his name. He twisted in his saddle. From the hillside, down through the rout of his army, a giant in armor was galloping, in a helmet crowned with a gold circle, looking all around him.

"Basil, false Emperor, I challenge you! Face me!"

At the thunder of his voice, the fleeing Romans stopped, turned, and stood, making a stand on the hill road behind him. The Varangians drew back, all at once, leaving Phokas in the open between the two armies.

Basil galloped his horse out before his men. His heart thundered; everything he saw seemed cast in a red smoky haze. Phokas had not seen him yet, and he shouted, "Phokas!

I'm here!" He flung his spear down. "Someone bring me a sword!"

Phokas reined his horse in. His helmet visor was down, and like a giant bird he searched around him. His horse wheeled suddenly in a circle. Basil's page rode up, holding a sword toward him, and Basil gripped it and thrust it over his head.

"Come—fight me! Fight me!"

Phokas lurched toward him. Then his horse reared again, and turned on its hocks, and galloped a little way off, aimless.

A great wail went up from Phokas's army, watching. The horse stopped, its head up, nose high. Phokas slumped forward. As the horse sidestepped around, Phokas's helmet fell off, and the crown, and the crown rolled off along the ground. Phokas slid bonelessly out of the saddle and lay still.

Basil roared. The Varangians with yells of triumph swarmed toward the fallen man. Phokas's army wheeled. In a single breath they were flying away again, the cataphracts galloping off into the hills, the infantry racing after in no order. Where Phokas had gone down was a seething mass of bodies.

Then out of the uproar came an upright spear, and stuck on it, a great bloody head. It took him a heartbeat to see it was Phokas's.

Michael and John Barbos came galloping toward him. Between them they held a big old-fashioned infantry shield. They reached him and bounded down from their horses, beside him, and held the shield between them. From all around them the men were running to grip the shield, holding it up toward him.

He stepped from his horse onto the shield. His heart was pounding. With feet wide apart to keep his balance on the uneven shifting surface he stood on the shield and they lifted him up, up above their heads. He looked out over a vast ring of men cheering and roaring his name.

"Sebastos! Forever! Sebastos! Forever! Basil! Basil Megalos Basileos! Megalos Basileos of Rome!"

He flung his fists up toward the sky, and threw his head back, and howled.

Later, in Abydos, alone, he hung the icon of the Virgin on the templon of the palace chapel and knelt before it, and put his head to the floor as everybody else had to do before him.

He thanked God for this victory. He fought against the gluttonous surge of triumph. It was Rome's victory, not his. He could not rejoice in it, only accept it as a charge on him, a sign of his purpose. His special place in the Divine Order. Now it began, the retaking of the world, the rebuilding of the Empire, not with gloomy old Nicephoros rooting up the pirates in Crete, or damned John Tzimisces, greasy-tongued, smiling always, mean as a cur dog, nearly recovering Jerusalem: it began here, with him, Basil, chosen by God. Because what had happened today, except that God Himself had struck Phokas down? God Himself had chosen the Emperor.

He would send Phokas's head around, to every city of the Empire, so everybody knew the civil war was over, and that Basil had won.

God had chosen him. He bent before the icon, half in ecstasy, doubled over to the ground, praising God, accepting this with his whole heart. He would never lay down his spear. He would retake the world for Rome, unify truth again: one empire, one God, and one Emperor, Basil Megalos Basileos, in whom all other men were ensouled.

—◦—

On the hillside, Raef saw Phokas fall. A shudder went through him. Basil had won his long war. Except maybe Rashid was right, and the war would never end for him. He glanced at Helena and saw her smiling.

"Are you glad he won?" he said, surprised.

She said, "I'm glad Phokas is dead."

She leaned on him, warm, stroking him, wanting him again. Something in her voice raised the edges of his nerves; he thought suddenly of the yellow crystal ring.

"You have to go back to your husband," he said.

"Not yet," she said. She was pressing her breast against his arm. Her lips stroked his chest. He turned toward her, and took her there on the grass, in the sunlight. It was different, this time, she did not yield utterly to him, she tried to master him, draw him on faster than he wanted. He felt in her a surge of greed, a dirtier feeling than lust. When they were done he did not meet her eyes.

He had known he would have her only for a while. He was beginning to be glad. His body still sang with the music of sex but it was over now.

She stroked him, her fingers sliding down over his balls, his thighs, trying to excite him. She said, "Come with me to Constantine. We have no sons, and I'll get him to adopt you. You could be Emperor."

He said, without thought, "Why should I be Emperor?"

She laughed, her eyes on him, unbelieving. She said,

"Master of the world? You would not be lord of all?" She licked his ear, her hands on him, and her words clung to him, sticky, like a web, and for an instant she held him.

"But Basil must die. You have to see that. Basil is evil. He is the true enemy of everything Roman."

She sat up, and in her anger at Basil she forgot about touching Raef. She moved away from him, and with a shake of his head he freed himself of her. She noticed nothing. She saw only her own way.

"Basil devours everything. He gives Constantine no power— his own brother. He will brook no rival. You should have seen him when I was pregnant. How he watched with hatred in his eyes as my belly grew. How glad he was, when they were girls. If they were all girls—I wonder sometimes, Eudoxia is so different from us all." She leaned on him again. She did not recognize the thing between them was broken. "He will let no one marry. He would not let even a sister marry. There are no sisters left, anyway, but twice he has promised away one to some foreign prince and instead sent some cousin—the German found out but the Rus still thinks his wife is Basil's sister. You should be Emperor. Kill him, and you will be, I promise it."

He said, "I loved you for the pleasure in it, and for the woman in you. Now you want to make a tool out of me." He untwined her arm from him and got up. "Stay here. I'll go to Abydos. I'll find someone to come out and bring you in, get you proper clothes, and a horse."

He got up and walked off down the hill, and did not look back. He thought he heard her call to him once and he quickened his steps away.

CHAPTER NINETEEN

Michael Lecapenus stood in the window of the palace at Abydos, looking down on the courtyard; Romanus Sclerus himself, governor of the city, had come to greet Helena.

Romanus had prepared the entrance well. There were pipes, and lutes, and a trumpet, and a great crowd gathered around the courtyard. Helena rode aside on a white horse, wrapped in a cloak of Imperial purple, and veiled in white, wearing a hastily concocted version of her crown. Romanus himself in a blazing red dalmatic with gold all over his wrists and ears led her horse in through the gate. After her came a cluster of servants and women, scattering flowers and sweets and money around to the crowd, as if she had ridden in luxurious triumph here from the City, and not been found alone and filthy on a hillside.

Michael looked in among her swarming retinue, and did not see a tall white head. He beat his fist softly on the stone sill of the window.

"What is it?" John Barbos said.

Michael gave a little shake of his head. "I'm wondering where the Varangian is."

John laughed, surprised. He looked out over the courtyard again. "She looks none the worse for her adventures. I wonder what she will tell Constantine." He turned toward Michael again. "What worries you about that one Varangian?"

"He's trouble," Michael said. He imagined the world like a ladder up to God, with the Emperor just under God, and all the rest of the world neatly stepped away beneath him, in order of rank. Raef had no fixed place in this order. He knew no higher nor lower, he belonged nowhere.

Michael had been there with Romanus when the messenger came, all excited, to say the Augusta was out in the hills, and needed an escort. The Varangian had not come himself to deliver this news. He had somehow gotten her away from Phokas and then he had dumped her on a hillside and disappeared. Michael hoped suddenly that he had gone on, as he had always said he would do, vanished into the emptiness of the west.

He had not even taken the huge yellow African diamond with him. They had found that on Phokas's finger, glued on with dirt.

"I doubt one Varangian can make much trouble now," John said. "We have all the armies—the tagmata and the themata. When Basil marches now, the earth will shake. The Varangians are only a little piece of that."

"We're going to cull them down to a Palace Guard, and send the rest back home," Michael said.

He tapped his fist again on the windowsill. John nudged him. "I think you just need something to worry about." He nodded toward the room inside. "Let's go, Basil wants us, we have this submission to plan."

⸺⚬⸺

Helena sat beside Constantine, under a pavilion of silk, and wound her fingers together ceaselessly. Her belly churned with rage and hate. Beside her, her husband drank wine, yawned, studied his fingernails, spat out olive pits, while out there before them his brother took all the power in the world unto himself.

They were on the field where Phokas had died. In front of her, at the center of everything, Basil sat, the great flared crown on his head, and one by one the generals and dynatoi who had waited to see who would finally win the civil war came in and submitted to him. His back was to her; she could not see the look of gloating and triumph on him, but she imagined it, and her heart seethed.

He had made sure she would be here. He intended her to see and suffer.

She looked carefully around her. The Varangians surrounded Basil's tent amd Constantine's pavilion in a great ring of axemen. She could not find the white Varangian there; she had not seen him in Abydos.

She hated him now, too. She remembered him walking away from her down the hill, leaving her, leaving all she promised him, without a backward look, and clenched her teeth. No other man had ever made such love to her, as if he knew her deepest lusts and exactly what she had to have; taking her to him he had freed her from herself. Now she longed to see him dead.

Up toward Basil came the last to submit, an old man, blind, with a boy on either side to support him. She leaned toward Constantine.

"Who is that?"

"Bardas Sclerus," Constantine said. "Romanus's father. See, he still wears the purple boots."

She saw, then, that the aged general, who had once declared himself Emperor, wore shoes of the Imperial color. He tottered up toward the throne where Basil sat.

She did not see what Basil did. He seemed to do nothing,

sat motionless on the throne, but suddenly the men around Sclerus were hurrying him off, were sitting him unceremoniously down and tearing the boots off his feet, and then leading him back, barefoot, stumbling, to do his obeisance before the Megalos Basileos.

Then the great ring of soldiers around them began to cheer, and thrust their axes into the air. "Basil! Basil!" And beyond them, the armies of those who had submitted, now his also, raised the thunderous roar.

"Basil! Basil!"

She lowered her head to hide her fury. And beneath her lashes she looked around at the Varangians again. The white Varangian had failed her. But she would find another weapon.

Leif the Icelander had the task of putting the Varangians back on boats, to go to the City. The harbor in Abydos was wide enough for fifty boats at once, and so the loading was going along well. He stood to one side watching half a century file onto the last dromon in the line. Most of them were hung with new silk, and gold rings; they whooped and laughed, but they were staying in their line.

From the other side Raef Corbansson walked up to him.

Leif blinked, startled. "Where did you come from?" His brows crumpled. "Did you fight here?"

Raef shook his head. "I just watched. Get me on a boat."

Leif said, "You can come with me." He looked Raef over. He still wore the ripped and filthy tunic he had first arrived in, but now he had a fancy dark blue cloak around him. He looked tired. Leif thought of some questions, but he only clapped one hand on the taller man's arm, and led him onto his own boat, where Raef lay down on the deck and promptly fell asleep.

—✦—

Raef sat in the taverna Do-Dokas eating dates. It was early enough in the afternoon that he was the only person there. Even old Maria was back in the kitchen; she sang when she worked, and now Laissa was singing with her.

He thought, I keep saying no and yet I keep saying yes.

He could not bring himself to leave Constantinople. He told himself he needed money, he had to get some money first, but he knew this was a lie. The hawk had warned him: the City was weaving a spell around him. He might never be able to go.

Laissa came out and laid a dish of meat and beans and bread on the table in front of him. She wore a new dress, which covered much more of her than the old one. He straightened, reaching for the flat round bread, and tore off a piece.

"Where did you get that dress?" he asked. He shoveled up the beans and meat with the bread and stuffed his mouth.

"Do you like it?" She backed away to show him the long skirt, sewn with figures across the hem. "Maria got it for me. I'm helping her. Leif said he would give me some money, too." She came closer; he was chewing a delicious mouthful, and she leaned over and sniffed his hair, and then recoiled away.

"You've been with a woman."

He glanced at her, his jaws moving. Carefully he scooped up another mouthful.

"Oh, come on, tell me who." She danced from foot to foot. "Was she beautiful? Do you love her?"

He shook his head. "This is good. I may never leave for the sake of this alone."

"Where were you? Who was it? Was she prettier than me?"

He shrugged.

"You heard about the fight. Basil won."

That made him laugh. "Yes, I know."

"He's always been our Emperor, though," she said. She sat down next to him. "You're lucky to serve him."

He started to say, "I don't—" and stopped. It occurred to him he did serve Basil, that somehow, without choosing, he had become one of Basil's men. He said, "He is a good king. There aren't many."

She laughed, disbelieving. "He's not a king, silly."

Through the doorway the Varangians from the palace streamed, Tryggve, Leif, and a dozen others. Their watch at the palace had ended. Laissa squealed and ran over to meet Leif, who ruffled her hair and gave her a fatherly hug. Raef watched her. He wondered if she had stopped whoring. She looked like a little girl now again. Leif came up and sat on the bench by him, and Tryggve came up on the other side.

Leif had three new arm rings, which he waved in Raef's face. "Plus," he said, "we're moving up to the palace now. We're going to be the Guards there, and live there." He gave Raef a long glance. "I'll bring you some scraps off the table now and then. I understand the leavings of the banquets are enough for everybody."

Raef grunted at him. "I can eat as well here. Without having to stand against the wall most of the day."

Tryggve leaned back against the wall. "It's not so bad. He

lets me watch them play on the sand table sometimes. I
showed them something I thought of today. They listened."
His voice rang with pride. He wore a new dalmatic. The gold
on it scratched his neck red under his ear. He said, "They are
sending Blud Sveneldsson back to Kiev."

Raef reached his hand out to Tryggve, who after a look of
surprise gripped it and shook it. He grinned at Raef.

"Maybe something will happen to Blud on the way."

"That won't matter," Raef said. "Not to us."

Leif said, "Something may happen in Kiev, once he gets
there." He turned to Raef.

"He wants you. When the gate opens in the afternoon. Go
to the Daphne, you know the room."

Raef said nothing, but his belly tightened. He had been expecting this. This was part of being Basil's man. His mind ran
ahead toward the Daphne, the sand table room. What would
happen there. They would expect him to submit. To kneel, to
put his face against the floor. He wondered what would happen
if he didn't.

Also he remembered what Helena said. He should tell that to
Basil. He would not. When he had taken her he had given himself to her. She had betrayed him but he would not betray her.

He thought, for a moment, he could kneel, once, to this
Emperor, but then something at the center of him rose up, the
stalk of himself that would not bend.

He went out into the back, to make water against the ancient
wall. The sun was moving down in the sky. The palace would
open again soon and he would go there and whatever happened
would happen.

Above his head, a hawk screamed.

He flung his gaze up there. She circled, in the blue sky,

higher than most hawks flew, sailed around him again, and then soared off to the west. He watched her go. He looked into the sky until his eyes ached but she did not come back. His heart cracked. She had left him.

⸺⸰⸺

He went in through the Chalke when it opened, as the bells in the big basilicas were ringing out the tenth hour of the day; rows of petitioners crowded in with him, and spread out toward the offices of the scribes and the Eparch's men. Raef went around the corner of the little church there and up onto the porch of the Daphne.

The day had been hot but up here between the arms of the sea the air was pleasant and sweet. The columns of veined stone on the Daphne's porch were like trees and like trees they kept the air around them cool. A breeze came in from the Bosporus. He walked along, past people sweeping and carrying and hurrying, the place familiar to him now, a known place.

He went in through the main hall of the Daphne and across the courtyard to the sand table room.

Ulf was at the door, his axe beside him, looking half-asleep. Raef's steps lagged a moment, his gaze going ahead of him into the room; he swallowed once, and then went in past Ulf, to whatever he was going to do here.

To his surprise, the room was empty. He went over to the sand table, looking down at the model of Abydos. It was much different from when he had seen it last. They had played out the battle on it, made the tracks of soldiers along the coast, and brought Constantine's army all the way down. Where the battlefield had been the sand was mixed to a great turmoil, and a marker stuck out off the little hill where Bardas Phokas died. Then he felt behind him something sharp moving in the air and he wheeled and ducked.

The blade of Ulf's axe swished over his head. He yelled, startled, and Ulf leapt at him again, bringing the great axe up over his shoulder. Raef had nothing but his belt knife. He put his hand on the table and vaulted up onto it, eeling his body out of the way as the axe slanted down again. It bit hard into the table, which cracked and broke, sinking inward. Raef braced himself against the sudden slope, scooped up one of the long sandbags that formed the hills, and as Ulf heaved the axe up again whipped the six-foot-long sand-filled sock full into Ulf's face.

The Norseman bellowed, his nose spouting blood, the axe wobbling in his hands. Raef jumped from the table onto his chest, both feet first, slamming him backward and down to the floor. Someone had come into the doorway. Raef kicked the axe away, and hauled Ulf up onto his feet again, the Norseman's back to him, Raef's left arm hooked around Ulf's neck, his right hand pinning Ulf's up between his shoulder blades.

He said, into the other man's ear, "It was Helena, wasn't it. Helena set you on me."

Ulf coughed, half choked, spraying blood all over the room. Raef looked toward the door, and saw Basil standing there, with Michael and Nicephoros behind him. He let go of Ulf's wrist; Ulf gave a groan of relief, easing his twisted arm, but Raef was just reaching for his knife. He said, "I'm doing you a favor," and sank the blade into Ulf's chest up to the hilt.

Ulf thrashed once in his grip. He let the body slide to the floor. Michael came into the room first, and then Nicephoros, the two swiftly looking around, making sure the room was safe;

Nicephoros picked up the axe. Then they both turned and knelt down and touched their heads to the floor.

Basil came in. "Stand." He came into the middle of the room. Raef stood where he was, and the Emperor faced him, with Ulf's body between thcm. Basil seemed hard and dark as volcanic glass. He beckoned Michael forward to talk for him.

Michael said, "We're late. We should have been here half an hour ago but Helena delayed us, so that he would catch you alone."

Raef said nothing. He thought of her in Ulf's arms, of her whisperings in Ulf's ear, and his belly knotted. His body burned with hate for her. He stared down at Ulf's body; when he raised his eyes, the Emperor was looking straight at him.

He gestured impatiently at Michael, who stood back, and Basil spoke to Raef himself.

"So this was certainly Helena's doing." Basil moved, getting between Raef and Michael. He wanted this quiet. Between them. Michael backed away, toward the door, with Nicephoros.

Basil said, "Why would she want to kill you? You saved her from Phokas, who apparently had spurned her. There are rumors you gave her a good deal of personal attention. Why suddenly want you dead? What do you know?"

Raef said nothing.

Basil said, gently, "Kill her for me."

Raef twitched, all over, startled. He said, "No."

"You did a fine job just now on him." Basil gestured toward the floor.

Raef looked again down at Ulf, on the floor between them, and at the Emperor through the side of his eye. He said, "He was my shipmate once. You'd have chewed him up. You're like cats, you people, you play with your meat."

Basil said, "We would have found out anything he knew. For instance—" His voice was still soft, almost tender. "She wanted you to kill me. Didn't she?"

Raef said nothing. He raised his gaze to look straight at Basil again, resisting him, angry.

"You refused her. Explaining much."

He said nothing. He thought, He has no more honor than she does.

"But you won't refuse me. Not this time. I will protect you from any consequences. I will make you chief of my guard. You will be lord over all the Varangians. One of the greatest men in Constantinople."

Raef said slowly, "Or I could kill you. For my sake, not hers."

He still had the knife in his hand, but something, maybe the look on his face, had warned the two men by the door. As he drew his arm back to strike, Michael crashed into Basil from the side and carried him flat to the floor, shielding him with his body, and Nicephoros plunged at Raef. The big Greek tripped over Ulf's body but his outstretched arm knocked the knife out of Raef's hand.

Michael was shouting for guards. Raef heard feet trampling toward them down the hall. Nicephoros was rising, and Raef kneed him hard in the face. Spinning around, he bounded out the window, and sprinted toward the nearest trees.

⊸⧟

Michael said, "Where in God's name is he?"

Beside him, John Barbos said, "Nicephoros will find him. My heavens, he's angry."

"It certainly spoiled his looks."

John murmured something sympathetic. They were standing on the edge of the grass, looking toward the Bucoleon, the
Daphne behind them. Nicephoros was tramping back up from
the seawall. His face, what was lcft of it, was a snarl of rage.

All the gates were guarded, all the men watching for Raef
Corbansson, and with Tryggve and several of his own Ouranians
Nicephoros had quartered the whole palace complex, but there
was no sign of the white Varangian. Michael gripped his hands
together in front of him. He remembered how Raef had looked,
in the instant before he started with his knife toward Basil. His
face like a blade, his jaw clenched, his whole body a weapon.
Michael had seen death on his face then, Basil's death. Michael
turned, and went back into the Daphne, to the war room.

Basil was there, watching the slaves repair his table. Two
Varangians leaned against the wall behind him. Ulf's blood still
splattered the room but his body was gone. Michael bowed, and
started to kneel down, and Basil waved at him to stand. Michael
rose, wondering if he needed to do penance for handling the
Emperor so roughly. He crossed himself.

"Have you caught him?"

"No," Michael said. "He's disappeared." Wizard's son.
"Sebastos, if I hurt you—"

Basil waved his hand at him. "You probably saved my life.
When you catch him, bring him here, and lay him on his face in
front of me."

"We have to assume he still intends to kill you. You have to
be careful. Please."

"We'll catch him," Basil said. He watched the slaves level
the table.

Michael licked his lips, wondering how to say this, and began, slowly, "Sebastos, if we corner him, he will be more dangerous."

"Bah," Basil said. "So you want to let him walk out of here? You like him." He stared at the table a moment. Then he turned his eyes on Michael. "Find him."

Michael gave up; he bowed. "Sebastos."

Raef stayed in the big basilica most of the rest of the day. The central dome of the church was so high and so big it seemed to float like heaven over everything; this was the great golden dome, he knew, but until he came inside he had not guessed at its splendor. The dome stood on two rows of massive columns, one on top of the other, and the light came through in long sheets from the windows along the top. The space swallowed him; he felt invisible, as if the dim light made him transparent.

He entered through a side door during a service, and hid behind the columns. When no one else was there, he went up to the main altar, with its wall of gold and silver icons, and slipped in through the door in the middle to a cool darkness scented with sharp smoke.

He sat down with his back to the icons. He had to get out of here. He had attacked the Emperor; he did not want to think what would happen to him if they caught him alive. Yet the more he thought of Basil the more he wished he had stuck his knife in him, Megalos Basileos.

He would not have another chance. And the problem was not killing the Emperor, anyway, but getting out of here.

Rashid had warned him. He wished now he had sailed past Abydos, before, and gone home.

They would be careful about the gates, they would have lots of men watching, men who knew him, but who would kill him for the gold arm rings. He thought of going down to the little harbor and stealing a boat, if there was one small enough.

If they trapped him against the seawall he was finished.

After darkness fell, there was another service; the priests shuffled into the space behind the icon wall, and he hid in a wooden stall in the back until the ceremony was over and everybody had shuffled out. Then he left through a side door.

Before him the palace spread out in the cool evening, the blue shadows strung with lanterns and lamps and torches, people moving here and there. The moon hadn't risen yet. He went down along the edge of the Magnaura, where he had seen the brass lions roar. They were still looking for him; he felt them, all around him, like a forest of knives, and therefore knew where to go, and when to stop and wait, between the blades of their awareness.

He went into the Daphne, which was empty. Even the war room was empty. Basil perhaps locked into his chamber with guards all around. The sand table had been fixed and more sand dumped onto it. He could smell blood in the air. He should have stuck him.

They would have killed him then.

He wandered around through the ancient palace, rooms on rooms. Gradually he began to see people around him; they paid no heed to him, except one woman who gave him a sharp look before she melted into the air. They wore the clothes of Emperors and Empresses, they went around in processions, and giving orders, as they had when they were alive. A disembodied head floated toward him along a corridor, a man with sharp eyes, frizzy brown hair, a thin brown beard.

Raef knew Helena was still in the Bucoleon, someplace, and the urge came over him to find her and break her neck. In the darkness, surrounded by ghosts, he thought he was becoming a grim man, like Basil. He had to escape, soon.

He had spent all his life refusing his deep senses. Now when he needed power he had only muscle. He remembered using the crystal to find Helena. Now he began to wonder if he could draw someone to him.

He had no crystal. He knew no way to do this. He thought of Michael Lecapenus. He had seen Michael take Basil down to save him. Michael would do much for Basil's sake. Wandering through the Daphne he imagined Michael, seeing him sharp in his mind, trying to summon up his voice. Trying to put his voice into Michael's head: Come. Come.

He doubted this would work. Nothing he tried of magic worked the way he expected. He cursed himself for not listening to the hawk, years before, when she told him to know himself. Through the dark old palace he drifted like one of the ghosts, and struggled to throw his mind to Michael Lecapenus.

Nicephoros said, "Well, maybe he got out of the palace somehow after all." And shrugged. They had cleaned the blood off his face but his lips were still split and raw, his mouth and left cheek swollen, the whole side of his jaw bruised black, and he had been spitting out teeth for hours.

Michael said, "He's still here somewhere."

"He can't get to Basil now, at least."

Michael made no answer to that. The palace was a maze of buildings, rooms and closets, basements and courtyards and storage, clumps of trees and shrubs. He thought how easy it would be to elude people in such a place for a man like Raef, quick and strong and clever, and impossible to sneak up on. And somehow, Michael thought, Raef could find Basil; if he could find Helena in a place he had never been then he could find Basil here.

But the order was to stop looking until sunrise. He and Nicephoros crossed the grass to the Bucoleon and Michael went to his rooms there.

He had a palace in the City, and various houses, but most of his life he had lived in this bare little room near Basil's, with a chest, a couch, a window on the sea. But this night he could not sleep. A deep uneasiness filled him. Basil was well guarded; the palace was secure. Nonetheless he was unable to be still.

It was dark, the palace around him quiet. He left his room almost without thinking, went through the narrow corridor that led outside, into the courtyard of the Bucoleon. Slowly he began walking almost aimlessly toward the other side of the palace, thinking about the Varangian, and where he might hide.

The great dome of the Holy Wisdom stood against the sky; he started toward the basilica, but then without his thinking about it much his steps strayed around, and he walked toward the Hippodrome. The Daphne rose before him, the little cluster of buildings, with the tower in back, the Kathisma, square against the Hippodrome wall.

He went in the first building; it was empty, felt hollow, smelled of dust. He saw no one, not even a servant or a guard. No one used this place now; that was why Basil had his war room here. His feet padded across the inner courtyard. The door to the Kathisma was closed, but it opened silently at his pull.

He came to the foot of the great twisting staircase that led up to the Emperor's box. Almost without willing it he began to climb the steps in the dark. As he went around and up the space grew lighter; the door up there was open, he realized, and his heart clenched.

He climbed step by step the rest of the way, and walked out the open door onto the box where the Emperor sat to watch the races. The Hippodrome spread out before him in the deep blue night, the track picked out in torches, encircling the enormous oval of the walls, darker, massive, jutting out over the end of the hilltop. He went to the front of the box; he could see the guards there, by the main gate, under the Horses of Delphi.

"Don't turn around."

He startled all over. The voice behind him was Raef's. His hands lay on the rail of the box and he looked straight ahead, wondering how he had known to come here.

But this was what he wanted. He said, "Give yourself up. Beg his forgiveness. Submit to him."

Behind him there was a low ragged laugh. "He and I have been enemies since the first time we met."

"Since you first defied him," Michael said.

"Since he tried to rule me."

"You must not kill him."

"I'm going to try," Raef said flatly. "Unless . . ."

Michael's mouth was dry; he was trying to imagine himself wheeling around, and overpowering Raef, and capturing him. He knew that was impossible. His mind jumped at the suggestion of some other way. "Unless what?"

"Get me out of here."

Michael was gripping the railing so tight his hands hurt. He said, "Promise me you won't kill him."

"If you get me out of the palace I won't kill him. I pledge you this."

Michael let out his breath in a sigh. Before him now he saw a way, not only to save Basil, whom he loved, but the white Varangian, whom somehow he loved also. There was a terrifying risk in it, but it was a chance. He crossed himself. God help me.

"I will," he said, and turned, and faced the Varangian. "I need to go find some keys."

Raef's eyes glittered; he said nothing for a moment. Michael supposed he was considering that Michael might betray him. But then Raef's long homely face creased into a smile.

"Go get the keys," he said.

Michael gathered himself; he felt a spurt of gratitude the Varangian trusted him. Part of their pact, he thought. He said, "In half an hour or so, the bells will ring. Be near that gate into the Hippodrome, you know the one, by the stables."

"Where the heads are," Raef said.

"Yes. Where the heads are." Michael swallowed. Like yours, he thought. Or mine. He went past the Varangian and on down the steps.

Finding the right keys was easy enough; there were dozens of copies, and the Eparch kept some in his offices. The harder part was getting rid of the guard on the gate. It was the middle of the night, the bells had just rung the fourth hour. He developed his story as he walked down to the gate there.

He was glad to see the three guards there were Varangians, all new men; this would be easier than if they had been Ouranians. He strode briskly up and said, "Quickly, go down to the Bucoleon. They have the murderer trapped there but they need everybody."

Two of the guards were half-asleep, but they all snapped upright at that, and bowed to him and went running off toward the Bucoleon. Michael stepped to the door, hoping there was no one outside, and put the key in the lock.

At once the white Varangian was next to him, taut, his fists clenched. Michael said, under his breath, "There is a little gate, in the side of the far wall almost directly across, under the stands. It won't be guarded, it's always locked and no one uses it. Here's the key for that—"

He held out that key and pulled the door before him open, but before he could say anything else the Varangian was gone, flying out the opening space, not even taking the other key. Michael's heart was hammering in his chest. His ears strained for sounds out there, shouting, any sign someone had seen him. He pushed the door shut and stuck the key in the lock, and then heard, behind him, men running toward him.

He wheeled. They had torches, and Nicephoros, with his swollen face and now seemingly permanent scowl, was leading them, a score of them. The gate guard had seen through his ruse.

Behind him was Basil.

Michael dropped to his knees, and put his face to the ground. He thought, Kill me. Let them kill me now.

Above him, the Emperor's voice was like ice. "Nicephoros. Take him away. I never want to see him again. Put him in the hot pit."

Michael clenched his eyes shut. In Basil's eyes he had betrayed him. That alone mattered. He went sick with shame. They walked past him, out the gate, and just beyond were shouting. Nicephoros bent down and yanked him up by the arm and pulled him away, back toward the Daphne.

After they had gone some little way, when Michael was walking along on his own feet, Nicephoros said, "Why did you do that? For the love of God, Michael—you're mad about this Varangian."

"He promised me he wouldn't kill Basil," Michael said. His shame had subsided into a steady fear of what was to come.

"Well, he might have another chance. Basil's out hunting him now."

"He promised me."

At least he knew it was true. He knew the Varangian would keep his pledge. He could face all the rest if that was true. He forced himself to hold that foremost in his mind, a shield against fear.

Nicephoros took him in a side door of the Daphne, and down steps, down into the basements, down more steps, down to the hot pit, at the very bottom of the palace, in the center of the cliff. There werc lamps on the walls of the corridor and Nicephoros took one. The guard there opened the door into the cell, and Nicephoros gave Michael the lamp.

Their eyes met. Nicephoros's eyes blinked. He said, "I'll try—I'll tell him it was for his sake. He must remember everything you've done."

"He won't let you," Michael said. He looked in the darkened doorway. He had been here before often enough, to see men punished for their sins, or torn open for their secrets. The heat of the room met him like a foul breath. "What will happen to me?"

Nicephoros blinked again, looking away. "Exile, certainly. I hope that's all, but . . ." He swallowed, his gaze turning toward the door to the hot pit. "I'll talk to him, Mica."

"He won't listen," Michael said. He knew Basil's darkness.

Impenetrable. That tiger's heart. He went into the hot room, the dungeon, with its braziers and pokers and knives and hooks, and the door shut on him.

⸺⸱⸺

Raef needed no key to the second gate, a narrow wooden frame set deep in the wall, but scaled it, flung himself over, ran down into the City. He knew they were coming after him. He wondered what would happen to Michael; but Basil loved Michael. He could not think of that now, he had to feel his way around the narrow, twisting streets.

Behind him, he could hear shouting.

He went swiftly down through the tangle of hovels and shabby tenements of the poor, toward the Golden Gate, which was always open, even at night. Where the narrow alley came up to the Mese, he stopped. Down there the street ran through the great double gate, and in front of the gate he saw six of Nicephoros's Ouranian Guards.

He backed quickly away, and ran uphill. He had no money. Nothing to eat. He was tired, and he had to think this out. He circled up and over the great spine of the promontory down to the gate near St. Mamas, where the beggars sat, and he had slept before. But when he crept into the deep shadows at the back, Laissa said, out of the darkness, "Raef? Is that you?"

He jumped; he reached out his hand and touched her. He heard the smile in her voice. "Afraid? You should be. Everybody in the City is looking for you." Then, quieter: "I'll bring you food. What else do you need?"

"Is there a prize for me?" he said.

"Yes," she said, and then her voice took an edge. "If they

catch me doing this, I'll be killed. Trust me, or I'll just go, I'll
be safer if I do."

He said, "I trust you." But he had been a fool to come here,
he realized, if she knew to look for him here, he was being too
predictable. "You know the old arch, up on the hill, with the
horses carved on it?"

"Of course."

"Meet me there."

He did not wait to hear her answer, he bolted away into the
dark street. Climbed wearily back up the hill to the arch. There
part of a ruined wall led off to the west, with a sunken lane below, and he went down into deep shadows and slept.

Her whistle woke him up. He sat, looking up at the sky; the
moon was riding high in the sky, sickle-shaped. It was still hours
until dawn. But he had slept enough, an hour or so, enough to feel
better. He climbed up the wall and found her sitting by the arch,
whistling, looking around, her back to him.

When he touched her shoulder she nearly flew out of her
skin. She wheeled, wild-eyed, and then laughed, and threw her
arms around him. He peeled her off. "Did you bring me something to eat? Come with me."

He led her in under the arch, where they could hide, and
they sat on the bottom ledge and she laid a basket of bread and
cheese on his lap.

"What did you do?"

Raef said, "Not enough." He ate the bread in gulps. "Thank
you, Laissa." He was remembering how she idolized Basil.

She smiled, pleased. She tucked up her knees to her chest
and put her arms around them, her back to the wall.

"Leif says you'll get out of this. He says you always do."

"I don't know about that. Don't tell Leif you saw me."

Her brows arched in surprise. "Leif likes you. It's Tryggve you should worry about. He found out Basil promised you his command."

"I like Leif. But if he doesn't know he can't slip."

She nodded. "Where will you go? If you leave here."

He grunted. "Right now I think just getting out is my main problem."

"But you are leaving."

"I have to. They'll kill me if I stay." He was breaking pieces off the cheese and eating them.

She shook her head. "Basil is Emperor. He can kill anyone he wants. Leif thinks he'll forgive you, though. Do you know where Frankish—where they speak Frankish?"

"Francia," Raef said. He handed her back the empty basket.

The girl's face was solemn, young, the eyes direct. "Leif says the words I remember sound—sound to him like Frankish. The people who lost me here—who I lost—" She stopped, her voice wobbling. She settled herself, and went on, "They were Frankish. I want to go to Francia. When you go, will you take me there?"

Raef said, "If I find a way out of Constantinople I'll take you to Francia."

She flung her arms around his neck, and this time he hugged her back. She said, "Thank you. I'll come again tomorrow, with more." Gathering the basket, she went quickly away. He thought that if he was not out of Constantinople by the end of the next day, he would likely be dead.

CHAPTER TWENTY

He sat under the arch. They would be watching all the gates. He could try the seawall, and swim out, although he knew the currents boiled there like a mixing cauldron, and he would likely drown doing it. Then he heard the watch coming by.

They had no lantern, which was strange, and no one called out, or sang, as they usually did, riding up the rutted street along the foot of the wall. Then he saw who led them, and his teeth clenched.

It was Basil, wrapped in his black cloak, four other horsemen with spears riding single-file after him. Not his officers; Varangians, most of them Kievite. The Emperor carried a spear across his shoulder and his horse was the big black he had ridden at Abydos. Raef watched them go by him, and a slow rage brewed in him. When the Emperor had passed, Raef got up and followed him.

The growing anger blurred his mind; he began to think if he could kill Basil it would be worth dying. He began to wonder again what had happened to Michael. He knew Michael had been caught.

He let them go a good way ahead of him, tracking them on a side road, and then over a ridge and between houses, while they went along the city wall. Then they were turning, going up the long rise toward the Mese. He picked his way along, closer now, the Emperor like an icy white blaze at the edge of his vision, climbing the steep hill. He came to a broad churchyard and had to circle around it, and for a moment, in the deep narrow lanes below the churchyard wall, following the blaze of the Emperor, he missed one of the lesser men, who had come down a side street.

A long stretch of open street lay between him and the guard, with houses and walls on either side, but when the other Varangian saw him he let up a yowl. Raef spun around and plunged into an alley that quickly turned to a flight of steps, leading up toward the height of the hill.

They were pounding after him. Basil on his black horse was already well ahead of the others. Raef could hear the galloping triple beat of his horse. At the top of the hill, where the arch was, he turned left and scrambled up over the ruined wall there, and dropped ten feet down into the sunken lane and ran back toward the oncoming horsemen, along the twisting grassy dirt.

He heard them gallop by him, up there on the road, and he wheeled, turning his eyes to follow where they went, although the wall rose between him and them. They stopped a moment, up near the arch. He drew in close to the wall, his hands behind him on the flaking stones. The moon was setting and the night was dark around him like a cloak.

Then they were galloping off again, up toward the Mese, shouting and calling. Raef frowned. For all their noise, he knew the Emperor had not gone with them. He knew Basil was still there, by the arch. He had sent the guards on as a bait.

If he was alone, Raef could take him.

He looked up at the wall on the other side of the lane; it was much higher here than by the arch, but many of the stones were broken out. He stepped into the lane, looking up at the wall, thinking how to climb it.

Then, with a crash of stones, Basil jumped his black horse onto the wall and then plunged down into the lane, his black cloak fluttering, and charged at him with his spear.

Raef whirled, startled, his mind full of the sudden crash and the thunder of the horse rushing down on him, the spear point aimed at his face. He wheeled and scrambled up the wall, up out of the way. The Emperor launched the spear at him, a coiling underhanded throw.

Three feet up the wall, Raef pulled back from the oncoming tip. He could not get all out of the way. The point jabbed in through his shirt and some of his hair and some skin and pinned him to the rock. Basil galloped past him and spun the horse on its hocks, coming back. Raef reached for the spear's haft, to pull free, and the rock gave under him and he fell into the lane on his back almost under the oncoming horse.

The horse's hoofs struck toward him. He rolled, and the hoofs smashed down just behind him, around him, and past. Basil wheeled his mount around again, rearing its forequarters up into the air, the hoofs cleaving the air like clubs.

Raef still had the spear. He jerked it up, point first, and lunged. In the saddle, his black cape swirling around him like wings, Basil swung the wild-eyed horse around and hauled it up into a rear, so its hoofs flailed at Raef's head. Raef dodged violently back, and one thrashing hoof cracked the spear shaft in two, sending the point flying.

He spun around, trying to keep his feet under him, trying to get behind the wheeling horse. Basil loomed over him, shouting, "I'll make you bend your neck, Goose!"

The name jolted him. The old insult. In a fury he lunged at the horse, got one step behind its spinning forelegs, and grabbed

Basil by the booted foot and hurled him up and out of the saddle.

The horse bolted away, spinning chunks of grass and stone behind its hoofs. Down on the lane, Basil had landed on hands and knees, was scrambling toward the fallen spear point. Raef cast quickly around for a stone, and Basil reached the long narrow point, and wheeled. Cocking up the foot-long stick, he cast it hard.

Raef dropped flat on the ground and the point passed over his head. He wheeled and lunged after it. A hard furious body landed on top of him. They wrestled on the ground, the spear point between them. Six inches of the shaft remained below the head; Basil clutched it in his fists. Raef got his hand flat against the flat side of the point and shoved it around, and reversed its angle, pointing it toward the Emperor's face.

For an instant they were braced against each other. Basil wrenched around on his back, struggling to turn the point up toward Raef. His face was contorted with rage, and from him Raef got such a wave of hatred he could not think, knew nothing but the white blast, could only twist the spear point back and back, toward the man beneath him. He jammed one foot against the ground for leverage, and twisted his elbow to ram it into Basil's chest.

In his mind, Michael's voice said, "Promise me you won't kill him."

His mind cleared like a mist before a sudden wind. He leapt back, casting himself away from the Emperor. He saw what he had been about to do. The guards were galloping back, too, and a lot more of them. Basil was already up on one knee, his eyes white with fury, and charging after him. Raef bolted down the lane and around the corner, bounding across a meadow, headed for the northwestern part of the City, where the crooked alleys were too narrow for horses.

—⟶—

Nicephoros drew rein. "Sebastos. You sent for me."

"I saw the Varangian," Basil said. He had caught his horse and mounted before they reached him. He reined the big black around in a close circle; if he kept moving Nicephoros might not notice how dirty he was. His black mood had melted before the high vigor of fighting. He wished he had won. He would win next time and hang that long hair from his gate.

"Where?" Nicephoros said. His mouth made his voice mushy. His eyes went over Basil; one of the torchmen had come back, too, with the soldiers, and in the light Basil saw Nicephoros interpreting the marks on his face. Basil stared blandly back at him, knowing he dared say nothing.

Nicephoros bowed, silent. Basil sidestepped his horse across the street, counting the men.

"He's gone that way. Half of you—Nicephoros, take them down that way. He can't get through the wall. We'll pin him up against it. The rest of you follow me." He led them at a lope down the street, chasing the Varangian.

—⟶—

They spent the rest of the night working through the narrow streets and finding nothing. After daybreak, when the bells rang the second hour, Nicephoros and the Emperor with their men met again on the Mese. Nicephoros tried to force himself to speak to Basil about Michael but could not break the lifetime discipline of saying nothing to the Emperor until he spoke first. Basil looked worn, and he had certainly fallen hard, or been in a fight, or both; his cheek was scraped raw and his hands were bloody. Nicephoros imagined what he would say, formed the word, rode up closer, tried to open his throat and speak.

Then the Emperor's horse reared straight up, shrilling.

An instant later all their horses were bucking and trying to run. Basil had sprung down from his saddle; Nicephoros dismounted also, clutching his horse's bridle, his feet widespread.

Under his feet the ground was rolling. All around them the City was thrashing as if it sought to throw them off. He heard stone falling, people screaming. The horses reared again. Basil had his black by the bit, his lips moving, trying to calm the maddened animal; two of the other men's horses had fought free and galloped off, even while the ground under them twisted and cracked and Nicephoros went to one knee, gasping.

It seemed to go on forever. The pillars of the Mese, one by one, were weaving back and forth and then falling gracefully apart in an elegant white tumbling. A statue fell and smashed on the filthy marble street. Then, abruptly, the earth was still again.

He lifted his eyes toward Basil. The Emperor met his gaze, his face wide with alarm. "Michael," he said, and flung himself into the saddle, and galloped away down the Mese toward the palace.

⟶⟨⟶

Raef slept a little, curled up in a dark corner of an alley, and when he woke, it was daybreak. He went slowly and carefully toward the harbor, where it would be crowded, and he might find something to eat. He had two coppers left. Maybe he could steal something.

Laissa would bring him something.

He had to stop her from that. They would catch her, and probably they would kill her.

The great harbor street was already packed with people, fish-wives screeching, the water carriers with their donkeys, and seagulls billowing into the air. On the harbor the boats were put-ting out to fish. He walked along toward the nearest fountain, to get a drink, his eyes sharp for guards or Varangians. He should cut his hair, he thought. He stopped at the fountain and put out his hand to the gushing water.

Then a distant rumble reached his ears, that sound he had heard before, and his hackles went up; an instant later the ground was shaking under him and the fountain tilted and broke in a spray of water.

He wheeled. The whole City was swaying and dancing be-fore him. He had been wrong. There was still magic here, the greatest magic, the jealous magic of the earth. Under his eyes a building collapsed, the walls sliding down into dust, the roof still whole on top. Screams and shrieks rose out of the mess. Other buildings sank down, as if they knelt, tipping their heads toward the harbor. The street waved like the ocean, popping up its paving stones. Rocks and chunks of wood flew through the air like cata-pult shots. People lay on their faces, screaming, and others ran and fell and rose and ran again. Raef felt water around his ankles, and looked down; the water of the harbor had sloshed up over the seawall. A crack opened in the seawall like a new door. A moment later the water drew back. Down more toward the mouth of the bay he saw a boat hung up on the top of the seawall, its hull smashed in.

He started toward St. Mamas, his knees watery, not even sure it was over. All along the harbor street every house seemed fallen in, walls crumbled, and clouds of dust rising. Screams and pleas for help rose from the piles of rubble. He broke into a trot, sure now the earthquake had passed, and ran down the desolated street through the gate and the little village to the bridge.

The span had cracked from side to side, and one part had moved several feet to the left, but he jumped across the gap. Beyond its low wall, the monastery of St. Mamas was on fire. The Do-Dokas taverna was a heap of fallen stones.

He went in over the battered wall, into dusty air and a stink of old lime. He felt them all there like sparks in a heap of ashes. Gregorios was nearest to him but Gregorios was dead, under there, a stone through his skull, his spark fading. Raef climbed over the shifting, crumbling stone to where he knew Maria was lying, groaning, but not badly hurt, one ankle broken, but her head safe under the angle of her kitchen table. He pulled away some roof tiles, and then the stones piled up on the table, and tore off the broken top of the table and hauled her out through the gap.

She clung to him, gasping. Her face was white with dust. She turned and vomited onto the ground. He stayed with her until she stopped heaving, and then shook her by the shoulder.

"Help me."

She lurched up onto her feet and limped with him across the crunch of the stone, over some buried dead men, to where a heap of roof tiles and a broken beam lay over Laissa, sobbing but alive. They heaved off the red clay tiles and the beam, and she crawled out, and hugged them, weeping. Then he took them to the corner of the taverna where Leif and Tryggve were.

"Gregorios," Maria said, clutching his arm.

"He's dead, Maria," Raef said. "I'm sorry."

She slumped over, weeping, sat down on a chunk of rock, her shoulders bent. Laissa turned to him, wide-eyed, and said, "You're in trouble. They'll catch you."

He pointed toward St. Mamas monastery, where the smoke was rolling off the roof in a thick brown cloud. "They have no time for me. I can get away now. Help me. Leif is under here. Tryggve, too, but Leif is here."

She helped him pry off a great slab of the wall, and push it to one side. The fallen roof was propped on what was left of the wall, and they dug out the small rubble that choked the opening under it. Leif shouted, in there, and Laissa began to laugh and cry at once.

"He's alive. He's alive."

"He's too fat to fit through the tunnel, the old tub," Raef said, and dragged away the pieces of the broken table, to try to push the roof back up a little. The rubble shifted, falling farther. "Come on—hurry up!"

Leif squeezed and groaned his way out from the dark. When he saw Raef, he said, "Thor's blood, Raef, we're supposed to take you on sight."

Raef said, "Isn't Tryggve alive in there still?"

"Either dead or not conscious."

"Good. Then he won't see me. Help me get him out." He knew Tryggve was alive.

"You're mad," Leif said, and bent his back to the task of hauling up the roof. "I think the table's pinning his legs."

They cleared away the big rocks, and finally, with a piece of rope, heaved the roof up and off the stub of the wall. Tryggve was mashed in one corner, but the angle had protected his head and shoulders. He was just coming awake when Leif dragged him out.

Raef turned to Leif. "Thanks. I'm leaving. Give me until the tide begins to ebb. That's all I need."

Laissa said, "Remember—you said—"

"Yes, I know. Meet me under this end of the bridge at high tide."

Leif said, "Run, you fool."

Raef walked away across the bridge. He thought in the ruin of the City no one would notice him, not even Basil, and it was true. All the people wherever he looked were digging out their friends and goods, or calling names, or just sitting in the open air staring glumly at the water. The fountains by the harbor were broken and dazed men were wandering around with empty buckets in their hands. There was a dead donkey against a wall. On one corner a smashed cobbler's box and a dozen half-made shoes. The seawall was piled up with wrecked boats. He looked out on the water and saw some other hulls sunken, and half-sunken, and began to look for one he could use.

⁓

Michael had taken his clothes off in the heat, but he could not bear to sit in the dark, although the lamp made the room even hotter. But then the lamp itself went out. He sat in the utter blackness and tried to pray. He dozed awhile. Then the earthquake began.

He pressed himself to the wall, into the corner. He heard the distant crash of stones and a deep terror swept over him. He had a horror of being buried alive. In the dark, he would go mad first, before he died. All the weight of stone above him creaked and swayed.

Then it stopped, and it was all still around him, and pitch-dark.

He forced himself to see the order here. Throughout his life, he had tried to make up for the sins of his family. His great-grandfather had usurped the throne; although Romanus repented, in the end, his sons, all but Michael's grandfather, had tried to keep their crowns. All of them had died. Soon he would die also, and the Lecapenoi would sin no more against Rome.

Then he heard people pounding, outside, coming closer. He got up in the dark, his back to the stone. Over there the pitch-blackness lessened. The door had sprung open. Someone was coming with a torch. He heard someone call out, alarmed, "Sebastos—the building could fall—" and Basil came in, the torch behind him, his shadow falling enormous over Michael.

Michael cast himself down on his face at Basil's feet. Roughly the Emperor seized him with both hands on his shoulders and pulled him upright. "There's no time for that. I need you. There's work to do. Come on." He whirled and strode out.

"Sebastos—it's not safe—"

Michael grabbed his clothes and followed, suddenly light-footed. As he let him go, Basil had touched his hair. He still felt the memory of that caress, the Emperor's beloved hand on his

hair. Nicephoros was there, ahead of him, smiling at him. They
followed Basil up to the light and the blue sky.

—⁘—

Raef at last went down the harbor street to Markos's compound.
To his relief those walls were still standing, and while everybody there was out in the open, nobody looked hurt. But when
Markos saw him in the gateway, he came running over, grabbed
his arm, and towed him away outside, around the corner of the
compound wall, where they had talked once before. "You've got
to get out of here," he said.

"Yes, I know," Raef said. "I need a boat. Let me take one of
your small boats. I saw they came through the quake."

Markos's face worked. "Basil hates you." His gaze ran toward the street, barely visible beyond the end of the wall.
"What did you do to him?"

"Markos," he said, "I need a boat."

"If they find out—"

"Tell them I stole it."

Markos turned to look toward the water, at the far end of
the alley. He said, "I can't." He faced Raef again, earnest. "I'm
an honest man now. He's the Emperor. I can't, Raef. He's the
Emperor!"

"Markos, this is my last chance to get out of here."

Then someone rushed in among them, and Markos jumped,
and Raef backed up a step, but it was Ruskas's widow, Irene.

She said, "What is this?" She cuffed Markos on the face.
"Are you saying no to him? After what he has done for us? God
have mercy on you." Apparently she wasn't as deaf as he

thought. She turned to Raef. "My last boat. In the harbor, right out there, moored properly, so it rode out the earthquake. Green with a red stripe. It's small enough for one man to row."

"Thank you," he said, and she gathered him up as if she were the tall one and kissed him on the forehead.

"Go."

He left, Markos wringing his hands behind him, Ruskas's widow wagging her finger under his nose, and her mouth moving fast.

He went up the harbor street. Now all over the City, plumes of thick dark smoke rose into the air. He passed a row of bodies laid on the ground before a heap of rubble, a priest going along murmuring and crossing them. Next door two men were trying to prop up a roof with poles. Streams of people walked by him, listless, dusty, crying, some in a hurry with desperate faces, some calling names in hoarse voices. He saw the City watch, but they were busy trying to dig people out of a burning building. At a bakery, under a big red awning, a woman was giving away bread and thrust a loaf into his hand as he passed. A child stood on a corner, screaming, "Mama! Mama!" At the only fountain still flowing, high on the slope, people with buckets stood as thick as at Mass. On the Mese several columns had fallen down. Down in the poor houses on the north side, fires burned on every street.

The earth shook again, and all over the City, shrieks went up, and prayers. A few more stones fell.

In the midafternoon he swam out into the harbor to the little green boat with the red stripe and climbed over the gunwale. Someone had been on board recently. Someone had put a sack of food and a jug of water under the front thwart. He ran out the oars and rowed up the harbor, into shallower, quieter water, to the bridge.

The sun was lowering. Its slanting light through the rolling smoke was turning the air orange. The water shone like brass. The tide was starting to ebb, burbling in deep eddies around the piers of the St. Mamas bridge. As the sea went out it would sweep them along through the Horn and into the Bosporus. Once there he could catch the steady westward current before the tide turned again and dragged the sea back in.

He bumped in under the bridge, and Laissa called.

"I'm here."

"I'm here, too." Leif came after her, out from under the dark hulk of the bridge. "I'm coming with you."

"I thought you liked it here," Raef said. Laissa had brought a cloak, some bread, another jug of water, and he helped her stow them. They would be crowded. But he was glad of Leif.

"I do," Leif said. "But I like you better. And her. Let's go. Tryggve says you have until nightfall, when he goes back on duty. He says hurry. He'll report you then."

Raef did not answer him. Leif's words touched him more than he wanted to admit. He busied himself getting them all onto the boat, and then sat down to the oars. With a few swift strokes he was out in the center of the withdrawing tide. They floated down the Horn in the murky yellow light. His back to the bow, he maneuvered them easily enough through the best draw of the ebb, through the packs of boats, some half-sunk, some drifting, that clogged the narrow bay. A cat yowled from a boat awash to the gunwales. Wood, leaf bits, scraps of cloth, dead fish littered the greasy water.

The boat glided smoothly along, past two of the Eparch's dromons; they were using their grappling hooks to pull wrecks off the seawall and paid no heed at all to Raef.

When the little boat breasted out onto the Bosporus the

sudden chop and lurch of the waves made Laissa yelp, frightened, clutching the side. Her fair hair blew across her face.
Raef rowed them strongly out away from the promontory, out
from the seawall where the currents lashed and ripped. The sun
was going down, and the sky had turned fiery red from horizon
to horizon. The long trails of smoke rising out of the City bent
to the north wind like the banners of a demon army. He could
see, now, against the vivid sky, the great golden dome of the
magnificent basilica, cracked halfway down.

My City, he thought, with a stab in his heart. My City.

His City was gone. It had never been his City, anyway. It
wasn't Basil's City. It hadn't belonged to the first Constantine,
whoever he was. Like the Millstorm it sat on a passage to the
center of the world, where the whole of the world went down
and turned around and fountained back up again, an irrepress-
ible whirl of life.

Leif was holding Laissa as she bent over the gunwale being
sick. Then, from the rolling ruddy smoke above him, came the
scream of a hawk.

Raef straightened, looking up, the oars cocked motionless
in his hands. In the rushing air she circled over him, her wings
wide. He gave a yell. He flung one arm up to her, who had not
abandoned him after all. Leif and Laissa gawked at him, startled. The hawk soared off, into the west, and he bent his back to
the oars, following her.

⚊⚬⚊

Michael followed Basil out onto the balcony of the Bucoleon,
where the first light of day was breaking; the Emperor sank into

the chair, exhausted, and shut his eyes. They had been in the saddle all the previous day and all the night, going around the City. There were hundreds of people dead, hundreds of buildings down. All the fires now were out, but they had to make sure everybody had enough to eat, get the water working, arrange the prayers for the dead, clean everything up before the inevitable plague followed, when the contagion seeped out of the ground through the cracks in the earth.

Here, in the palace, it was quiet, calm, under control. Michael had bathed, was dressed again in clean and proper court clothes. The waves of the unsoilable sea churned against the wall below the balcony, and the light cool air of sunrise touched his face. He looked out toward the sea, hazy with rising mist, his muscles aching with fatigue, waiting for Basil to tell him what to do next.

Basil said, "Michael. Any word of that Varangian?"

Michael licked his lips. They had not spoken of any of this yet. He had vowed silently never again to be false to Basil in any way. He said, "Tryggve thinks he has escaped the City."

"Either that," Basil said, without opening his eyes, "or dead. Maybe the City crushed him."

Michael gathered his breath, relieved. "Possibly."

"Certainly," Basil said. "It's God's will. God struck him down. A lesson. I should not have left it to God. I should have killed him when he first resisted me."

Michael was staring away down the sea. Far down there, in the daybreak, he thought he saw a sail. For an instant the heart yearned out of him, tugged after, but with an effort he turned his back. He shut down that quiver of self in him. He was

Basil's man forever. Yet he was glad, somehow, mysteriously, for that distant sail. He said, "I will bring you some wine, Sebastos."

"Drink it yourself, Mica," Basil said. "I'm going to sleep."

HISTORICAL NOTE

The Emperor Basil II (958–1025) ruled for nearly fifty years and never stopped fighting. Once he had destroyed his rivals for the throne, he turned to his real work: restoring the Eastern Empire. A long, bloody war in the West secured the Danube, the ancient northern border, for the first time in four hundred years, and took Croatia, Bulgaria, and Serbia to hold all the Balkans. Turning east, he defeated Khazaria and forced Armenia to submit to him, so that he controlled the Crimea and the Caucasus. His friend Nicephoros Ouranos served as his viceroy in the East, and Byzantine policies dominated the Aegean and Syria.

Basil is best known in the popular mind for putting out the eyes of the fifteen thousand Bulgar prisoners he took at the battle of Kleidon, leaving a single eye in every hundredth man to lead them all home. He did this again, after another battle; the Byzantines were prone to mutilation. Basil also built the strongest army in the Middle East, and his policies humbled the great families of the Empire, shifted the burden of taxation onto the rich, and restored the lands local elites had misappropriated from the ordinary farmers. He was terrible, but he was just. The Empire never saw his like again.